whisper sweet NOTHINGS

ROSEWOOD RIVER

ALSO BY LAURA PAVLOV

Rosewood River

Steal My Heart
My Silver Lining
Over the Moon
Crazy In Love
In a Heartbeat
Whisper Sweet Nothings

Honey Mountain

Always Mine
Ever Mine
Make You Mine
Simply Mine
Only Mine

Magnolia Falls

Loving Romeo
Wild River
Forbidden King
Beating Heart
Finding Hayes

Cottonwood Cove

Into the Tide
Under the Stars
On the Shore
Before the Sunset
After the Storm

whisper sweet NOTHINGS

ROSEWOOD RIVER

USA Today Bestselling Author
Laura Pavlov

Entangled Publishing, LLC
644 Shrewsbury Commons Ave., STE 181
Shrewsbury, PA 17361
rights@entangledpublishing.com

Amara is an imprint of Entangled Publishing, LLC.
Visit our website at www.entangledpublishing.com.

Edited by Sue Grimshaw
Cover design by Hang Le
Cover images by tomograf/iStock and Keola/Depositphotos
Edge design by Bree Archer
Edge image by Nongkran_ch/GettyImages
Interior design by Britt Marczak
Interior images by Vasilyevalara/GettyImages
and MartinaVaculikova/GettyImages

ISBN 978-1-68281-616-5

Manufactured in the United States of America

First Edition February 2026

10 9 8 7 6 5 4 3 2 1

Because following this girl was like following
the sound of my own heartbeat.

—Archer Chadwick

Whisper Sweet Nothings is a sweet and sexy small-town romance with all the feels. However, the story includes elements that might not be suitable for all readers, including an absentee parent by choice. Readers who may be sensitive to this, please take note.

1

Archer

"I cannot stress how important it is to make education the number one priority, and that needs to start at home, Mr. Chadwick," Mrs. Groucher said, and it took everything I had in me not to roll my eyes. "College is getting more and more competitive with each passing year."

Was she fucking kidding me?

My daughter was five years old, and this was kindergarten.

Mrs. Groucher had been my teacher back in the day, so this wasn't her first rodeo, and I sure as hell wasn't going to argue with her.

But did I agree with her?

Hell no.

"I do understand the importance of academics." I cleared my

throat. "However, we'll be in Paris for my cousin Rafe's wedding, so it's a long way to travel, and we'll be staying for the week to do some exploring."

"Tsk." She pursed her lips and made no attempt to hide her judgment. "Leave it to Rafe to get married abroad. That one always was a bit over the top."

Mrs. Groucher had taught all of my cousins, Bridger, Rafe, Easton, Emerson, and Clark, as well as my younger brother Axel and me. I was fairly certain she had come with the building here at Rosewood River Elementary, because the woman had been a part of this school since it opened.

I chuckled. "Yes. He does enjoy a production, and Paris has special meaning to him and Lulu. And Melody is their flower girl, so it's important that we have this time with family."

"It's all about choices, and Melody is a bit of a—*whimsical* girl. A daydreamer, if you will." She tapped her finger against her chin as she thought over her next words, and I fought the urge to bite back because this wasn't the first time she'd insinuated that my daughter had her head in the clouds. "It will be up to you to keep her focused."

"I'm not concerned," I said, my voice coming out harsher than I meant it to. "She's five years old, and I wouldn't change a thing about her."

Mrs. Groucher sighed. "This is where Melody having two parents would come in handy. You're going to have to be both good cop and bad cop." She shrugged.

Clearly there were no boundaries to the advice that my daughter's kindergarten teacher felt inclined to give me.

"Daddy, are you staying at school all day today?" Melody came running over to me, her lips turned up in the corners as she blinked at me with those big brown eyes of hers.

The kids were allowed to be dropped off for free play on the playground before school started. Today they were playing inside the classroom because it had just started raining outside, and I'd come to speak to her teacher about our trip to Paris in two weeks.

Welcome to fall in Rosewood River.

"Nope. I've got to get going in a little bit, but I was just telling Mrs. Groucher about our trip to Paris." I scooped my baby girl up and settled her on my hip.

"You're going to miss three days of school, so I'll send the work home with you, and I'll expect it back after Thanksgiving break," her teacher said, crossing her arms over her chest as the words left her mouth.

"Hey, you could come with us to Paris, Mrs. Groucher. Mrs. Dowden can't nannies for me no more, because she's too tired. Daddy's finding a new lady to come live with us today." Melody spoke with the slightest twang, which was fucking adorable.

But her teacher seemed far from impressed with this new information.

"I won't be coming to Paris with you because I'm your teacher, Melody." The older woman's tone was harsh, but my daughter wasn't even remotely fazed.

"Well, that's just sad, because we love each other, right? Right, Mrs. Groucher?" she asked, and I couldn't help but chuckle as she stared at the strict woman in front of her.

"Teachers love all their students." She looked between us. "A new lady is moving into your home?"

"Oh, it's not like that," I said, shaking my head at the insinuation. "Oscar and Edith's niece has moved to town, and she's looking for part-time work, since she does some sort of remote work as well, apparently. I actually have an interview set up with her in an hour."

Thankfully, Josh Barker started yelling about Tommy Jordan stealing his markers, and Mrs. Groucher left to torture someone else for a little bit.

"Do you think my teacher is sad that she can't come with us to Paris, Daddy?" Melody placed a hand on my cheek. "Are you sad she can't come?"

Fuck, no.

"No, angel face. I think she's fine, and she'll be here with her family for Thanksgiving, and we'll be in Paris with ours."

"Yeps. And I'll be the flower girl. And my Beefcake will carry the rings and walk with me."

My nephew Cutler liked to go by his handle, "Beefcake," which Melody seemed convinced was his real name.

"Yep," I said, kissing her cheek and setting her down on the floor. "I've got to go meet the new nanny and see if we like her."

"I like her, Daddy."

I laughed. "You've never met her, so how do you know?"

"'Cause Uncle Bridger told me she's a big provement." She shrugged.

Fucking Bridger.

My brother and cousins had all given me shit for keeping Mrs. Dowden employed for as long as I had.

But they weren't wrong. It was time for a change.

"We'll see. If it works out, I'll have her come back and meet you today, all right? If not, I've got my feelers out to find someone else."

"Melody, why is your daddy so tall?" Bernice Warner asked as she tipped her head all the way back and pushed her glasses up on the bridge of her nose as she looked at me.

"He said he was born this way," Melody said.

"Wow," Bernice gasped. "Your daddy must have been a very big baby."

I chuckled. "Hey, Bernice."

"God doesn't create us all equally, does he, Archer?" Sarah Lynn Schwartz walked over, and I tried not to wince. The woman was relentless, and her daughter Justine was in Melody's class, so there was no escaping her. She tweaked Melody's nose, her voice a little too sugary sweet for me. "He shined his light a little brighter on your daddy."

"Daddy, you've got the lights shining all over you?" Melody asked.

I sighed. "Hi, Sarah Lynn. How are you?"

I tried to avoid her most mornings at drop-off, but she always seemed to be there when we'd arrive.

"Well, I'm still single and waiting for that phone call." She laughed a little too loudly. "Hey, I'm free right now for coffee, if you want to go?"

"Aren't you a shameless flirt," Bethany Jordan said. Her son Tommy was also in kindergarten and a friend of Melody's. "You're supposed to have coffee with me this morning."

Thankfully the bell rang, and I gave Melody one last kiss on the cheek and told her to get to her seat before turning to the two women standing in front of me. "I've got a meeting to get to. You ladies enjoy your coffee."

Sarah Lynn shouted out for me to call her as I hustled out of there.

Once I was in my truck, I turned on the wipers to clear off my windshield just as my phone rang, and Bluetooth announced an incoming call from my mother.

"Hey, Mama," I said.

Her voice came through the speaker. "Hi, honey. Are you

meeting with the new nanny this morning?"

My family had been urging me to get more help for months. My business was taking off, and balancing work and being a single dad didn't leave time for much else.

I wasn't complaining. I loved being with my daughter, but the reality was that I couldn't be in two places at the same time, and I needed help.

"Yes. I'm meeting her at the office now."

"Why didn't you meet her at the house? Doesn't she need a place to live? I thought you were going to offer up your casita? It wouldn't be a bad thing to have someone at the house if you get called out to a meeting," she said. "Dad and I feel terrible when we travel that we aren't there to help you."

"Mom, you do plenty. It's all good."

"But I know you're expanding the office and growing your business, and you can't do it all, Archer. You need help."

"And I'm getting it. But I need to meet her first. I know nothing about this woman, other than she graduated from college two years ago, which means she's young. She could be a party girl. I can't just move some stranger into the house until I know she's a good fit. It's always harder to get someone out once they're in."

Loud laughter echoed through the cabin of my truck. "You don't say? I mean, you kept Mrs. Dowden for far too long, and she wasn't even living there."

"Agreed. I'm being more cautious now. I'll get a read on her and go from there."

"If she's a good fit, you should bring her to Paris with us. It would be good for you to have some adult time and get out a little. Who knows, you might meet a nice Frenchwoman," she teased.

Nothing like having your mother tell you that you need to get out and date.

It had been a while.

"Let's first see if it's going to work out before we move her into my home and travel with her," I said as I pulled into the parking lot at my office. I glanced through my windshield to see the rain coming down harder now. "All right, I'm at work. I'll call you later."

"Love you, honey," she said, and I replied with the same sentiment before ending the call.

I walked into the office, noting that a few people had beaten me here this morning. I was a commercial broker, and land was a hot commodity out here. I'd opened my own brokerage a few years back. Business was booming, and I'd just brought on a few new brokers.

"Hey, boss," Lucy said. "The rain is really coming down this morning."

"Yes, it is." I nodded. "Are we set for the staff meeting?"

"Yep. I've got bagels and coffee ordered. Do you need anything else?"

I glanced down at my watch. I was meeting the potential new nanny in five minutes, and then I had our weekly company meeting in an hour.

"Nope. That sounds good. I have an appointment in a few minutes, so just send her back when she gets here."

"The new nanny, right?" she asked as she followed me to the staff lounge. I poured myself a cup of coffee, and then she tagged along as I made my way to my office.

Lucy was the best personal assistant one could ask for, but she was nosy as shit most of the time. Her husband Marcus was a good friend of mine, and we joked about it often.

"Yes. We'll see how it goes."

"And she's Oscar and Edith's niece?" She crossed her arms.

"Correct."

"Well, I noticed on your calendar that her last name is Smith. Winnie Smith. But I could have sworn Edith said her name was Winnie Wilson. How could she have two last names?"

I pinched the bridge of my nose. "I don't know their family tree, Lucy."

"Hmmm... Maybe she used her maiden name when she booked the appointment, but she's actually married. But why would a married woman need a place to live? I wonder if she's single?" She waggled her eyebrows.

"How the hell would I know?" I groaned. "All Edith told me is that she graduated from college two years ago. That means she's young, so get your mind out of the gutter. I'm looking for a nanny, not a date."

"That would probably make her twenty-four years old. Hardly too young."

I blew out a breath. Why did everyone feel the need to try to set me up? I was doing just fine on my own.

"That would make her a decade younger than me. In my book, that's too young." I glanced at the door, an invitation for her to find her way out.

"Fine. I'll send her in when she arrives."

"Appreciate it," I said as I opened my email.

And I spent the next hour catching up on admin and taking a few phone calls.

My nanny turned out to be a no-show.

I knew it wouldn't be easy to find a replacement for Mrs. Dowden, but I'd expected her to show the fuck up for an interview.

Or at the very least to have the decency to cancel the interview.

I made my way to the staff lounge, and Lucy threw her arms in the air. "Did she at least call to say she wasn't coming?"

"Nope."

"What should I do if she shows up now?" she asked.

"Tell her the position is no longer available. I can't hire a nanny who can't show up for the initial meeting. I'm going to need someone I can count on to pick Melody up from school."

"Should I check those job boards I was telling you about on the *Rosewood River Review* website? There are plenty of people looking for work in town."

"Sure. I need to find someone quickly," I said. "My family is covering for now, but I can't keep asking everyone for favors."

My life was far too busy to waste time on an employee who didn't have the decency to make a phone call to say she wasn't going to make it.

Time to find a new nanny.

2

Winnie

Of course my piece-of-shit car decided to give out on me the day I had an interview.

In the middle of a rainstorm.

The universe clearly hates me.

I glanced around from where my car had died on the side of the little country road about a mile from downtown. It was pouring rain, and I dug in my purse and pulled out my phone.

I looked at my watch and chewed on my thumbnail as I tried to figure out what to do. I could call my uncle Oscar and see if he or Aunt Edith could come pick me up. I'd never make it on time now.

My phone had no signal.

"Shit!"

I needed this job if I wanted to start a new life, which I was desperate to do.

I squeezed my eyes closed as my father's words filled my head.

You don't quit. You're Winnie fucking Smith.

I was happy to be Winnie Smith again. I'd lost my mojo when I was Winnie Wilson.

And the mantra worked better this way.

They weren't the typical words one says to a five-year-old kid, but he'd been saying this to me ever since my mom walked out on us.

My father, Sam Smith, was a man of few words, but he made sure the ones he said counted.

I pushed myself out of the car, then reached in the back seat for an umbrella and opened it. I held it over my head as I made my way around to the front of my Mustang.

A large blue truck driving far too fast down this back road flew past me, and the tires crossed a puddle in the dip in the asphalt and doused me in brown, filthy water.

My mouth hung open with surprise as I gaped down at my cream suit that was now filthy.

A lump formed in my throat, and I blinked a couple of times.

I will not cry.

My father was a mechanic and I knew my way around a motor, so I popped the hood of my dated car. I inspected the engine, and nothing looked out of place. At the end of the day, this car was older than dirt, and it most likely just needed a jump.

I couldn't do that on my own without another vehicle, and as I turned to look down the long road, I didn't see anyone in sight.

Time for plan B.

I reached up and adjusted the bow I wore in my hair; a bow

was my reminder to keep moving forward. However, the fact that I was covered in soot water made it highly unlikely that the bow would do much for me now.

Jaden would love to see this. My ex-husband was a spiteful man. He loved nothing more than to see me fail. I blew out a breath as my heels clanked against the unstable pavement beneath my feet.

And I walked.

The rain pounded against my umbrella as I glanced out at the mountains and trees and just kept on moving.

I'd be ridiculously late, but at least I'd show up.

Finally, I saw some buildings up ahead.

I'd just arrived in town last night, and I hadn't been here since I was a kid, but I was fairly certain I was approaching downtown Rosewood River.

I checked the time on my phone just as my heel caught on a pothole, and I went tumbling to the ground, my umbrella flying from my hand, along with my purse.

This day just keeps getting better.

I rubbed my knee, groaning when I saw the big hole in my favorite dress pants, and I stood before retrieving my purse and my now-broken umbrella.

I sniffed multiple times, desperate to keep the tears away as I brushed my scraped hands together.

A few heads turned to look at me as I walked down the sidewalk. I tipped my chin up and ignored the fact that I clearly looked like a walking disaster. I was no longer sure why I was even pursuing this job, but at the end of the day, I wasn't a quitter. And as a parent, wouldn't you want to know that the person caring for your child wouldn't throw in the towel every time they hit an obstacle?

Checking the numbers on the buildings, I finally spotted Chadwick Brokerage.

I blew out a breath, closed my umbrella (which was no longer offering any protection anyway), and pulled the door open.

The woman behind the desk looked up, and her eyes widened as she took me in.

"May I help you?" she asked.

I tucked my soaking-wet hair behind my ears and forced a smile. "Yes. I'm Winnie Wilson. I have an appointment with Mr. Chadwick."

"I believe the position is already filled." She winced as if she felt bad telling me. But of course it was filled. He probably had several applicants and didn't want to waste his time waiting on someone who was very late for her appointment.

I sighed. "I know I'm late. My car broke down. My phone had no service. I guess I'm not surprised that he's already filled the position."

I could feel my bottom lip start to tremble, and her gaze softened. "Give me a minute."

She pushed up from her desk before disappearing in the direction where voices were coming from the hallway. Several people walked past me, holding coffee cups in their hands as they glanced my way. No one said anything, and I couldn't even feel any embarrassment or shame. I just felt numb at this point.

After they'd passed, I took the opportunity to adjust the bow holding up the front part of my hair before grabbing some tissue from my purse and dabbing at my face.

"Your knee is bleeding," a deep voice said, startling me as I looked up.

He was tall, with sandy-brown hair and the greenest eyes I'd ever seen. His white dress shirt showed off his broad shoulders.

I followed his line of sight down to my knee and groaned when I realized my filthy cream dress slacks were now stained with red blood.

"Oh, um, yeah, I tripped. But I'm fine. I just…" I shook my head. "Are you Mr. Chadwick?"

"I'm Archer Chadwick." He stepped closer, and the woman who'd been behind the desk moved back to her chair. "And you're Winnie."

It wasn't a question; it was a statement.

"Yes. And I know I'm late, and you've potentially filled the position already, but I just wanted the opportunity to explain why I was late. And to apologize."

"Follow me," he said, his voice deep and commanding.

I looked over at the woman behind the desk, who gave me two thumbs up and motioned for me to follow him.

He stepped into an office that was fairly large, and he shut the door after I'd stepped inside. The room had cherrywood bookshelves and a matching desk, with two leather chairs on the back side and one tall leather chair where he obviously sat.

"Sit down," he said as he moved to a cabinet and pulled out a black box with a handle.

I sat on the leather chair, mortified at how badly my knee was bleeding now, before dabbing it with tissue because I didn't want it to drip onto the carpet in his office.

I startled when he bent down in front of me and reached for the hem of my pants. "May I?" he asked.

My breath caught in my throat.

When was the last time a man had been down on his knees in front of me offering anything?

Not in a very long time.

I cleared my throat and nodded. "Yes, but I can also clean it up myself. I don't want to bleed on your carpet."

His eyebrows cinched together with confusion. "I don't give a shit about the carpet. You're bleeding, and you're soaking wet and shaking."

Just then the door opened, and the woman from the front desk walked in with a blanket. "Found one. I'm Lucy, by the way. I run the office for the big guy here."

She wrapped the blanket around my shoulders, and I was almost too stunned to speak.

It took me a moment.

"Thank you," I said, my words wobbly as I blinked back the tears that so desperately wanted to fall.

I could deal with obstacles—hell, I'd dealt with them my entire life.

But kindness from strangers.

That was a different story.

Archer rolled my pant leg up, and his eyes widened as he took in the gash on my leg. Apparently, I'd fallen harder than I'd realized.

"Thank you, Lucy," he said, and she nodded before leaving the office and closing the door. "This is going to sting."

"It's fine. Seriously, I can do it myself. It's not your job to clean me up."

"How'd you fall?" he asked as he slipped on a pair of rubber gloves from the first aid kit before pouring some peroxide onto my knee and then dabbing it with the gauze.

"My car broke down about a mile away, and I walked the rest of the way. My heel caught in a crack in the asphalt on my way here, and I fell." I blew out a breath as he covered it with what he explained was an antibacterial spray. He was unusually gentle, and then I remembered he had a little girl. The reason that I was actually here. "You keep a first aid kit at your office?"

I was raised in a home where you brushed things off. My father was big on duct tape instead of bandages.

We certainly didn't keep a medical supply kit at home or at work.

"Yes." He held my ankle with one hand and inspected the wound before applying a layer of Neosporin and covering it with a large bandage. "You never know when you're going to interview someone, and they're going to trip and fall on their way in."

"I'm terribly sorry about all this and sincerely apologi—"

He waved me off and quickly asked, "Does this happen often?"

I chuckled, appreciating his teasing tone. This was *so* not what I'd expected. At least he wasn't angry. Regardless, I was sure he wasn't going to hire me.

"You're the first to walk through the door soaking wet and bleeding." He pulled down my pant leg and set my foot back onto the floor. "I think these pants are done, though."

I shrugged. "Great. I've lost my favorite pants, and I apparently lost the job, too."

He stood and laughed as he pulled off the gloves and dropped them in the trash can. "No, Winnie. I didn't replace you in the last hour. I thought you'd flaked on the interview, and I told Lucy that if you showed up to say that the position was filled."

"Why would I set up an interview and flake on it? What if I'd been kidnapped or murdered? You just assumed that I no-showed?" I teased as he settled in the chair on the other side of his desk so he could face me.

"I figured you're young and you met up with some friends. I wouldn't blame you. I just wouldn't hire you." He smirked.

My God. The man oozed sex appeal. The deep voice, the

green eyes that felt like they were looking straight into my soul.

The gentle touch and care.

His jaw was chiseled perfection beneath a light layer of day-old scruff.

Who the hell is this guy?

So, being an author, these were the traits I always included in my heroes.

Because I wrote fiction.

But this guy—he appeared to be what book boyfriend dreams were made of.

"I'm young?" I asked, feigning irritation.

He held his hands up in defense. "Your aunt told me that you graduated from college not that long ago. I just assumed you'd found something more exciting to do than go interview for a part-time nanny position."

"First off, I graduated from college over two years ago. I'm not some co-ed party girl. My father always jokes that I was born a forty-year-old woman," I said with a laugh. "So I assure you, I'm not going to be off partying. I take my responsibilities seriously. But the car breaking down was unexpected. It got me all the way here from Chicago, and then it decided to die on me when I was only a mile from town."

He studied me for a long moment and then nodded. "Fair enough. So, tell me what your experience is with children? Your aunt Edith said that you're great with kids."

"Ahh… they were both singing my praises, weren't they?" I asked as I thought over how I could best answer the question.

"They were. And you're clearly deflecting. Just give it to me straight. Do you have experience with kids?"

Damn. The guy was good at reading people.

"I haven't been a nanny before, per se."

"'Per se'?" He raised a brow, the move so sexy I shifted in my seat, pulling the blanket around myself a bit tighter.

"I like kids." I shrugged.

He laughed. "All right. Did you grow up in a large family? Do you have a lot of siblings? Nieces and nephews?"

"I'm an only child." I cleared my throat. "No nieces and nephews."

He leaned back in his chair and crossed his arms over his chest. "So you have zero experience with children?"

"No. I just don't have siblings or nieces and nephews."

"Nor have you been a nanny before." He shook his head. "Why would Edith tell me you were great with children?"

"Because I love children. I just haven't been around them all that much." I shrugged. "But my ex-husband has the mentality of a toddler, so I have experience with grown men who behave like children."

Loud laughter bellowed from him. "I'm sure that took some patience."

"You have no idea." I shrugged. "Listen, Mr. Chadwick—"

"You can call me Archer. But let me be straight with you. I don't think this is going to be a good fit," he said, and my heart sank. "I can't hire someone with no experience."

I needed this job.

I could do this job.

I just had to convince him that I was qualified.

3

Archer

The woman had tenacity, I'd give her that. She'd walked in the pouring rain, even after ripping her pants and with a large gash on her knee. But even though I felt bad for her, she had zero experience with kids, and I couldn't hire her just because her ex-husband was a man-child.

"Listen," she said, just as a knock on the door had us both pausing.

"I'll be wrapping things up shortly, Lucy," I called out.

The door sprang open, and my cousin Bridger waltzed in like he owned the place. "We've got lunch plans."

I looked down at my watch and gaped at him. "In an hour and a half."

"Well, I called to see how the interview went, and Lucy told me that you were getting a late start, and I was visiting Emilia at the Vintage Rose, so I thought I'd come meet the new nanny." He dropped into the chair beside Winnie.

Emilia was Bridger's better half, and she owned an interior design firm, but she also ran her family's flower shop, just a few doors down from my office.

"Dude. We're in the middle of an interview here," I hissed.

"*Dude.* Melody is my girl, and I need to meet whoever you hire. You can't be trusted after your last pick."

Winnie stood up and sighed. "Well, isn't this interview over? You've already decided that you aren't hiring me, right?"

Was her bottom lip quivering?

"That's harsh." Bridger gave me a look before turning his attention to where Winnie had just tossed the blanket on the chair. "Geez, is that blood on your pants? My God, what the hell happened to you?"

"You know what? " She threw her hands in the air and turned her attention to me. "Let me tell you why I'm more than qualified for this job and why you're missing out big!"

Now she was leaning over my desk. I couldn't help but notice the way her wet cream blouse clung to her chest, accenting the two hard peaks poking through her bra. She was stunning, with her long brown hair falling all around her shoulders as her honey-brown eyes found mine. Normally, this sort of aggression would've pissed me off, but instead I found myself intrigued.

"Ah… I came at the perfect time," Bridger said under his breath, though we both clearly heard him.

"First off, my car broke down in a rainstorm, yet here I am. I didn't throw in the towel, find a phone, and call and reschedule. I was determined to get here, today, because I want this job."

"And that's reason to hire you, even if you have zero qualifications?"

"Zero qualifications and zero experience are two very different things. You only asked my experience with children, not what my qualifications are," she hissed. "I don't have siblings, which doesn't make me unqualified. Your daughter is also an only child, so clearly, she and I already have something in common. And we were both raised by a single dad." She paused and blew out a breath. "Yes, my aunt and uncle told me you're raising Melody on your own, so I know this bit of information, even if you didn't bother telling me anything before deciding I was unqualified."

Bridger leaned forward and grabbed the apple sitting on my desk and took a bite, causing us both to turn and look at him, before he directed his attention to Winnie. "Continue. So far, I'm on your side," he said.

This fucking guy.

"My point is, if I broke down in a rainstorm with your daughter in my car, I wouldn't fall apart and give up. I would do whatever it took to get her where we needed to be. I'm quick on my feet." She held her hand up when I started to interrupt. "I've volunteered at the nursing home near my apartment in Chicago for years, so I have experience with caring for people, just not children. I have a degree in English literature and a minor in psychology, which means I love to read and I understand the value of reading to children. I graduated top of my class, which means that I'm driven and determined to be the best at whatever I do. So, you should be so lucky to hire me because I will be the best nanny Melody has ever had."

"I mean, she makes a good point, and the bar is certainly not high in that department," Bridger said, and I flipped him the bird.

"Bridger, zip it. Winnie, can you please sit down and let me have my say now."

She shrugged before dropping down in the chair beside my cousin.

"I didn't mean to offend you. My daughter is my whole world. I just want to make sure I'm hiring someone who can handle the responsibility of caring for a child, because work is getting busier than ever, and there will be times when I'm not able to be around. That would make you the primary caregiver." I sighed before continuing. "This means cooking for her, bathing her, driving her—and you clearly don't have a reliable vehicle."

"I've been cooking for my father and myself since I was eight years old, and I'm a damn good cook. I bathe people at the nursing home, and I assure you, bathing an elderly person is not easier than bathing a child." She tipped her chin up. "And I can't help that my car is old and unreliable; however, I'm saving up for a new car now. I can ask my aunt and uncle if I can use their car when I need to drive Melody. I was told that the school was close to the house, and I didn't realize a lot of driving would be involved."

"Pfft. Your last nanny didn't even drive Melody, nor could she walk her anywhere, since she barely got off the damn recliner," Bridger said before chucking the apple core into the garbage can like he was a professional basketball player.

"Bridger." I pinched the middle of my nose. "Can you please stay out of this. I'm trying to do things differently this time."

He just smirked like the whole thing was hilarious. "Well, let me just say that I have more cars than I need, so Winnie, I'll drop a car off at the house for you to use when you drive Melody. Sound good?"

Her mouth hung open, probably wondering if he was serious.

Turning to my cousin, I rolled my eyes. "Are you done now?"

"I am. Hire the girl. She went through hell to be here. That already trumps your last hire." He stood and smirked at me before turning his attention back to Winnie. "And we've got a spot for you on the plane, so plan on coming to Paris for my brother's wedding in a few weeks. We want the big guy to have some fun, so having help will make that a hell of a lot easier on him. See you at the Honey Biscuit Café at noon, Archie."

Did he seriously just tell her she got the job and that she's coming to Paris?

Winnie was still gaping at the door when he pulled it closed after he'd walked out, and then she turned to me. "At least one of you thinks I'm qualified."

"I'm sorry if I insinuated that you weren't."

"You didn't insinuate it—you actually said that it wasn't going to work." She looked like she was trying to hide her smile. "Listen, Archer, I really want this job. I promise you, I will take the best care of your little girl. I'm extremely reliable and capable, and if you want to do a trial run, I'm happy to do that."

I scrubbed a hand over my face. "All right, let's try it out for two weeks, and if it's going well, we can make it permanent. It's hourly pay, which I'm happy to discuss, and free room and board is included, as long as your hours are flexible."

"My hours are very flexible," she said. "I'm an author, and I can write when Melody is at school and in the evenings. I can be available whenever you need me."

This did seem like a perfect solution.

"You're an author?"

"Correct. I'm still pretty new to this profession, but I'm having fun with it."

"Good for you. And you're okay with making meals if I don't

get home in time for dinner, or occasionally breakfast?"

"I'd actually prefer to do the cooking, especially if you're offering to feed me." She chuckled. "I took cooking classes for a few months when I did a summer abroad in France. I promise you, I'm a good cook."

"Wow. Seems like you know how to do just about anything," I said, pushing to my feet.

"Well, aside from walking in the rain without falling." She shrugged as she moved to stand. She extended her hand. "Thank you for the opportunity. When do I start?"

I chuckled. Did she think I was going to just leave her here when we both knew she didn't have a working car?

"How about we go jump your car, get the thing running, and then you can meet me at my house after I pick Melody up from school this afternoon, and you can meet her and see the casita, and make sure it'll work for you. It's not a huge space, but it's got its own bedroom and bathroom, and you'd have access to the kitchen and laundry room in the main house."

"Thank you," she said, her voice quieter now, as if she was surprised by my words.

I led her out of my office.

She carried the blanket with her and handed it to Lucy. "Thank you for letting me use this."

"Of course. Bridger said things went well?" Lucy asked, and I had to laugh.

"Next time, how about we don't let the guy barge into my office during an interview."

"Have you ever tried to stop your cousin from doing something?" She pursed her lips. "I asked him to wait, and he just chuckled and walked right past me."

"Sounds like Bridger," I said, trying not to laugh because the dude was an asshole, but I loved him. "I'm going to give Winnie a ride to her car, and then meet my pain-in-the-ass cousin for lunch. I'll be back in a bit."

"See you soon. Bye, Winnie," Lucy said.

"Thanks again." Winnie waved before following me to my truck as I pulled the door open.

"Thank you," she said, her voice quiet again.

I pushed the door closed and made my way to the driver's side. Once I was in and buckled up, I glanced over at her. "Where'd you leave the car?"

She directed me to River Bend Drive, where I saw the Mustang parked on the side of the road up ahead. The rain had finally stopped, and I pulled up in front of her car, so our engines were facing one another.

It surprised me when she got out of the truck at the same time I did, and we both met between the vehicles, holding our own jumper cables.

"I'm impressed. You carry a set with you?"

"I do. I told you that I'm more than capable of handling different situations." She chuckled as she moved forward and popped her hood, and I did the same. She started attaching the wires, which again caught me off guard.

She not only carries them but also knows how to use them.

I must not have hidden my surprise very well, because after she'd connected the wires to my car, the corners of her lips turned up when she looked at me.

"You don't think a woman knows how to jump a car?"

"No. Of course I do. I guess I just didn't expect you to do it so confidently." I laughed. "Maybe it's the bow in your hair and the all-white angelic outfit that's throwing me off."

She rolled her eyes. "Hey, this was my good luck interview

outfit before I destroyed it by falling down. And get used to the bows… They're a staple for me. They give a little something, don't you think?"

I shook my head and tried to hide my smile as I jumped in my truck and started it up. I got out, and we both stood there staring at the jumper cables as if we could will them to work.

"My dad owns a mechanic shop, so I grew up around cars."

"That explains the vintage Mustang," I said as I moved to walk around her car. I whistled. "She's a beaut."

"Right? I saved up for years for this car. Unfortunately, she's seen better days as far as reliability goes. But she's easy on the eyes."

She wasn't the only one.

Get your mind out of the gutter, asshole. She's far too young for you, and she just interviewed to be your daughter's nanny, for fuck's sake.

"We'll get her up and running, and then my cousin offered you one of his cars to use while you're driving Melody."

She nodded. "What's Melody like?"

"She's the best. Sweet and strong all at the same time. She's got a huge heart, feels everything. She's creative and loves to paint and draw. She sings and dances and enjoys playing outside. She's taking riding lessons from my brother's girlfriend, and she's obsessed with horses. She loves big, and she's very tenderhearted, which always worries me," I said, wondering if I'd overshared.

"I think she sounds amazing. I can't wait to meet her. My aunt and uncle adore her." She moved to the side of her car before climbing inside and starting it up.

It roared to life, and I removed the cables from both of our vehicles before handing them to her.

"How about you meet me at my house after I pick Melody up

from school. You can meet Melody, take a look at the casita, and we'll go from there."

"Great. Text me your address. And I'll have time to get cleaned up." She smiled up at me.

"Sounds like a plan."

"I think this is going to be a great fit, Archer." She slid the seat belt across her body, and I nodded.

"I hope so. See you soon."

As I climbed into my truck, I glanced in my rearview mirror, getting one more glimpse of her before she drove past me and waved.

She'd impressed the hell out of me.

She was more than qualified, and we both knew it.

But now there was a bigger issue I was concerned about.

How the hell would I survive having this gorgeous woman living in my house?

4

Winnie

When I pulled up to his house, I took a moment to take it in. It was stunning. The single-story ranch-style home sat on a corner lot, right on the river, with the perfect mix of water and mountain views.

The front yard was massive, with plush green grass and large trees. A paved walkway led to the front door of the house, which was a mix of stone and siding.

The air was cool when I stepped out of the car, but coming from Chicago, I was used to cold weather. And it was only fall, so I knew the winters here would get much colder than it was right now. I made my way to the front door, and just as my knuckles were about to knock against the dark wood door, it swung open.

"Hi, Winnie. I'm Melody," the little girl said, and I couldn't help but smile at the cutest little thing standing in front of me. Large dark eyes flanked with the longest black lashes, and two little brown buns on the top of her head, along with the sweetest smile on her face.

I bent down to get eye level with her. "Hi, Melody, it's so nice to meet you."

She threw herself into my arms. "I think we're going to be besties for sure."

I chuckled as a deep voice startled us both. "What did I tell you about opening the door when I'm not with you?"

I pushed to stand as Archer scooped her up.

"But it's Winnie, Daddy. She's my new nanny, and I can open the door for my best friend, right?"

He blew out a frustrated breath. "Like I said. She loves big."

"I can see that."

"Come on in," he said as I followed him through the gorgeous home.

It wasn't what I'd expected. He was a single guy, so I figured it would be less—homey.

But this place looked like it could be straight out of an interior design magazine.

Wide-planked wood floors ran throughout the space, its walls a warm mix of taupe and gray. We stepped into the massive kitchen, and I gasped. I was a woman who enjoyed cooking, and this kitchen was an absolute chef's dream. The cabinets were white oak with a large black island in the center, and white stone counters covered every surface. The appliances were top of the line, and it smelled heavenly in here. I turned slowly as I took in the wall of windows and French doors along the back of the house.

The river flowed in the distance, looking like an actual painting.

"Wow. The river view with the mountains in the back is breathtaking."

"Yeppers. Daddy built this place for me and him to grows up in, right, Daddy?" Melody beamed up at her father like the man set the sun.

I knew the look.

It was the way I looked at my father.

He chuckled. "I purchased the land before Melody was even born. I knew it would be a good spot to build on. We finished construction before she even started walking. She took her first steps right here in this kitchen, probably trying to sneak a cookie."

Her head tipped back in a full-bodied laugh as he set her back down on her feet. "I do love my cookies, right, Daddy?"

"You sure do, angel face."

These two were something. It was clear that they adored one another.

"Let's show Winnie the casita and see if she thinks it will work for her," Archer said as he motioned for me to follow. Walking behind him gave me the perfect opportunity to take him in. He was wearing a black sweater tonight, with dark jeans. He was tall, and the man just had this presence about him.

"Winnie, you're very pretty. And I love the bow in your hair. I like bows, too." Melody slipped her hand into mine as we walked to the far side of the house.

She was a little bundle of sweetness, and I knew watching over her would be great fun.

"Thank you. I've always loved bows." I chuckled just as Archer pushed the door open, and my eyes widened.

"Did you decorate this place?" I asked as I stepped inside the cutest room I'd ever seen. Wood flooring, with big windows looking out at the river. Cotton-white roman shades decorated the windows. We moved to the bathroom, which was equally spectacular. Small but very quaint, with the cutest claw-foot tub with antique gold feet and a little chandelier hanging above it.

I couldn't get over how adorable it was.

"No. When I built the place, my mom helped me pick all the finishes in the main house. My cousin Bridger's girlfriend, Emilia, is an interior designer, and she just did a refresh on the casita for me last month. So, I've had a lot of help."

"Well, it's stunning. This will definitely work." I immediately thought about what a beautiful space this would be to write in. I could sit out on the patio looking at the river. It didn't get any better.

"Obviously you'll have full access to the kitchen any time you need it, since there's a door attached to the house. But you also have your own entrance to come and go as you please when you don't want to use the interior door." He shoved his hands in his pockets, and I noted the two doors. It was a nice touch.

Melody clapped her hands together. "Can Winnie eat dinner with us tonight, Daddy?"

His green gaze locked with mine, and I tried to place the color. They were this deep emerald green with pops of caramel and gold. "I made some chili and cornbread, if you'd like to stay for dinner?"

"I'd love that. I knew it smelled good when I walked in," I said with a laugh.

We spent the next two hours eating and chatting, and were now enjoying dessert. Melody told me all about her teacher and her classmates. She was adorable. She had this infectious laugh and sweet disposition. She talked about all of her uncles and aunts and asked repeatedly if I could come to Paris with them.

I was surprised when Archer's cousin had extended the invitation as well, since I didn't know that traveling to Paris would come with the job.

I'd certainly never turn that down. It was one of my favorite places in the world.

"Do you have a boyfriend, Winnie?" Melody asked as she scooped a bite of apple pie into her mouth.

"Melody, that's not something you need to be asking," Archer said.

"How come? Tommy says I'm his girlfriend."

"You're far too young to be anyone's girlfriend," Archer grumped.

I chuckled. "Well, Tommy has great taste."

"Don't encourage this." He shook his head and laughed.

"It's innocent. She's five."

"He's really just my good friend, but he likes to call me his special girlfriend."

"I've got my eye on that kid," he said as the corners of his lips turned up in a mischievous smile.

"You don't gots a boyfriend?" she asked me again, and Archer shot her a look that only made her head tip back in a fit of giggles.

"I do not. I went through a breakup a while ago, and I like being single," I said, trying not to give her all the gory details.

By "breakup," I meant "divorce."

I'd married my high school sweetheart when I was far too young.

We completely outgrew one another.

And he hadn't taken the divorce well, so I'd basically left

with my car, my clothes, and my dignity.

He'd kept our apartment and all the furniture, and he'd managed to spend the advance checks from my publisher for the first two books I'd released shortly after they'd hit our account.

But I was free now, and I could rebuild both my bank account and my life.

"Daddy likes being single, too. He doesn't go on no dates," she said as ice cream dribbled down her chin. I instinctually reached for my napkin and wiped it away, just as Archer did the same thing.

My gaze caught his, and he smiled.

And holy hotness, when Archer Chadwick smiled at me—my entire body reacted.

When was the last time my body had reacted to anyone?

Years, maybe?

"Doesn't go on *any* dates," he said. The way he corrected her was gentle and sweet.

"Right." Melody's head fell back with a laugh. "That's what I said, Daddy."

"And that's not completely true. I've been on plenty of dates. Plus, I've got my favorite girl right here. I don't need anyone else." He winked at his daughter.

"That's 'cause I've gots the best daddy around," Melody said as her father got up and cleared our dessert plates from the table. I'd already attempted to do the dishes after dinner, but I'd been turned down. He'd made a joke about me not being on the clock tonight. "Do you gots a good daddy, Winnie?"

"I have an amazing father. He's my favorite person in the world," I said without hesitation.

"Do you gots a good mama, too?"

I noted the way Archer's shoulders tensed at the question

from where he stood at the sink. So maybe I was staring a little—the man was very captivating in that quiet, understated sort of way.

"I don't really know my mom. She left when I was five," I answered honestly. I figured honesty was an important part of being a nanny, right? And I was a straight shooter, so I'd tell her the truth. I didn't know their situation, as my aunt and uncle hadn't mentioned Melody's mother, only that he was raising her on his own. I wondered if I'd be interacting with her on weekends or just occasionally.

Melody gasped, and her hands came over her mouth. Maybe I'd been too forthcoming.

Was there a rule to how you shared your own abandonment?

"Daddy. Winnie doesn't know her mama, either," she whispered, as if we were sharing something sinister.

Archer dried his hands with a towel and came back to the table. He didn't take his seat; instead he bent down and faced his daughter, taking his hands in hers. The act was so sweet, it made my heart ache.

"I heard that. And you remember what we've talked about. That it doesn't matter how many parents you have, just that you're surrounded by love, right?" The concern in his voice was impossible to miss.

"Justine Schwartz said that it does matter if you don't have a mama," she said, eyes wide as she looked up at her father. "She said it means that I'm not special like her. 'Cause she gots two parents that love her."

I noted the way his jaw tensed, and the way the vein strained against his neck, but he kept his features calm and cool. "Justine is a child. She doesn't know what she's talking about, so I would not listen to that nonsense, okay?"

"Well, my best friend Winnie is very special, and she only has a daddy like me."

Kids could be cruel. I'd lived it. I'd survived my fair share of comments and questions about only having a dad attend every school event over the years.

"You know what I've learned?" I said, surprised that I was injecting myself into this father-daughter moment, as that usually wasn't my style. But she'd mentioned me, and I had experience with this.

"What did you learn, Winnie?" Melody turned and smiled at me, eyebrows cinched together with curiosity.

"I learned that having a rock star dad was the best thing ever. My dad and I talk about everything. We've always been close, just like you and your daddy. And some people don't have that with either of their parents. So we're lucky to have someone who loves us that big, you know?"

She nodded, flashing me her little white teeth. "We're lucky, Winnie. And now I'm lucky that you're going to live with us."

"I feel like the lucky one." I shrugged as I stood up. "I should probably get going."

Melody jumped up and gave me a hug, and Archer told her to go get her jammies out and he'd meet her in the bathroom for bath time.

He walked me to the door.

"Sorry, that got a little heavy," he said, scratching the back of his neck. "She's never talked like that before."

"That's all right. I want her to feel comfortable with me. So I'm guessing we're giving this a shot, right?" I said with a laugh. "Or is this still going to be a trial basis?"

"Yeah. Let's do it. Are you comfortable with the living conditions?" he asked before quickly adding, "That interior door to the house locks, so you'll have complete privacy."

"I'm not worried about you sneaking into my room in the middle of the night, Archer," I teased, but I realized that it probably sounded flirty. "Oh my gosh. That's not what I meant."

He chuckled. "It's fine. There will be no sneaking into anyone's room, I assure you."

Ugh. I'd just made this so awkward.

"Of course. So when should I plan on moving in and starting?"

"The sooner the better for me, so whatever works for you."

"Okay. How about I start immediately. What time do you take Melody to school?"

"Eight a.m."

"I'll be here at seven a.m. tomorrow and observe your morning routine, and go with you to take her to school so I can get the hang of everything. I can get my things moved into the casita while she's at school."

"That would be great. Thank you."

"Sure. See you tomorrow. Thanks for dinner," I said.

He nodded. "See you tomorrow."

I walked to my car and slipped inside, noting that he was still standing at the door, as if he was waiting to make sure my car started. Or maybe I was making that up in my head, and he was just staring at the moon or something more exciting.

I blew out a breath and pulled out of the driveway, and I couldn't help the smile that spread across my face.

Because this was a fresh start.

And I was ready for it.

5

Archer

The doorbell woke me from a sound sleep, and I sat up in bed. Fuck.

My alarm hadn't gone off, and I'd overslept.

I had a full day of meetings, and I couldn't afford to be late. Not to mention Mrs. Groucher didn't take kindly to being late, and I didn't have time for a lecture on my lack of responsible parenting this morning.

I tugged on my sweatpants and heard Melody shouting from her bedroom, asking who was here.

"My alarm didn't go off. Get up, angel face. We need to get moving." I jogged to the front door and tugged it open.

Winnie stood on the other side wearing a white sweater, some baggy faded jeans, and cowboy boots. Her eyes scanned my chest, and I remembered I hadn't pulled on a tee.

"Sorry, I uh—we overslept. Come in." I stepped back as she walked past me. "I need to grab a shower, and get Melody dressed, and make breakfast. So you can chill on the couch or go bring your stuff into the casita if you want."

She chuckled. "Relax. I'm the nanny, remember? You don't need to entertain me. How about you go shower, and I get Melody dressed for school and make breakfast?"

It hit me at that moment that I hadn't had a nanny who actually helped me with anything before now.

"Really?" I shrugged. "Yeah, that would be great."

"Winnie? Is that you?" Melody called out from her room.

"It's me. And I'm coming to get you ready for school, and we're going to make a delicious breakfast together."

And just like that, I made my way to my bathroom and shut the door. I took my time in the shower for the first time in a while. I was always hustling and in a hurry, but the fact that I didn't need to get Melody dressed this morning or make breakfast meant I didn't need to rush.

I dried off and slipped on some dark jeans and a dress shirt before combing my hair and getting myself ready.

When I stepped out into the hallway, I heard Melody giggling and the sound of pots and pans being moved around. Country music played softly in the background on Alexa, and the smell of bacon flooded my senses as I came around the corner.

"Daddy!" Melody ran over to me. "Good mornin', handsome."

I chuckled and scooped her up. "Good morning, angel face. How'd you sleep?"

"I had all the dreams, Daddy."

I set her back down, noting that her hair was braided in a way I'd never be able to manage. She had a bow at the end of her braid that matched one Winnie was wearing. She had her back to me as she stood at the stove, cooking eggs and bacon. She glanced over her shoulder and smiled. "I hope it's okay that I grabbed what was in the fridge to make breakfast?"

"Yeah, of course. We don't usually get this fancy of a breakfast unless it's the weekend." I walked over to where she'd made a fresh pot of coffee.

Damn. I could get used to this. I always had to make Mrs. Dowden's coffee for her and bring it to her.

My family was right. I needed help, and this was much better than the situation I'd been in for the past two years.

Winnie and I had discussed her salary, which she seemed very pleased with. But she'd agreed to be flexible with her hours, and I needed that right now. Room and board was also included, and at the moment I was very grateful that she was going to be living here at the house.

It would make life much more manageable on mornings like this.

I poured myself a cup and held up the coffee pot, offering to top her off, and she nodded. After I filled her coffee mug, I pulled out some plates from the cupboard and asked Melody to set some forks and napkins on the table.

The three of us sat down after Winnie had plated our food, and I groaned when I took the first bite, as did my daughter.

"Daddy, Winnie's eggs don't taste like yours. These are so yummy."

Winnie had just taken a sip of coffee, and she coughed over her laughter before dabbing her mouth with her napkin. The smell of lavender surrounded me as she sat in the chair beside me.

This was also a change for me.

Having a beautiful woman in my home was slightly overwhelming in a way I hadn't expected.

I'd shake it off because this was a good fit.

She was exactly what we needed.

"Thanks," I grumped, and they both laughed some more. "But I agree. This is delicious. You said you took some cooking classes abroad?"

"Yes. I spent a summer in Paris during college, and I took a few classes while I was there. I've always loved to cook." She reached for a strip of bacon.

"Can Winnie come with us to Paris?" Melody asked for the second time in two days. Between my daughter and Bridger, they were putting both of us on the spot. "I'm the flower girl in my uncle and aunt's wedding."

"If she would like to come with us, she's more than welcome. Let's see how the first few days go. We don't want to scare her off." I chuckled. "Did Winnie tell you that she's a writer?"

Melody's eyes grew wide. "I love to write, too, Winnie. Do you write books or letters?"

"I write books. I'm working on a new one now." She shrugged, as if it was no big deal.

"That's impressive," I said. "This should work out well because you'll have your hours free to write while Melody's at school."

"Yeah, that sounds like the perfect schedule. And I also write a lot in the evenings before bed," she said.

We went over the schedule, and I told her that Melody had lessons today with my brother's fiancée, Wren, who had a horseback riding school for kids. They could walk there from school and then walk home, since we lived close to everything. So there was no need to drive today, though Bridger had already texted to say that he'd have a car dropped off this morning. That would come in handy when it got colder outside.

We finished up breakfast, and Winnie loaded the dishes in the dishwasher while I got Melody's lunch in her backpack and grabbed her jacket.

We got into my truck because I'd be going to work after we dropped Melody at school. I introduced Winnie to Mrs. Groucher, who acted completely unimpressed to meet her. We'd had a late start getting out of the house, so the bell rang shortly after we'd arrived, and we were hurried out the door after a quick goodbye to Melody.

"Wow, her teacher is a real delight," Winnie said.

I laughed. "Yeah, she taught me and my brother and all of my cousins. She's been the kindergarten teacher here since the beginning of time."

She snorted as we made our way to the parking lot.

"All right, well, I'll plan to be here early for pickup, and then I'll take Melody to her horseback riding lessons. Just text me that address so I can save it in my phone."

"That sounds great." I shoved my hands in my pockets. "I can drop you by the house on my way to the office?"

"That's all right. It's nice outside, so I can walk, and that way I'll get my bearings for the area."

"Sounds good." I glanced down at my phone to see a text from my cousin. "Bridger just texted to say that he dropped a car in the driveway. The keys are under the mat on the driver's side. There's an extra car seat in the front closet for Melody if for any reason you need to go anywhere in the car. Just text me so I'll know where you are."

"You got it. Thank you. I'll see you later," she said, holding up a hand as she started walking.

I climbed in my truck and glanced down at the endless group chat with my brother and cousins.

Rafe: *I heard Archie hired the new nanny.*

Me: *Bridger, I thought you were a man of few words. When did you get so gossipy.*

Bridger: *Fuck off. Wasn't me, dude.*

Rafe: *I had breakfast at the Honey Biscuit Café this morning. Oscar told me you hired his niece.*

Easton: *This is great news. What's she like?*

Bridger: *He likes her. <winky face emoji>*

Me: *Fuck off. I don't like her.*

Axel: *You hired her to take care of Melody, and you don't like her?*

Me: *Shit. No. I like her, but not the way he insinuated. And she's young.*

Clark: *So you like her, but you don't like her? <laughing face emoji>*

Rafe: *How young could she be if she's qualified to be a nanny?*

Me: *She's 24.*

Axel: *For fuck's sake, you're acting like you hired a teenager. News flash… 24-year-olds are adults.*

Easton: *I'm just happy you hired someone who can actually get around and take care of Melody.*

Bridger: *She walked her ass all the way to his office after her car broke down in the rain, and he almost didn't hire her. I had to step in.*

Clark: *Seriously?*

Me: *I didn't know if she was qualified. She proved she was.*

Easton: *I mean, the fact that she can make a sandwich for Melody makes her more qualified than your last nanny.*

Me: *She doesn't have experience with kids, so I wasn't sure that she could handle it.*

Rafe: *I didn't have experience with kids before Melody came along, and you let me watch her.*

Me: *You're family.*

Axel: *So what happened?*

Me: *She made a good argument and convinced me that she was the right person for the job.*

Clark: *I'm glad you came to your senses during the interview.*

Bridger: *He didn't. I showed up when he was sending her out the door. I got involved. You're welcome.*

Axel: *How did you even know she was qualified if you'd just walked in?*

Bridger: *Because she looked like she'd fought a bear to get there. Clearly, she wanted the job, which is more than I can say for Mrs. Dowden.*

Rafe: *So when does she start?*

Me: *She started this morning.*

Easton: *That was a quick turnaround. You went from not hiring her, to hiring her, and she's already working today?*

Axel: *When is she moving in?*

Me: *Also today.*

Bridger: *He likes her. He's nervous to have her in his home, that's why he was hesitant.*

Me: *Fuck off. That's not the reason that I was hesitant.*

Clark: *But she's qualified, right?*

Bridger: *She's got a college degree, and she can figure out what to do when she breaks down in the middle of a rainstorm. She also doesn't take Archie's shit. She's more than qualified.*

Rafe: *Let me get this straight. You had a nanny who barely stayed awake during the day, and you were fine having her in your home. Now you have a woman who is clearly overqualified, and very capable, and you're nervous to have her in your home?*

Bridger: *You want the truth?*

Me: *No.*

Rafe: *Yes.*

Clark: *Please.*

Easton: *Give it to us.*

Axel: *Absolutely.*

Bridger: *She's hot. He's horny. It's a terrifying combination.*

Me: *<middle finger emoji>*

Me: *I didn't notice her looks. She's my fucking nanny.*

Easton: *So you can't tell us if she's hot?*

Me: *I haven't noticed.*

Bridger: *You've got two eyes. You definitely noticed.*

Me: *I'm done with this conversation. Axel, let Wren know that Winnie will be bringing Melody to her riding lesson today after school.*

Axel: *Winnie. Good name.*

Rafe: *I love Winnie the Pooh. Speaking of Poo, I tried the turbo clean on the new toilet and let's just say it's equal parts fabulous and terrifying.*

Bridger: *I don't fuck with the turbo setting.*

Easton: *He has a sensitive ass.*

Axel: *I'll let Wren know Winnie's coming today.*

Clark: *That's what she said. <winky face emoji> Sorry. Couldn't resist.*

Rafe: *Just wait till the new nanny sits on your fancy shitter. She'll never want to leave.*

I set my phone down and chuckled. Rafe had introduced us to the world's best toilet several months ago, and I couldn't deny that it had changed the whole bathroom experience for me. But we spent far too much time talking about the shitter.

My phone vibrated, and I rolled my eyes, thinking it was the group text again, but instead I saw Winnie's name on the screen. I'd saved her number in my phone last night and asked her to do the same.

Winnie: *Hey, it's Winnie.*

Me: *Yep. I've got you saved in my phone.*

Winnie: *Okay, just making sure you knew who it was.*

Winnie: *How do you feel about slow cookers?*

Me: *In general? As a product?*

Winnie: *<head exploding emoji>*

Winnie: *As a form of cooking.*

Me: *Never tried one. I always thought they were weird in concept.*

Winnie: *Weird in concept?*

Me: *You asked. <laughing face emoji>*

Winnie: *Well, I have one that I just unpacked, and since I'm taking Melody to riding lessons, I thought it might be a good idea to get dinner prepped ahead of time so it's ready when everyone gets home.*

Me: *Sure. That sounds great. I've got an account in my name at the Green Basket if you want to grab groceries for the next few days.*

Winnie: *Got it. I'll head over there now.*

Me: *Thank you. Be careful of the owners' son, Josh. He's a tool.*

Winnie: *Worried about me already, boss? <laughing face emoji>*

Me: *Just need to make sure you don't run away with the grocery store douchebag.*

Winnie: *You need not worry. I've sworn off all men at the moment. Douchebags in particular. <winky face emoji>*

I set my phone down, but for whatever reason, I couldn't wipe the smile from my face.

6

Winnie

It had been one week since I'd started working for Archer Chadwick.

I'd gotten a lot of writing done during the day while Melody was at school, and I enjoyed my time with her when I'd pick her up. She and I had a ton of fun when we were together, and she'd helped me make dinners this week. I'd taught her some of my tricks of the trade.

Archer was appreciative of the meals I'd prepared this week, yet he always remained very professional around me. As soon as we'd finish eating, he'd tell Melody to say good night to me, which was my cue to leave. We didn't spend any time together when she wasn't around, which was probably very normal for a nanny. This was my first time in a gig like this, so I was following his lead.

I'd make breakfast, and he'd thank me, and then he'd take her to school, and I'd start writing. He wanted that time with his little girl, and I respected that. And then I'd pick her up from school and take her to her riding lessons, or dance class, and we'd come home and get homework done before we'd start dinner.

I'd even made my first friend in Rosewood River.

Wren Waterstone was Melody's riding instructor, and we'd hit it off immediately. Melody went over to the ranch twice a week, and I loved hanging out and watching her.

Archer had asked me last night if I was certain it was okay if I joined them in Paris, and of course I was more than okay with it.

I mean, it's Paris. Who wouldn't be okay with it?

So Wren had invited me today to the Honey Biscuit Café, which my aunt and uncle owned, to join her and her friends for what they called a "boozy book brunch." She wanted me to meet them, as they were all going to Paris for Archer's cousin Rafe and his fiancée Lulu's wedding.

Lulu was in this group, and she was obviously the bride, and the other women were all going as guests.

I was going as the nanny.

But it would still be nice to know them before we traveled together.

She'd asked if I was a reader, and I'd shared that I was an avid reader. She'd inquired about my writing, since obviously Archer had mentioned it to his brother. I'd told her that I was working on a new book, but I was fairly private about my career as a romance author, mostly because it was still new and I was still finding my footing with it, even though the first two books that had released had been more successful than I'd ever imagined.

Thank you, BookTok.

I pulled the door open, and my aunt Edith came walking

over and opened her arms before I stepped in for a hug. My aunt and uncle had always been great to me, as my dad and his brother had always been very close. They visited us a couple of times a year, and I'd always looked forward to seeing them.

"It's so good to see that beautiful face," Aunt Edith said.

"Now she's so busy with her new job and working on her book, we'll barely see her," Uncle Oscar grouched as he came around the corner and pulled me into a bear hug.

"I saw you both yesterday," I said, laughing, because I'd come by to have lunch with them.

"Well, we know if we pour on the guilt you'll keep coming around." He chuckled. "I'm happy to keep coming around."

"Is that ex-husband of yours leaving you alone?" my uncle asked, his tone more serious now.

I sighed. "Yep. The divorce is final, so there's nothing left to discuss."

"Good. I never liked him," he said.

"Stop giving her a hard time. Let her go enjoy brunch with the girls." Aunt Edith swatted him in the arm before she turned to greet some customers when they walked in.

"All right. They're in the booth in the back. It's where they always host their little club meetings," he grumped as I gave him a kiss on the cheek and made my way to the back of the restaurant.

Wren jumped up when she saw me, and she started the introductions. Wren was gorgeous with long blonde hair, and she also happened to be the eventing world champion. She was retired from competition now and lived with Archer's brother, Axel, and they were engaged to be married.

"Winnie, this is Henley. She's married to Easton." I knew Easton was one of Archer's cousins, since I'd been filled in on the family tree from Melody. She gave me a hug and squeezed my hands as if we were old friends.

"It's so great to meet you. We're absolutely thrilled that Archer found a new nanny, and that you're coming with us to Paris."

"Me too," I gushed.

"Speaking of Paris. I'm Lulu, and I'm the one getting married." She stepped out of the booth wearing a black jumpsuit. Her hair was in a loose knot at the nape of her neck as she leaned forward and gave me a hug. "We're thrilled that you're going to join us. So, meet the rest of our little boozy book club—this is Emilia."

Emilia slipped out of the booth next and hugged me as well. I knew she was Bridger's girlfriend, and she owned the flower shop, from what I'd gathered. But Archer had mentioned that she was also an interior designer, and she'd decorated the casita for him.

"Emilia, it's great to meet you. I heard you're responsible for making the casita the cutest guest room I've ever seen." I leaned forward and gave her a hug.

"Thank you. I loved working on that project. It's such a charming space, and it's got its own vibe from the main house, right?" she asked with a laugh.

"It sure does. I love it."

"And this is Eloise," Wren said as the last woman slipped out of the booth. They all started sliding back in as she smiled and gave me a hug as well.

They were a warm group.

"Nice to meet you," I said. "Melody told me that you fixed up her uncle Clark when he was broken."

The table erupted in laughter.

I'd learned that Clark was one of the best hockey players in the NHL, and Eloise was the team physical therapist.

"Something like that, yes." She smiled as she motioned for me to slide in beside Wren, and then she took the other seat beside me.

"So, Wren said that you're a big reader, but we're dying to know what you read," Emilia asked.

"I read everything, really." I shrugged, because I'd dipped my toes into a lot of genres.

"How about we cut to the chase. We've heard you're an author, and we're dying to know what you write." Lulu held her hand up as Aunt Edith dropped off a mimosa for me. They were all sipping theirs, and we quickly paused to place our orders.

Lulu rubbed her hands together as if she was waiting for an answer once my aunt stepped away.

"I actually write romance."

They all smiled.

"That's our favorite genre," Henley said.

"Okay, I have to confess…" Lulu reached for her mimosa and took a sip before continuing. "I googled you and I couldn't find any of your books. So tell us how to find you."

"I can't believe you just said that. We just met her," Henley said as she pressed her hand over her forehead.

"She lives with Archer. She's practically family. She writes romance and we read romance." Lulu shrugged. Everyone chuckled and turned to me, as if waiting for a response.

Thankfully, six plates of pancakes and eggs and French toast were set down, along with a few refills on the mimosas. It was the perfect distraction as we all dug into our food.

"Did anyone read 'The Taylor Tea' this morning?" Emilia asked.

"Yes. You're the hot news of the week, Winnie," Eloise said with a big smile on her face.

"'There's a new lady in town, and she's just been hired by Rosewood River's favorite single dad,'" Lulu said, her tone dramatic as she waggled her brows at me and glanced down to read whatever she'd pulled up on her phone. "They just added that little part in at the end, so everyone knows you're here."

"What's 'The Taylor Tea'?" I asked.

"It's this gossip column in the local newspaper that my parents own. Some people hate it. Others love it. And we've all been in there at one point or another." Emilia shrugged.

"And we don't know who writes it?" I asked before reaching for my drink and taking another sip.

"Nope. And it's not for lack of effort." Eloise shook her head and winced. "We nearly got arrested for breaking into the *Rosewood River Review* and trying to find out not that long ago."

"We escaped easily," Lulu said over a fit of laughter. "But back to the original question—how do we find your books?"

"Well, I only have two books out right now. The third is written and releasing in a few months, and I'm writing book four now. So I'm still very much a newbie author," I said, clearing my throat because for whatever reason, talking about my writing career still made me nervous.

My ex-husband had deemed me a failure, and that negative voice still found its way in my head sometimes, even after I'd achieved success.

"So how do we find the first two?" Lulu pressed.

"Lu, maybe she doesn't want you to read her books," Henley said, giving me an apologetic smile. "There's no pressure to tell us anything you aren't comfortable with."

"No. It's not a big deal. I just still get a little nervous

because it's new. I write under a pen name." I blew out a breath. "Hannah Chase."

"Shut the motherfucking front door!" Lulu whisper-hissed, keeping her voice low so no one would hear her but making no attempt to hide her surprise. Eloise and Emilia squealed, Henley gasped, and Wren stared at me with her mouth hanging open.

My gaze moved around the table, taking them in. "What am I missing?"

"We're superfans!" Lulu threw her hands in the air. "We're anxiously waiting for *Whisper Sweet Nothings* to release."

"It's Hunter's book, and I cannot wait for it," Wren said. "I just reread the first two books again. That's how obsessed I am."

"Same." Eloise used her hand to fan her face. "I cannot believe we're eating brunch with Hannah Chase."

"You don't put your face on your social media," Henley said. "We've been stalking you, and here you are at the Honey Biscuit Café?"

My mind was blown. Truly blown. I still couldn't wrap my head around the fact that people were actually reading my books.

"Are you okay?" Henley put a hand on Emilia's shoulders as she just sat there gaping at me.

"I'm speechless. I was searching your website for any upcoming events because we wanted to meet you," she said.

"Well, now I'm speechless." I chuckled. "And if you want, I'll have my publisher send you an early copy to your Kindles."

Lulu leaned forward on the table. "I'm a vault. We all are. Please, send the book. We're dying for it."

I could feel my cheeks heat. I couldn't believe they knew who I was.

This was beyond surreal.

"And that title," Henley said. "*Whisper Sweet Nothings.* I cannot even wait."

"It's perfection. And we get to read it early." Emilia fell back in the booth and shook her head with disbelief.

"I am so here for a single-dad romance with Hunter. Let's go," Lulu said, holding up her mimosa and waiting for us to join her.

"Cheers to meeting our favorite author and new book bestie," Wren said.

"I'll drink to that," Eloise squealed as we all clinked our glasses together.

I'll drink to that, too.

This fresh start was feeling better every day.

7

Archer

My cousin Bridger had chartered a private jet large enough to accommodate our entire family to fly to Paris for the wedding. He owned his own plane, but it wasn't the type of aircraft that could travel this far.

Melody had started out seated beside me and moved to sit in the seat across from me, beside Winnie, for the second half of the flight, and they'd both fallen asleep. After we'd all grabbed our bags, a car service was waiting to take us to the hotel.

Once we arrived, we made our way to where we were staying. I'd upgraded to a two-bedroom suite. This way, if I had plans in the evening, Winnie would stay with Melody, and she could put her to sleep in my room.

The level of stress that had been removed from my shoulders

in just the first two weeks with this woman was surprising, to say the least.

She'd stepped up in more ways than I could have imagined. She picked Melody up from school, and she handled homework, cooking, laundry, and taking her to her activities. I hadn't felt pulled in twenty different directions lately. When I was home from work, I was able to just spend time with my daughter. Everything around the house was taken care of.

Even more than I'd asked her to do, which surprised me.

And having her on this trip would be a game changer, because I could go out and have some adult time after I gave Melody her bath and got her ready for bed.

I struggled with giving up control, which had caught me off guard. I'd been doing this solo for such a long time that having someone consistently step up to the plate almost felt foreign to me.

Maybe I'd kept Mrs. Dowden on for so long because I'd been able to stay in control of everything.

Even though I desperately needed the help.

I'm sure there was some Freudian reasoning behind it.

But now that I had help, really good help, I realized how much I'd needed it.

I pushed the door open, and we stepped inside the room.

"Wow. I like this place, Daddy." Melody hurried over to the window to see the view of Paris down below.

"This is gorgeous," Winnie said as she glanced up at the crystal chandelier hanging over the living room area.

We were staying at the hotel where the ceremony was going to be held, which made it all very convenient.

We'd flown through the night, so we'd have the day to rest and recover before the rehearsal dinner this evening.

"How about I order some lunch while we unpack and we can get some food in our systems," I said as I walked over to grab the room service menu.

"I'm hungry, Daddy," Melody said, her voice sounding sleepy. She made her way over to the couch and curled up. Winnie grabbed the throw blanket and placed it over her.

"Rest your eyes, angel face." I handed the menu to Winnie and asked what she wanted to eat, then quickly placed the call and ordered some food.

I dropped Winnie's bag in her room, then took the luggage Melody and I had brought to our room to get us unpacked.

The food arrived shortly after, and the server placed the trays of food on the dining table.

"Should we wake her up?" Winnie asked.

"Let's let her sleep for a bit longer. She's got a long night ahead of her."

"Listen, you can just text me, and I'll take care of bath time and putting her to bed tonight," she said as she picked up her burger and took a bite. "I'll have my phone on me and will just wait here to hear from you, and I will come get her when you're ready."

I narrowed my gaze. "What? You're coming with us to the rehearsal dinner."

"Oh. I know you wanted me to attend the wedding, but I figured the rehearsal dinner was just family." She shrugged.

"The wedding is basically just family, plus a few friends, and everyone is invited to both events. It's like two weddings, which is very on par for Rafe and Lulu." I laughed.

"Lulu showed me pictures of her dress, and it's absolutely stunning. This is going to be a gorgeous wedding."

"Yeah. This city has a special meaning to them, as they lived here for a while when they were first together. But I've been warned that her family is—a lot."

She laughed. "She told me that, too."

"So you said that you're recently divorced," I asked, because I was curious as hell about it. She was fairly young to be married, so I was guessing there was a story there. "Did you have a big wedding?"

"No." She shook her head and sighed. "I married my high school boyfriend. We'd been together for years. I went to college, and he didn't. He had an issue with us doing the long-distance thing. So he showed up and proposed my junior year of college, and we eloped when I was twenty-one years old. Not my best choice."

"That's pretty young. Did you just outgrow one another?"

"Yes. We were already so different, but I think I felt almost obligated to get married when he asked, you know? Like we'd dated so long, and he was so lost after I went away to school, and he was sort of floundering, and I felt bad about that."

"So you married the dude because you had your shit together and he didn't?" I gaped at her.

"Well, when you put it that way, it sounds crazy." She chuckled. "But in a way, it's the truth. Jaden has this great family, and I really loved them, and I think I wanted it to be this fairy tale—and it just wasn't."

"What happened?"

"We truly just grew in different directions. Or maybe I continued growing and he stayed still. He was the same guy he'd been when we were in high school. But back then, me being a type A overachiever and him being a hipster, pot-smoking mellow guy was appealing to me. But when you have bills and dreams and things you want to achieve, and your partner doesn't want any of those things, or at least he doesn't want to work for those things—it gets old quickly. Probably a good reason to hold off on getting married until you're older." She let out a soft laugh. "Anyway, the deal-breaker was when I got my first book published. He didn't handle it well, and I just knew that I had to walk away if I wanted to chase my dreams."

"What did he do when your first book was published?"

"I think maybe he felt threatened by my achievements? I'm not really sure. But he told me it was a fluke that a publisher had taken a chance on me, and that I shouldn't get my hopes up, because no one would ever read my books. He thought it was a ridiculous dream, even after I'd written the book and signed with a publisher. Interestingly enough, he didn't mind spending the money that I received for the advance, all while telling me daily that I was going to fail."

"What a weak man," I said before wiping my mouth with my napkin.

"Yeah, I can't argue that. But I came to Rosewood River for a fresh start, and so far, it's been a really good change."

"I'm glad to hear that." I reached for my water and took a sip.

"How about you?" she asked, her honey-brown gaze meeting mine. "I haven't heard anything about Melody's mom. Is she in the picture at all?"

"No." I blew out a breath. I didn't talk about Scarlet much. There wasn't much to say. I would eventually tell the whole story to Melody, but for now she knew that she had a daddy who loved her more than anything in the world. "She came to town for a year to work remotely, and we started dating. We were both very career-focused and spent all our free time together. Seemed like a fairly normal love story up until then. Until it wasn't."

She studied me as if this was riveting information. "And then what? She robbed a bank? Went on the lam?"

"'Went on the lam'?" I laughed, then glanced over to see that Melody was still sleeping on the couch.

"Yeah. You know, she traded small-town living for a life of crime." The corners of her lips turned up, and it was hard not to stare at her pretty face.

She's your nanny.

She's far too young for you.

She's newly divorced.

"You're definitely an author. And by the way—the girls are all big fans of your work, apparently. We've been hearing about these books for months."

She wagged her finger at me. "Nope. You don't get to deflect with compliments. I gave you my sordid details—let me hear it, Archie."

Archie.

It was the first time she'd called me that.

"She found out she was pregnant when she was pretty far along, and when she told me, I was thrilled. It wasn't planned, but it was a child conceived from love, and I'd always known that I wanted to be a dad at some point." I cleared my throat. I could still remember the conversation. The panic in her eyes. The realization that we were on completely different pages. "She told me she did not want to be a mother. She'd had a tough childhood, and she was very career driven, which I respected, but we'd never had the conversation that probably should have been had before getting to that point."

"So what happened?" she asked, eyes wide and filled with empathy.

"She told me that we had two options. She would have the baby, and together we could give the baby up for adoption, or I could keep the baby, but she would not be involved."

"She knew what she wanted, and it's good that she gave you the option, but I'm sure it was very painful."

"It was. And there was zero hesitation on my end, because I also knew that Melody was mine, long before she'd even entered the world. The day she shared her pregnancy news was the day I became a father."

"You just knew it was your path, huh?"

"I did. And she was very determined to be the best home to our daughter while pregnant, and she left Rosewood River the day after Melody was born. Our relationship had obviously ended months earlier, when we both realized we'd be going in different directions. But I appreciated that she stayed until after she gave birth so I could be involved, and be present in the delivery room."

"And you don't keep in touch?"

"Nope. It was part of the deal. No contact. She left town to head back to New York, and we said our goodbyes. There was no drama or hurt feelings by the time Melody entered the world," I said, keeping my voice low.

Winnie's eyes welled with emotion. "Wow. I love that you knew without hesitation that you were supposed to be her dad. And you aren't resentful about her leaving?"

"No. I mean, it hurt at first, just like a normal breakup would hurt. I loved her, and she didn't want the same things that I wanted. I couldn't fault her for that. And she gave me my greatest gift, so I can't be angry about it."

"That's really incredible. People come into your life for a reason," Winnie said with a sigh. "And she really stuck to the agreement and never reached out?"

"Nope. We agreed it would be better that way. It'll be up to

Melody if she wants to find her when she's grown up and able to make that decision for herself."

"That had to be scary. A single guy becoming a father and doing it all on his own," she said, shaking her head with disbelief.

"The beginning was overwhelming. I didn't know what I was doing. But I have a very supportive family, and I learned as I went. All that really matters at the end of the day is that I love my little girl. The rest I'll figure out."

"She's lucky to have such a good father," Winnie said as a single tear trailed down her cheek.

I leaned forward and swiped it away with the pad of my thumb. Her skin was soft beneath my touch. "Trust me, I'm the lucky one."

"Well, I'm glad I'm here. So now you can start having some fun. The girls told me you hardly ever go out. You're still young—you've still got it." She wiggled her eyebrows, and her cheeks pinked.

"I'm still young?" I laughed. "What about you. You're plenty young. I don't see you going out much."

"I've been separated for a year, divorced for six months. Honestly, I'm just happy to be by myself. I have no desire to go out. So use me in the evenings. I'm happy to stay with Melody while you whoop it up."

"'Whoop it up'? Aren't you twenty-four?"

"Your point?" she said with a sexy smirk.

"Aren't you supposed to say 'get lit' or something hip like that?" I teased.

"My dad says I'm an old soul. So no one is getting lit over here," she chuckled.

"Looks like we're two old souls, then. But I'm probably going to be forced to go out tonight, so I'll take you up on the offer to stay in with Melody tonight."

"Yeah, I heard that there's a woman who works for Lulu's company here in Paris who wants to meet you." She raised a brow. Damn, she was cute. "A little French romance does not sound like a bad thing."

"And you're sure you don't mind staying in after Melody goes to sleep? We are in Paris, after all."

"I'm your nanny. You literally pay me to stay in," she said over a full-bodied laugh.

"All right. But you've got my number if you need anything. Her sleep schedule is going to be off with the time difference, so she may not go to sleep as easily, especially this first night."

"We'll binge-watch Disney and eat snacks. You need not worry about us," she said. She set her plate on the tray as she stood up. "I'm going to go grab a shower and a nap, if that's okay?"

"Of course. We don't have to leave for a few hours."

She smiled at me, then disappeared into the second bedroom and pulled the door closed behind her.

I'd need to rally tonight, as everyone would be excited to be out in Paris.

But a part of me wished I could stay in the hotel room bingeing Disney shows and eating junk food.

Of course I wanted to be with my daughter.

But I'd be lying if I didn't admit that I enjoyed hanging out with my new nanny, too.

8
Winnie

The rehearsal dinner had been so much fun, but Melody and I sneaked out right after we ate. She was exhausted, and I knew Archer wouldn't relax until she was in the room resting.

And of course, when we attempted to sneak out, he followed us all the way back to the suite to make sure we'd made it back safely.

I encouraged him to get back downstairs, because a gorgeous Frenchwoman named Sabine was clearly interested in him—she'd pulled up a chair at our table and attached herself to him.

I'd given Melody her bath, and we'd both slipped into our jammies before climbing into her bed and turning on *Dumbo*, which was her favorite movie.

"I like snuggling with you, Winnie," she said as her little hand found mine. We were both sitting with our backs pressed to the headboard.

"I like snuggling with you, too," I said, stroking her little hand with the pad of my thumb.

She scooched closer to me and slid down on the bed a bit, and I knew she was getting sleepy. "Will you go with me to get my hair dones tomorrow for the flower job? I don't think daddies are supposed to go in that room."

"Of course I will. Are you excited?"

"Yeppers. And I'm happy I'll have my Beefcake with me when I walk down that island with my flowers."

I chuckled. She was damn cute.

Speaking of cute... Cutler, a.k.a. "Beefcake," had more game than most grown men I knew. He'd introduced himself to me, kissed the back of my hand, and told me I was his girl.

"He will definitely be right there with you."

"Will you stay with me in here tonight until Daddy gets back, Winnie?" She squeezed my hand as her little eyes fell closed.

"Of course I will. I'm not going anywhere. I'll be here watching *Dumbo*."

I listened to the sound of her breathing until it settled and she fell into a sound sleep. Her hand slipped from mine as she rolled onto her side. Her arm came over my waist as if she was hugging me and making sure to keep me there.

Melody was the sweetest kid I'd ever met. I continued watching as the cute little elephant on the screen started flying, his ears flapping around him.

My phone vibrated, and I looked down to see a text from Archer.

Archer: *How is it going over there?*

Me: *We're good. She just dozed off. And I'm watching Dumbo get his redemption on all the haters.*

Archer: *Fabulous movie.*

Me: *We're fine. Get back to your date.*

Archer: *I'd rather be watching Dumbo.*

Me: *Suck it up, Archie. You know what they say… when in Paris.*

Archer: *No one says that. It's when in Rome, and we aren't in Rome.*

Me: *Just go have some fun. You're only young once.*

Archer: *If I'm young, what does that make you?*

Me: *Younger than you. <winky face emoji>*

Archer: *Fine. I won't be too late.*

I chuckled and was just setting my phone down when it vibrated again. I was going to tell him to stop texting me and go have some fun when I saw my ex-husband's name on my phone.

He hadn't texted in a few weeks, and I was hoping now that I'd left Chicago, he'd move on as well.

Jaden: *Hey. How's small-town living?*

I didn't want to give him any information about where I was or what I was doing. He hadn't made this divorce easy on me. He'd dragged it out, and financially he'd hit me hard.

We weren't friends anymore.

We hadn't been in a very long time.

Me: *All is good.*

Jaden: *I'm sending you a screenshot of the bill for the BMW. It broke down and needs some work.*

He loved to word it as "the BMW," when it was very much his car.

A photo of a bill for $1700 came across my screen, and I rolled my eyes.

Me: *Why would you send me a bill for your car? We're divorced. This is your problem not mine.*

Jaden: *I would never have gotten this car if we hadn't been married. We had two incomes when I bought it.*

Me: *We actually had one income when you purchased that car, because you were between jobs. And if you remember, I kept the same car that I'd had since high school. You chose to buy a car that you couldn't afford. That is on you, Jaden. I wish you nothing but the best, but we need to not speak for a while. I've asked you to stop texting me numerous times.*

I'd made this request during our very messy divorce.

But every few weeks, Jaden liked to have a few cocktails (which was a nice way of saying "a dozen cocktails") in the evening, and then he'd start rage-texting me. I'd tried blocking his number, but he'd always have his mother message me. She'd then beg me to unblock him and promise that he'd just text to check in and nothing more.

But here we were again, and it was a pattern that wouldn't

change unless I gave him no option.

Jaden: *So I'm supposed to pay a bill I can't cover because you chose to leave our marriage?*

Jaden: *How fucking selfish are you?*

Actually, I was the opposite of selfish when it came to this man. I'd stayed with him much longer than I should have.

He'd been unkind and, I suspected, unfaithful.

I'd paid his bills and left him everything that we'd purchased together, even though I'd paid for most everything we had.

So I was done engaging.

I set my phone down and stared at the TV in hopes he'd go away.

I opened my Kindle and started reading and ignored the next dozen angry texts from Jaden.

My eyes grew heavy, and I set the Kindle beside me to rest my eyes.

And I let the darkness take me.

• • •

I felt a hand graze mine, and I startled, sitting up with a jolt.

"Hey, hey, it's just me. I was just setting your Kindle and your phone on the table," Archer said, his words slurring a little bit, and he looked good.

Really good.

His hair was a bit tousled, and he had this lazy smile on his face.

Plump, kissable lips. A little bit of scruff along his chiseled jaw.

"Your phone keeps vibrating," he said, glancing down at the screen as his eyes widened. "Who the hell is this?"

My phone was locked, but the first few words of a text from Jaden showed on the screen.

Jaden: *You're a selfish fucking bitch.*

I took my phone from him. "Sorry. That's my charming ex-husband. He's a real peach, isn't he?"

I got out of bed, taking my Kindle and my phone with me, and he followed me out to the living room area.

"I thought you were divorced?"

"We are."

"Yet he texts you shit like this?" he asked as he sat on the couch and patted the space beside him for me to sit.

"Not every day, but sometimes. He gets drunk and angry, and he's got a gift for rage-texting." I dropped to sit beside him as I rubbed my eyes, since I'd just been in a deep sleep.

"Block him."

"I did. But then his mom called me and asked me to unblock him. She promised he'd stop harassing me."

"And he hasn't. Shame on her for asking that of you. You gave it a shot, and he didn't change. You should block the asshole."

He was right. Meredith would have to understand. She shouldn't have gotten involved. I clicked on his name, blocked him, and held up my phone to show him.

"I agree. He's blocked."

"Good girl," he said, his voice deep and gruff. My body responded, and I quickly jumped to my feet.

It was dark and late, and things suddenly felt—too close.

I made my way to the door. "How was your night? Did you have fun with Sabine?"

"Not particularly." He held my stare. He was standing now, his muscular frame highlighted by the light from the moon.

"Thanks for staying with Melody."

"Of course. I'll see you in the morning. If you want to sleep in, just send her into my room with me, and we'll get breakfast and walk over to the park."

"I think you might be too good to be true, Winnie," he said as he winked at me.

I nodded before hurrying to my room and closing the door behind me.

I needed space and air.

I climbed into my bed and squeezed my eyes closed, and all I saw was Archer Chadwick's emerald green eyes.

My boss.

And I hoped like hell that sleep would take me, and I'd wake up tomorrow and forget all about how sexy my boss had looked tonight.

• • •

The sun came through the curtains, and I sat forward in bed and grabbed my phone, surprised that it was already after ten o'clock in the morning. I sprang out of bed, surprised to see that my door was closed. I pulled it open to find Archer and Melody sitting at the dining room table, eating pancakes.

"I thought I left my bedroom door open? Why didn't you wake me up? You could have slept in," I said as Melody jumped off her seat and ran toward me.

"Daddy shut your door, and he said that we should let you sleep." She smiled up at me.

"I feel like I've failed as the traveling nanny."

"Listen, I was up, and you were out. You need sleep, too. This isn't boot camp. You've been doing everything for us since we arrived. You're allowed to have some downtime, too." He motioned to the plate beside his that had a silver dome over it. "I got you eggs and bacon."

I sighed. "Let me brush my teeth real quick."

I hurried into the bathroom, gaping at myself in the mirror when I realized my tank top was completely see-through. I brushed my teeth and my hair, pulled it into a bun on top of my head, grabbed the robe from the closet, and slipped it on over my pajamas.

I came back out to join them and made my way to the chair beside Archer.

"How did everyone sleep?" I asked.

He wore a fitted black sweater and dark jeans, and he looked all polished and put together, per usual.

"I slept reals good. Did you fall asleep with me, Winnie?" Melody asked, that little twang making me smile every time she said my name and held the last syllable longer than necessary.

"I did, sweet pea."

"I like when you call me 'sweet pea.'" She flashed me her white teeth and then cinched her brows together as if she was thinking about something. "Hey, it's Thanks Turkey Day soon, right, Daddy?"

"Yes. And we'll be here in Paris for Thanksgiving."

"What about Winnie's daddy?" she asked, and my chest squeezed at how thoughtful this little girl was.

"Do you usually spend Thanksgiving with your father?" Archer asked, and now he mimicked his daughter's concerned look.

"Yes. But he knows I'm in Paris, and he's going to be just fine. We always cook for all the guys at his mechanic shop, and he'll just do it this year without me. I sent him our favorite recipes, and I told him I'd FaceTime him on Thanksgiving and help him get things prepped."

"I should have asked you if you were okay leaving over a holiday," Archer said, and I could see the anguish in his gaze.

"You did! You asked if I wanted to go to Paris with you, and I said yes. You didn't force me," I chuckled. "I'm happy to be here."

I always missed my father when I wasn't with him, but he understood that I'd moved to Rosewood River to make a new life for myself, away from Chicago and away from Jaden—and he was the one who'd encouraged me to do it.

"All right. Well, you know if you want Christmas off, or any particular days or weekends, you just put it on the calendar."

"You're already trying to get rid of me, and we're only a couple of weeks in?" I teased.

"Not a chance." He winked, and my stomach fluttered again with a rush of butterflies.

I'd gone years without butterflies.

Years without any excitement.

Years without my body reacting to anyone.

And now I land a job, and I start getting all the flutters around the one man I can't go there with?

They say karma is a bitch, but I think working for the hottest single dad I've ever met is the worst kind of torture.

I'd take karma any day.

9

Archer

The wedding was very heartfelt, with not a dry eye in the place. They'd kept it small and intimate, and Lulu's family had gone all out on the reception, which took place in a swanky ballroom with floor-to-ceiling windows and views of the Eiffel Tower.

Lulu and Rafe had arranged for a dance company to perform, and it was like something straight out of a Broadway show.

The music, the dancing, the costumes.

Sabine was planted in the chair beside me. She hadn't left my side since we'd arrived. Nothing had happened last night, outside of a few cocktails and good conversation.

She was nice enough, but I wasn't feeling it.

I glanced over at my nanny, who was standing on the edge of

the dance floor with my daughter and her cousin. Cutler twirled Melody around, and Winnie chuckled.

Winnie wore a black dress that hugged her curves in all the right places. Her hair was pulled into some sort of loose knot at the nape of her neck, with a little silk bow tied around it.

She always wore bows, and now Melody was wearing them every day as well.

"I'm going to go grab us a slice of cake," Sabine said as she winked at me.

I was still bothered by the text that I'd seen last night on Winnie's phone, but I hadn't brought it up today, because it wasn't really my business.

Yet, it felt like it was.

"Thanks for being here, Archie," Rafe said as he walked over and dropped in the chair beside me, the one Sabine had just left.

"Where else am I going to be?" I laughed. "I'm happy for you and Lulu. Wouldn't want to be anywhere else."

He clapped me on the shoulder. "Winnie's quite the hit, huh? She's making life easier on you?"

"She is. I should have jumped on that sooner."

His eyes widened, and he smirked. "Literally and figuratively?"

"No. Oh fuck, that's not what I meant." I shook my head and took a sip of my whiskey. "I meant that I should have gotten good help sooner."

"Well, you had a soft spot for Mrs. Dowden, and thankfully she finally retired." He chuckled. "But Winnie's definitely what you needed."

"What are we talking about?" Bridger asked as he slipped into the chair on the other side of me.

"The improvement in his nanny situation."

Bridger nodded. "It's night and day, huh?"

"Yep."

"So how about Sabine?" Rafe asked. "She told Lulu she was really into you."

"She's nice enough. But I'm here for a week," I said, shaking the ice around in my rocks glass.

"This is Paris. French flings are the norm here." Rafe waggled his eyebrows.

I rolled my eyes as I blew out a breath. "It's not really my thing."

"What? All you've had is flings since you've had Melody." He held his hands up defensively when I glared at him. "I'm not judging you. I know you don't get out often. But I just meant that you aren't looking for a relationship, so an international fling seems perfect. And you have a nanny to stay with Melody."

Bridger snorted, and we both turned to look at him as he finished off his cocktail.

"Read the room, brother." Bridger stood. "His eyes haven't been on the Frenchwoman once. Probably because they're always on the nanny. I'm getting a refill. I'll be back."

He dropped a bomb and then walked off like it was no big deal.

That was Bridger's style.

"Pfft. This fucking guy doesn't know what he's talking about." I shrugged. "My nanny is with my daughter. My eyes are on Melody. I'm making sure she's okay."

"You're making sure she's okay? You're in a ballroom with security outside the doors, and it's just family and friends in here." Rafe arched a brow. "You sure it's Melody that you're watching?"

Lulu's family was big in the political world, and they always traveled with security.

He was right. I wasn't worried about Melody.

But it didn't mean I didn't naturally keep my eye on her.

If I happened to get a glimpse of my pretty nanny at the same time, it wasn't a big deal.

"Don't be ludicrous. She works for me. And she's a decade younger than me, for God's sake," I hissed, unsure if I was trying to convince him or myself.

"Wait till you try this cake, handsome," Sabine said. She sat in Bridger's seat before handing me a slice of cake.

"Thank you so much for grabbing that for me." I smiled as I forked a bite at the same time she did.

"I've already had two slices," Rafe said, rubbing his hand across his stomach.

"Well, we don't want to eat too much—we want to save our energy for after the reception," Sabine purred, her French accent heavy as her blue gaze locked with mine.

Why the fuck don't I feel anything?

She was stunning and smart and easy to talk to.

"Daddy, did you see me getting twirled by my best cousin, Beefcake?" Melody asked as I pulled her onto my lap.

"I did, angel face."

"I want to dance with you now." She smiled up at me.

I glanced out on the dance floor, where Cutler had dragged Winnie. Everyone was laughing as he poured on the charm.

She went right along with it, kicking her shoes off as she took his hand and they danced. Lulu, Henley, Emilia, Eloise, and my cousin Emerson all made their way out on the dance floor as well, then all joined hands and danced to "Dancing Queen" by Abba.

My nephew was having the time of his life, and Rafe and I

chuckled. I glanced at Sabine.

"Will you excuse me for a moment?" I asked, and part of me hoped she would move on to someone else while I was gone.

"Of course. I'll be waiting right here for you." She crossed one leg over the other and licked her lips.

Rafe's eyes widened, and he stood up beside me. "I'm going to grab my bride out on the dance floor."

Sabine was unfazed. She was eating cake when Lulu's mother walked over to speak to her.

I held Melody on my hip and joined everyone on the dance floor.

We were having a good time, and we stayed out there for three or four songs, until we were all overheated and ready for a drink.

"Why don't I take Melody back to the room, and you stay and enjoy yourself?" Winnie said.

"You tired, baby?" I asked my daughter.

"I'm tired, but I'm having the super-most fun ever. But my tummy doesn't feel so good." Melody yawned, her eyes barely open as she rested her cheek on my shoulder.

"All right. I'll walk you both upstairs and get you settled."

"I'm fine to take her," Winnie insisted, but I shook my head no. I wanted to make sure they made it upstairs safely.

I stopped by the table where my parents were sitting and let them know I was taking Melody upstairs. They both kissed her cheek and told her they'd meet her for pancakes in the morning, and my mom gave Winnie a big hug and thanked her for the millionth time for being here.

We stopped at the table where Sabine was sitting. A group had gathered around her, so I didn't feel too bad about leaving her on her own.

"My little girl is exhausted, so I'm going to walk her and Winnie upstairs," I said, and she turned to look at me before directing her attention to my nanny.

"Isn't *she* capable of taking her to the room by herself?" Her tone had a bite, which caught me off guard. I didn't know Sabine well enough to know if that was the norm, but it was out of left field and out of line.

"I, er, I offered," Winnie said defensively, her eyes glancing between the two of us, obviously trying to figure out what was up.

"I would like to take my daughter upstairs and put her to bed," I said, my words coming out harsher than I meant them to, but I didn't appreciate the way she'd spoken to Winnie.

"Fine, Archer," she snipped.

What the fuck was this about? I barely knew this woman. I was at my cousin's wedding. I had my daughter with me.

She was acting like we'd arrived at this wedding together and I'd ditched her for another woman.

I motioned for Winnie to follow me, and we walked out of the ballroom, making our way to the elevators. No fucking way I was coming back down here. Sabine had just shown me who she was, and I didn't like it.

"Seriously, I'm more than happy to take Melody upstairs by myself," Winnie said as she reached for my daughter. "You don't need to escort us."

"I don't feel so good, Daddy," Melody moaned. Her head popped up just as the elevator doors closed.

Before I could respond, projectile vomit had left her lips, and she doused the elevator in puke. She heaved three times before bursting into a fit of tears.

Fuck.

Winnie took her wrap from her shoulders and dabbed it along

Melody's mouth and chin, cleaning up her little face. "You're all right, sweet pea."

The elevator doors opened, and thankfully, someone in a uniform was standing there. I stepped off and explained that my daughter had just gotten sick, and he told me not to worry about it. The guy immediately called someone on his walkie-talkie and stepped on the elevator.

Melody was crying hard now, and Winnie pushed the door to our suite open and hurried toward my bathroom. "How about I run her a bath and get her cleaned up."

"Thank you," I said as I carried my daughter to the bathroom while Winnie started filling the tub. "Do you need to throw up some more?"

She shook her head and sniffed several times. "No. My tummy feels a little better."

A tear ran down her face, and I set her down on the counter and grabbed a washcloth to get her cleaned up.

"I'm going to order some ginger ale and see if they have some crackers they can send up," Winnie said as she left the bathroom.

I hung my jacket up on a hook and quickly got Melody undressed. I checked the temperature of the water before helping her into the tub. Her hair was already tied up in a bun, and she sank down and rested her back against the cool porcelain.

Melody had only been sick a handful of times in her life, but it always scared me.

I hated to see her suffer.

I turned off the water when it was halfway full.

Winnie walked in with Melody's favorite plastic pink cup, then held the straw to her lips. "Take a sip, sweets. It'll help your tummy."

Melody took a small drink, and Winnie set the cup on the

side of the tub.

We sat there quietly as my daughter held her arms up. "I'm ready to get out."

While Winnie left to get her jammies, I grabbed a towel, lifted her out, and wrapped it around her. Between the two of us, we had her dressed, teeth brushed, and tucked beneath the covers in a matter of minutes.

"I'm going to set these crackers on the nightstand in case she wakes up during the night and she's hungry," Winnie whispered to me. Melody had already rolled to her side and was sound asleep.

I nodded and motioned for her to follow me out of the room.

"You should go back down to the wedding. I can lie in there with her," Winnie said.

"No. I'm not going back downstairs," I said. I typed out a text in the family group chat to let them know where I was.

"Archie, this is the reason you brought a nanny with you to Paris." She crossed her arms over her chest. "Plus, I think Sabine might gouge my eyes out if you don't go back down."

"First of all, I didn't bring you to Paris so you could sit with my daughter when she was sick. Secondly, I want to be here," I said, my gaze locking with hers. "And Sabine should not have spoken to you like that, so I have no desire to go back down and meet up with her."

She blew out a breath and chuckled. "You don't need to protect me from your French lover."

I didn't find it funny. Sabine had been rude, and that wasn't okay with me. "If someone disrespects you, I'll damn well say something. So I suggest you get used to it."

"Trust me. I can take care of myself. I've been doing it for a very long time." She glanced in the bedroom. "Do you want me to go lie in there with her for a while?"

I want you to stay out here with me.

But I didn't say that.

"No. I've got it. You go get some sleep." I took a step back, because her lavender scent was doing fucked-up things to me.

"All right. Let me know if you need anything."

"I will." I cleared my throat. "Did you block that asshole ex-husband of yours?"

She appeared surprised that I'd remembered, arching an eyebrow as she turned around to look at me. "Yes. He's blocked."

Good girl.

I nodded. "Glad to hear it. Good night, Winnie."

"Night."

I was both relieved and bothered when she disappeared into her room.

And that scared the hell out of me.

Time to get myself in check.

10

Winnie

We had Thanksgiving at a beautiful restaurant that Lulu's family had rented out in Paris, and though it was strange not to be with my father, I'd had a wonderful time.

Melody had felt fine the morning after she'd puked in the elevator. I was quickly learning just how resilient children were.

We'd been back in Rosewood River for two weeks, and everything in town had shifted from fall to Christmas. White twinkle lights wrapped around every light post downtown, with white-and-red flowers hanging from each one.

It took me some time to get back on a normal sleep schedule after Paris.

I'd also grown close to Lulu, Henley, Emelia, Eloise, Wren, and Archer's cousin Emerson since our trip, and they'd all read

Whisper Sweet Nothings for me. They'd also been very discreet about my pen name, which I appreciated.

My mornings were back to normal: breakfast with Melody and Archer, and then she'd go off to school and I'd go to the writing cave. I looked forward to picking her up every day from school and taking her to her activities and just spending time with her. She was such a special little girl, and I adored her.

Her teacher, on the other hand, was a different story.

"I was hoping Mr. Chadwick would be picking up Melody from school today," Mrs. Groucher said.

Her name was very fitting.

"Well, I've been picking her up every day for several weeks, so I'm not sure why you were expecting him." I glanced over at Melody, who was retrieving her backpack from her cubby, and when she looked at me, I noticed that her eyes were puffy. "Has she been crying? Did something happen?"

"Yes. Something happened," Mrs. Groucher grumped. A few of the parents hustled out of the classroom, as if they didn't want to have to speak to her. "Melody chose to talk during work time today, so she missed Fun Friday."

I'd heard all about Fun Friday, and personally, it didn't sound all that fun. Mrs. Groucher allowed them to work silently in centers during Fun Friday. So I couldn't imagine what one did when one actually missed it.

Sit in a closet in the dark?

Walk on a floor covered in tacks?

Watch paint dry?

Melody walked over and slipped her hand in mine. "I'm-I'm-I'm sorry, Mrs. Groucher." The tears started rolling down her cheeks, and the unpleasant woman showed zero emotion.

I bent down and held both her hands in mine. "Tell me what happened, sweet pea."

She loved the nickname, and it was very fitting, so it had stuck.

"Josh Barker asked me to help him," she said, her voice wobbly. "He didn't know what to do on his math paper."

"And you helped him?" I asked, my thumb stroking over the back of her hand.

She nodded and sniffed a few times. "I just whispered that he needed to count the shapes and write the numbers."

"And he would have known that if he'd made the choice to listen to the directions," Mrs. Groucher said as she crossed her arms over her chest. If I hadn't been so pissed off, I would've been intimidated by her.

I stood up, facing the woman head on. "So let me get this straight. One of your *five-year-old* students didn't pay attention while you gave the directions, and he asked a friend for help." I watched her reaction, which was null and void. Amazing. "Melody didn't turn him away; she whispered the directions. And then she sat out Fun Friday because she helped a friend?"

"Tommy missed Fun Friday, too," Melody croaked.

"He sure did. And if either of them gets another violation this coming week, they will be missing our holiday party next Friday," her teacher said, and I could swear the corners of her lips turned up the slightest bit.

She was enjoying this.

Way to spread the holiday cheer.

My free hand fisted at my side, but I kept my composure.

"I see, *Mrs. Grouch*." I forced a smile.

"It's Mrs. Groucher," she snipped.

"Oh yes. Sorry about that. The name really does suit you. Have a wonderful weekend." I took the backpack from Melody while the older woman studied me as if she wasn't sure if I'd just offended her intentionally.

I'd definitely offended her intentionally.

I'd be writing her ass into a book and torturing her in the future.

How dare she break the spirit of this little angel.

I turned, and we walked out the door, Melody's hand in mine. Once we were outside, I bent down to face her again. "Look at me, sweet pea."

"Okay, Winnie. I'm looking at you," she said as a tear rolled down her cheek. "Do you think Daddy's going to be mad at me for getting in trouble at school?"

"I don't think so. You were helping a friend. And I understand that there are rules, but sometimes there are gray areas. And this was a gray area." I swiped the tear away with the pad of my thumb.

"What's a gray area mean?"

"It means sometimes you need to do something that might get you to miss Fun Friday because it's the right thing to do." I pulled her in for a hug. "You helped a friend who was asking for help. That's never a bad thing."

"Tommy wasn't in the class when she gave the 'rections. He came late to school, so he didn't know what to do."

He wasn't even there?

My blood was boiling. How could he have listened if he wasn't even there?

"Did Mrs. Groucher know that he missed the directions?"

"Yep. She said it was his choice that he was late, and his choice that he didn't listen." She shrugged. "And he was sniffing like he was trying not to cry. And my daddy told me to always help someone if they're sad."

"How about we have our own little Fun Friday?"

"You want to do centers and not talk to each other?" she asked, and I laughed.

"I don't want to do that." I pushed back up to stand. "I want to go get hot chocolate and cookies at the Honey Biscuit Café and then go pick out some gift wrap at Strawberry Fields because I told your daddy I'd help him wrap some Christmas presents this weekend."

"That sounds like the best Fun Friday, Winnie."

A gust of wind blew past us, and I zipped her coat up to just beneath her chin and took her hand in mine. I had access to the car that Bridger had loaned me, but we usually walked most places because everything was so close. We were only a block from downtown, and then it was just a short walk home.

"It sure does. Let's do this."

I sent a quick text to Archer to let him know that we were stopping for hot chocolate, because the man loved to know what we were doing. We texted all day, even when Melody was at school. He was always checking in.

He'd text to ask about dinner or activities, or he'd inquire about holiday shopping.

We'd become friends, and we spent a lot of time together.

But every night after we'd all have dinner, he'd end things fairly abruptly, which always made me wonder if maybe he was sneaking a woman in once he put Melody to bed. But I'd woken up a few times in the middle of the night when I couldn't sleep and I'd come into the kitchen to get a snack, and it had always been very quiet.

Maybe Archer Chadwick was a quiet lover.

Somehow, I doubted it.

And shame on me for wondering what type of lover my boss was.

He responded with a thumbs-up emoji, and we started walking to the Honey Biscuit Café.

"Winnie!" Melody came to a stop and looked up. "A snowflake just landed on my nose."

The snow started to fall, and I chuckled. It had been cold these last few weeks since we'd returned from Paris, and everyone was shocked that it hadn't snowed yet.

And here we were, walking down the sidewalk hand in hand, both of us smiling as the snowflakes fell all around us.

"This really is the best Fun Friday," I said. I pulled the door open as my uncle Oscar hurried us inside.

"Well, if it isn't my two favorite girls," he said, hugging us both. "Do you want your favorite booth?" he asked Melody, and she shook her head yes.

"Did you get your words today?" he asked me, and I was grateful that he understood this profession that I'd chosen. Hell, he'd been the one to encourage me to do it.

"I wrote five thousand words, so it was a good day," I said.

Melody gasped. "Five thousand words is lots of words, Winnie."

"It's a good writing day, that's for sure." Uncle Oscar winked at me. "Proud of you, Winnie girl."

"Thank you."

"Are you bothering these gorgeous girls?" Aunt Edith teased as she walked over and gave me a hug.

"Nope. Just asking if she got her words today and taking their order."

"We're going to have two hot chocolates, extra whipped

cream and sprinkles, and a couple of cookies." I helped Melody out of her coat as we settled in the booth.

My uncle said he'd go let the kitchen know, and my aunt chuckled as he walked off. "I think that man is living vicariously through you these days. He misses writing, even if he won't admit it."

"He should start writing again," I said, knowing that it was his passion.

"After he made the decision to retire, he just said he was done with it."

"He's so talented. He could just write for fun, if he doesn't want to do it as an actual profession anymore."

"That's a good idea. I think you could probably talk some sense into him." Aunt Edith shrugged before heading back to the kitchen.

"I wants to be a writer someday like my Winnie." Melody smiled up at me, and my chest squeezed.

"You can be whatever you want to be."

"Mrs. Groucher says you can't be whatever you wants to be." She shrugged. "Josh Barker said he wanted to be a candy cane, and she said he couldn't be one."

"Well, he could make candy canes if he wanted to." I chuckled. "And trust me when I tell you, Melody Chadwick: You can be whatever you set your mind to."

"I want to be just like you, Winnie." She leaned her head against my arm just as my uncle set our hot chocolates down with a big plate of cookies.

"I think we're going to need one more hot cocoa, Oscar," a deep voice said, and I turned to see Archer approach.

"Daddy!" Melody shouted. "You came to Fun Friday?"

He raised a brow at me in question, and I replied with a look that said I'd fill him in later.

We'd started communicating like this around Melody.

"I sure did. I heard you two were here, and I came right over."

My uncle disappeared into the kitchen and returned with another hot chocolate.

And the three of us sat there talking about our days. We filled him in on what had happened at school, and I watched with absolute awe as he smiled at his daughter and told her that she'd done the right thing, even if it meant having to deal with a consequence that she didn't like.

He didn't disrespect her teacher.

He didn't scold her for getting in trouble.

He just loved her.

I knew that kind of love from my own father.

Archer didn't try to talk us out of stopping at Strawberry Fields for gift wrap. In fact, I caught him looking around as if he was actually interested.

And when we arrived home, they both said how good it smelled in the house, because I'd left a roast in the slow cooker.

"Admit you were wrong about the slow cooker," I said with a laugh when Melody ran off to wash her hands.

"I didn't say they weren't good, just that I hadn't used one."

"You said they were 'weird in concept,' yet every meal I've made in this thing you've devoured."

"Listen, you're basically a gourmet cook. If you were cooking in an old-school hearth, it would still be good." He laughed. "I don't think it's the slow cooker that's making magic. That's all you, Winnie."

My breath caught in my throat at his words as he turned to grab a beer from the fridge.

When was the last time a man had made me feel like I was talented or special?

It had been a long time.

He held up a bottle for me, asking if I'd like a beer, and I shook my head no.

Alcohol did not mix well with the hot single dad in the house.

I knew myself way too well.

11

Archer

I'd tossed and turned all night.

Christmas was around the corner, work was crazy busy, and my nanny was consuming my thoughts.

I was horny as hell and tempted to take a shower so I could give myself a little fucking relief.

It was the one place I let my mind wander about the beautiful woman who was living in my home.

The woman who was great with my daughter, even getting defensive about how tough her teacher was.

Winnie was funny and witty and didn't hesitate to give me shit when needed.

I couldn't remember the last time I'd actually looked forward to spending time with a woman.

And this woman wasn't mine.

She was my daughter's.

But we spent a lot of time together, and the lines were definitely graying.

I fucking hated gray lines.

I was a black-and-white guy. I followed the rules. Stayed in my lane.

The day I brought Melody home from the hospital, I'd made a commitment to my daughter. One she wouldn't have been able to comprehend at the time, but I sure as hell did.

She was my priority. My life was forever changed, and I was going to be whatever she needed me to be to give her the best life.

So I'd date occasionally. Obviously I was a man with needs. But I was a straight shooter with the women I'd spent time with. I never lied about what I had to offer, which was nothing more than a casual thing.

Good dinner, easy conversation, and mind-blowing sex, if that was what they wanted.

And now, I was fantasizing about my daughter's nanny.

A woman Melody had quickly grown close to.

A woman who was a decade younger than me.

She worked for me, for fuck's sake.

I scrubbed a hand down my face.

I glanced at my phone when it vibrated, letting me know a new text had arrived.

Samantha: *Hey handsome. I just got home from a work trip on the east coast, and I was thinking about you. Can you get a babysitter this week, and I'll make you dinner? And maybe we can both scratch an itch. <winky face emoji>*

I looked at the time and saw that it was just after two a.m. It wasn't out of character for Samantha to text me this late. We'd hooked up several months ago. She was a flight attendant, and when she wasn't working, she was traveling. She'd gone through a nasty divorce a few years back, and she wasn't looking for anything serious, which had worked well for me.

Maybe that's what I need?

To get Winnie out of my head.

I didn't answer her. I wasn't sure how I wanted to respond.

Instead, I decided to go get a bottle of water and a snack. I was wide awake, and maybe that would help.

I set my phone on the nightstand and made my way down the hallway.

Melody wouldn't be up for several hours, so hopefully I'd still be able to get a few more hours of sleep.

I came around the corner and startled at the sight of her.

Winnie was standing with her back to me, staring into the freezer, wearing a pair of tiny shorts and a tank top. The curve of her peach-shaped ass was peeking out of the hem of her shorts, and my dick instantly reacted.

I quickly turned to get out of there before she saw me, but my arm hit the wall and made the slightest sound, causing her to turn.

"Oh, hey," she whispered. "I'm so sorry. Did I wake you?"

"No. I couldn't sleep. Came for a snack."

She pulled out the quart of ice cream that she'd picked up at the market and opened the drawer, then held up a spoon for me. "Want some ice cream?"

I shrugged. "Yeah, sure."

Her eyes scanned my bare chest, and I was grateful that I'd at least tugged on a pair of gray joggers over my briefs.

She handed me the spoon, my fingers grazing along hers as I reached for it. She sucked in a breath, and I noted the way her chest rose and fell rapidly once I'd moved closer.

Looking at her was a mistake.

A big fucking mistake.

Because her nipples were poking through the thin material of her tank top.

It took everything in me to look away.

She appeared unfazed as she jumped up on the counter of the large kitchen island. She dipped her spoon into the green minty ice cream and wrapped her lips around it.

All I could do was imagine those lips wrapped around my cock.

My cock that was currently raging beneath my joggers.

I made sure to stand close to the cabinets so she wouldn't notice as I faced her.

"Couldn't sleep, either?" I asked.

"Nope. But that happens a lot to me."

"Why?" I pressed.

"I think it's the book that I'm writing. My brain can't shut off sometimes, and I'm just sort of stuck right now." She dipped her spoon back into the ice cream and made a little humming sound when she placed it between her lips.

Fuck me.

Winnie eating ice cream was the sexiest thing I'd ever seen.

"What are you stuck on? Maybe I can help?"

"Do you read a lot of romance, Archie?" she teased.

"No, but I've been around a bit longer than you, so I'm sure I can at least help."

She chuckled. "Why do you always make age references? You're not even old."

Because I need to remind myself that I'm too old for you daily.

"Agreed. But I'm older than you, so I might have a different perspective."

"Fine." She rolled her eyes. "So, my hero, his name is Luka, and he's a single dad."

"Interesting. A single dad for your hero?"

"Don't get a big head—I started it long before I met you."

"Single dads are hot, aren't they?" I waggled my brows.

"Sure." She licked the ice cream off her spoon, and I swear I nearly came right there in the middle of the kitchen. "Anyway, he's crazy about a woman who he can't have. Her name is Francesca."

"Why can't he have her? She's not into him?"

"No. She's totally into him." She laughed. "She's his best friend's little sister. She's off limits."

I rubbed my jaw, noting that it was time to shave. "Ahh… got it. Well, he should do the right thing and stay the fuck away from her then."

She gaped at me. "That's terrible advice. We want them to get together."

"I don't think they should be together." I leaned closer, scooping another bite out of the container.

"Why?"

"Because I would assume that his best friend knows him better than anyone. He doesn't think he's good enough for her, so he probably isn't."

"His best friend is being ridiculous. Barbaric and controlling. He's a total hypocrite," she said, in the most defensive voice.

"Fine. Put them together. People love a happy ending."

She gave me a look. "Archie. That could be taken two different ways."

I laughed. Like I said, she was funny and witty.

And maybe I had a happy ending on my mind.

"You know what I mean."

"Do I?" she teased, reaching up to tighten her ponytail, and I noticed the ribbon tied around the elastic. Did she sleep in them, too?

"What's the deal with the ribbons? I notice you wear them every day."

"That's very observant of you." She smiled. "It's kind of my thing."

"Meaning?"

She pointed to my chest, where my daughter's name was inked over my heart.

"My father has my name tattooed over his heart. And when I was young, after my mom left, I guess I had a hard time for a while. I barely remember it." She shrugged. "Apparently, I didn't want to get out of bed because I was blue, and he told me that whenever he felt sad about something, he'd look at my name on his chest, and it became like his own little superpower. He told me that I had to find something to use as my superpower. To remember how strong I was when I wasn't feeling strong."

I'd moved closer to her without even realizing it.

Wanting to comfort her.

Wanting to touch her.

"I could see how he would find his strength in you. I've experienced that with Melody. Times where I struggle and question if I'm failing at this whole dad thing—and all I have to do is look at her and know I'm doing all right. She's my motivation.

I guess she's my superpower, too."

Her lips turned up in the corners. "Yes. It shows."

"So how did you decide on a bow?"

"My dad had bought me a bunch of bows to try to cheer me up. If you knew this man, you would know that he is not the kind of guy to go to the store and shop for hair bows." She chuckled, and her eyes were wet with emotion. "And he ended up buying me one in every color of the rainbow. So I guess in a way, these represent him. The fact that he stayed and he was there every step of the way. I put one of the bows in my hair that day, and I swear I felt like I suddenly had a superpower. And from that day on, I wore a bow in my hair every day, just to remind myself that I'm not alone. That I can do anything I set my mind to."

Fuck me.

This girl never stopped impressing me.

And now I moved even closer, stepping between her legs that hung a few inches apart. I reached up and touched the back of her head. "It's your superpower. I should just start calling you Winnie Woman instead of Wonder Woman."

She chuckled as her gaze locked with mine.

"It's a lengthy nickname, Archie," she whispered, and her cheeks turned a soft shade of pink.

My hand moved to the side of her face, my thumb gliding along her bottom lip.

Had I ever wanted to kiss a woman more than I did right now in this moment?

Her chest was rising and falling rapidly. Her lips parted when I pulled my thumb back.

I was going to kiss her.

I wanted it.

She wanted it.

That was all that mattered.

I tipped my head down as her hand moved to the back of my head and tangled in my hair, tugging me closer.

Our lips just a breath apart.

"Daddy!" Melody's voice startled me, and I jumped back, just as she came around the corner.

"Hey, what's going on, angel face?" I asked as I hurried toward her and scooped her up, settling her on my hip.

"I had a bad dream, and I went to find you in your room, and you weren't in there?" she whimpered.

Winnie was already off the counter and on her feet, slipping the ice cream back into the freezer and filling my daughter's cup with water. "Are you thirsty, sweet pea?"

Melody nodded, and Winnie reached for a paper towel and ran it under water before cleaning up her tear-streaked face. "I used to have bad dreams, too."

"You did, Winnie?"

She nodded. "Yep. But then I would remind myself that they aren't real, and usually when I'd go back to sleep, they were gone."

"I hope this one goes away. I don't remember what it was, but I was running from a bear, I think," Melody said, her eyes wide as her bottom lip trembled.

Winnie reached behind her head and untied her bow, placing it in my little girl's hand. "Here. Keep this with you. I'm giving you my superpower."

"I love your bows, Winnie. I'm going to keep this with me and scare away all the bad bears." Melody smiled.

"Sleep well, sweet pea." Winnie kissed her cheek, and then quickly headed for her bedroom.

She glanced over her shoulder, and my gaze locked with hers before she turned away.

I almost kissed my fucking nanny.

The woman my daughter had grown attached to.

What kind of selfish prick was I?

I would have crossed a line that I shouldn't have crossed.

And I would not make that mistake again.

12

Winnie

I'd tossed and turned the rest of the night after almost kissing my boss.

My mind was reeling.

I was painfully attracted to the man—but he was my boss.

And that would certainly complicate everything.

He couldn't even look at me after Melody had come out and stopped things before they'd gone too far.

I stood at the stove flipping pancakes as holiday music piped through Alexa. I'd gotten Melody dressed in the cutest reindeer costume this morning, and her hair was tied up in two little buns with red bows tied around each one.

Today was the final day before holiday break at Melody's school.

Personally, I couldn't wait for a break from her grouchy teacher.

Melody and I had baked cupcakes for the party and brought them this morning.

"Winnie, are you excited to see me be a real live reindeer on the stage today?" she asked from where she sat at the table, munching on fruit while I prepared her breakfast.

"I cannot wait to see you in the play today. You feel good about all your lines, right?" I plated the food, wondering where Archer was.

I had this sinking feeling he was going to be uncomfortable around me now.

"Yeppers. We practiced so much," she said, smiling up at me when I set her plate down, and her eyes grew wide. "Are those reindeer pancakes?"

"It's a special day today to be a reindeer, right?" I teased.

"Good morning." Archer's deep voice boomed as he came around the corner. He paused to kiss Melody's cheek, then moved past me to pour his cup of coffee.

He didn't meet my gaze, which was definitely not the norm.

So, he clearly regretted the near kiss.

I turned to pour the syrup over Melody's pancakes and felt my cheeks heat with embarrassment.

What was I doing? I'd sworn off men, and here I was nearly kissing the man I worked for.

"Are those reindeers?" he asked as he stood behind me and leaned over my shoulder to check out her pancakes.

I quickly moved out of the way. "Yes. It's a big day today."

I set plates down for Archer and myself with just regular pancakes.

"I don't get reindeer pancakes?" he asked, and now his gaze

locked with mine, and I saw something there that I couldn't put my finger on.

Guilt? Maybe shame or disappointment.

Either way, there was no doubt that the near kiss was a massive mistake.

One I'd make sure I wouldn't repeat again.

"Well, you're not a reindeer in the school play today, are you?" I asked, forcing a smile.

"Fair enough." He winked at Melody and took a few bites of pancakes before abruptly pushing to his feet. "Are you still okay taking Melody to school this morning?"

He'd asked a few days ago if I'd be able to take her today, as he was going to get to the office early so he could take a half day to attend her play.

"Yes, of course." I forked a bite of fluffy goodness and popped it in my mouth.

"Great." He kissed his daughter's cheek. "I'll see you both at school in a few hours."

"I can't wait for you to see me up there on the stage, Daddy," Melody said over a mouthful of pancake.

"Me either. Love you, angel face." He slipped his coat on, since it was cold as hell outside now, and then turned to me. "Thank you, Winnie."

I nodded and turned away, because I could feel his discomfort.

I'd done this. I'd come out to the kitchen in my jammies, and he'd been caught off guard. The man probably felt like he couldn't even come out of his room for a midnight snack now.

I'd clearly made him uncomfortable in his own home.

Had I tried to kiss him?

Had he even been interested?

I was trying to replay the events in my head when Melody

grabbed my hand. "I'm going to miss you when you go home."

I set my fork down and reached for her, pulling her onto my lap. I'd grown so attached to this little angel in the month and a half that I'd been working here. We spent a lot of time together. I wrapped my arms around her. "I'll miss you, too. But I'll just be gone for a few days to see my dad. And that'll give you and your daddy some time alone, too."

"I like when you're here, too." She tipped her head back and looked up at me. "I always like when you're with me, Winnie."

My chest ached. I needed to remember why I was here.

I was here for Melody.

Not a fling with her father.

This wasn't a freaking romance; it was real life.

"I like when you're with me, too, sweet pea." I sighed and held her close to me. "Okay, we need to get you to school. It's a big day. I'll go start the car and load the cupcakes."

"Yes!" Melody jumped to her feet and did a fist-pump. "It's going to be the best day."

I warmed up the car, since Archer was adamant that we not walk in this weather. He'd come looking for me two days ago, when I'd decided to walk to the grocery store. He'd freaked out that I could have gotten frostbite, but I reminded him that I grew up in Chicago and was very familiar with cold weather.

The man could be ridiculously protective.

I was still mortified that I'd misread things with him, but I wouldn't let that happen again.

I bundled up Melody, and we drove the short distance to school.

Sarah Lynn Schwartz did not hide her disappointment when I walked into the classroom this morning. The woman had made an effort to befriend me, but I'd quickly realized she was just trying to find a way to get invited over to the house and had no interest in me whatsoever.

"Oh. You don't usually do morning drop-off. Where's Daddy Chadwick?" she purred, and I tried to hide my irritation.

I noticed the way Mrs. Groucher turned her head with disapproval, as she'd clearly heard it as well.

Calling someone a "daddy" in a romance book was one thing, but saying it in the middle of a kindergarten classroom was another.

Especially when it was the man I'd nearly kissed last night.

"Archer is at work. He'll be here this afternoon to see his daughter in the school play," I said, my tone coming out harsher than I meant it to, but I wasn't mad about it.

Mrs. Groucher moved beside me, and I could swear I saw the corners of her mouth turn up when she looked at me.

She'd clearly found the "Daddy Chadwick" comment offensive as well.

"May I speak to you for a moment, Winnie?" she asked, and then she raised a brow at Sarah Lynn as if it was time to excuse herself.

"Yes, of course." I bent down and kissed Melody's cheek and told her to go unpack her backpack and hang her coat in her cubby.

Sarah Lynn left in a huff, and I turned my attention to Melody's teacher. "What can I do for you?"

"I just wanted to tell you that whatever you're doing with Melody at home..." She paused and cleared her throat. "Keep doing it."

I probably didn't hide my confusion very well as I studied her. "Keep doing what?"

"I don't know, but Melody is sounding out words all the time now and asking for books during free time. She's also writing stories every chance she gets, and I've been very surprised, because she's got quite the imagination." She chuckled.

My chest squeezed at her words. We read together every day, and she liked writing, so we'd come up with stories in the car ride home or after her riding lessons.

"That's so wonderful to hear. She's a talented little girl." I glanced over at Melody, who was helping her friend Bernice tie her shoes.

This little girl was all heart.

"Agreed. We'll see you in a few hours?" Mrs. Groucher said, and she winked at me.

Mrs. Groucher winked at me.

I guess I hadn't completely failed.

I made my way out to the SUV that Bridger had loaned me. I climbed in just as my phone rang, and my father's name came through the Bluetooth speaker.

"Hey, Dad," I said, always happy to start my day talking to him.

"Hi, sweetheart. I'm looking forward to seeing you soon," he said, and just the sound of his voice comforted me.

"Me too. Did two big boxes arrive at the house for me?" I asked, because I'd shipped my Christmas gifts home.

"They did." He chuckled. "I don't want you spending money right now while you're catching up from that asshole ex of yours bleeding you dry."

"I received my first royalty check since being officially divorced. Luckily Jaden signed off on future earnings if I'd agreed to give him what the books had already earned."

"Luckily? That shithead doesn't deserve one penny of that money. He should get off his lazy ass and get a job. It's despicable that he's taken your hard-earned money," he hissed.

My father was ridiculously protective, and I loved him for it, but I didn't want my divorce to be dragged out for longer than it had to be, and Jaden was a guy who wanted instant gratification. He saw the money in the account and he wanted it, and he didn't believe the books would continue to make money.

"It's over now, and that's what matters. Now everything that I make is mine, and there's freedom in that, you know?"

"Proud of you, baby girl. I'd still like to put my fist through his face," he said.

"That's the holiday spirit, Dad." I chuckled.

"All right. Enough about that. You've got the holiday show for Melody today, right? She's going to be a reindeer?"

"Yes. Cutest reindeer around. I'm so excited to watch her onstage. She's worked really hard on memorizing her lines. She's just the cutest thing ever."

"This is good for you. You're away from all the drama that surrounded your divorce, you can focus on your writing, and you're enjoying your time with Melody. Uncle Oscar said Archer is a good guy, and you know he rarely has anything good to say about anyone." He laughed.

"He is a good guy. And a really great dad."

"It's nice to hear. See, there are still good men out there. Don't let the one you married scare you off for the rest of your life."

I pulled into Archer's garage. "Are you seriously giving me dating advice?"

He chuckled. "No. I'm just saying, don't close yourself off completely. Finalizing this divorce and moving away was the first step, but you're young, and I don't want you to be so guarded that you're afraid to be happy just because things didn't work out with the asshole."

"Says the man who's been single most of my life." I turned the ignition off and held the phone to my ear as I walked inside.

"Hey, I get out plenty. But I'm way too old to be looking for forever. I'm slightly set in my ways. Plus, I have you, so I don't need anyone else. You don't have a Winnie, so you need to keep looking."

I dropped my purse on the counter and turned on the lights to the Christmas tree as I made my way to the kitchen. "Okay. This is starting to feel like an episode of *The Bachelor*."

He laughed some more, and I heard a bunch of voices in the background. "All right, sweetheart. I'll see you in a few days. I'll pick you up from the airport, and we're going to meet Nana and Gramps for dinner that night at Carlino's."

Carlino's was my favorite restaurant back home. And I loved my grandparents and couldn't wait to see them.

"That sounds great, Dad. Love you."

"Love you."

I ended the call and pulled out the mixer, because I wanted to make a bunch of cookie dough to refrigerate so Winnie and I could make and decorate holiday cookies tonight to celebrate her finally being on holiday break.

Alexa was blasting Mariah Carey through the speaker when my phone vibrated on the counter.

Archie: *Hey.*

Me: *Hi. How's work going?*

I was trying to just act normal. Things had been weird this morning, and I hated it.

Archie: *I'm sorry if I made you uncomfortable last night.*

Me: *You didn't.*

Archie: *It shouldn't have happened.*

Me: *Nothing actually happened.*

Archie: *It almost happened.*

Me: *Okay. Well, I'm sorry it almost happened.*

That was the best I could come up with. I was clearly the one who wanted it to happen, and he was clearly horrified by the almost kiss.

Archie: *I wanted to see if you were available tonight to stay with Winnie. I have plans and thought I'd check with you before I ask my mom if she's free.*

Me: *Why would you ask your mom? I'm your nanny. You literally pay me to be available.*

Archie: *So you're okay with working late tonight?*

Me: *Yes. Melody and I are making holiday cookies tonight to celebrate her being on break. I'm happy to stay with her.*

Tonight was Friday night. He clearly had a date. Why did I care? He didn't owe me anything. Nothing had happened between us. He'd admitted he didn't want it to.

Archie: *Thank you. I'll see you at the show.*

Me: *I'll see you there, boss.*

Why did I write that? Maybe to remind myself that he was my boss.

And he was completely off limits.

13

Archer

I was sitting on the end of the row, as far away from Winnie as I could get. She didn't seem to notice or care. My entire family was here to see Melody in her holiday show, and Winnie was sitting between Wren and my mother on the opposite side.

My mother adored her, as did my aunt Ellie. Winnie attended Sunday dinners with us, and she'd go over early and cook with them.

It was her passion.

She'd become a part of this family, and I'd almost fucked it all up.

"What's your deal?" Bridger said, keeping his voice low as he sat beside me.

"What do you mean? I don't have a deal."

"You seem—uncomfortable."

I rolled my eyes. "I'm fine. Stop overanalyzing me."

"Did something happen?" Rafe leaned in from where he sat behind me. "You seem a little off."

I glanced over my shoulder. "I'm not off. And nothing happened."

"I'm not buying it," Bridger said, chuckling. "Something is definitely going on."

"Why do you say that?"

"Because you took the farthest seat in the room from your nanny, whom you're usually attached to at the hip."

"I didn't even notice where she was sitting," I lied. "And be quiet. The show is starting."

Mrs. Groucher came onto the stage and introduced her class, and for the next forty-five minutes, we listened to several holiday songs, and they did a little skit. And that was when Melody moved to the front of the stage. This was her big part in the show. Only a few kids had lines, and Melody had taken it very seriously that she'd been chosen to recite some facts about the holidays.

Her gaze found mine in the audience, and I gave her a thumbs-up, and then I was surprised when her gaze moved down the row and she found Winnie.

Even my daughter couldn't keep her eyes off our nanny.

And as she started reciting the facts that I'd heard every single day for the last two weeks, I glanced over to see Winnie's lips moving as she recited them silently along with my daughter.

"And we wish you all a very happy holiday!" Melody shouted, and the crowd erupted with applause.

Mind you, half the people in the audience were my family members, so Melody drew a large crowd. And the first one to jump up on her feet was Winnie. She was clapping and jumping up and down as if Melody had just won a Pulitzer Prize.

Trust me, I got it.

I was proud as hell of my little girl.

It was brave to get up in front of all these people and speak.

But I wasn't used to anyone outside of my family responding in this way.

All the kids left the stage to go find their families, and I stood.

"Well, even if you don't want to admit something's going on, at least Melody isn't ashamed to admit it," Bridger said with a laugh as my daughter rushed off the stage into Winnie's arms.

"We did it, Winnie!" she said.

"*You* did it, sweet pea," I heard her say to my daughter.

"Daddy, why are you all the way down there?" Melody asked as she ran toward me and jumped into my arms.

"It was a good seat to take pictures," I said, earning an odd look from my dad, who was only a few seats down from me.

Clearly this was a terrible seat for pictures. The fifteen-foot-tall Christmas tree sitting beside the stage was blocking my view and made for very awkward photos.

The truth was, I was a man who couldn't stop fantasizing about his nanny, and I needed to stay the hell away from her.

Desperate times call for desperate measures.

"You guys want to grab a beer tonight?" Easton asked as he walked over to me.

"I've actually got a date. I'm taking Samantha Moth to dinner." I cleared my throat, waiting for them to give me shit.

Bridger chuckled, in that sarcastic judgmental way he often did. "Got it. Now I know that I'm on to something."

I ignored him and made my way over to my mother, pulling her in for a hug.

"Wasn't that just amazing?" she gushed as she lifted Melody up and settled her on her hip. "My little granddaughter is such a superstar."

My gaze moved to Winnie's, and she quickly looked away from me.

She was clearly uncomfortable around me now.

I'd obviously freaked her out.

She seemed thrilled about staying home with Melody tonight and had encouraged me to go have some fun.

Her words, not mine.

I'd told her that what almost happened was a mistake, and she'd agreed.

I just needed to stay clear for a little bit until I could shake off this attraction.

She'd be going home for a few days, and the distance would be good for us.

Hell, it would be great for us.

That was exactly what I needed.

Distance from Winnie Smith.

• • •

I'd managed to keep my distance from Winnie for the rest of the day. I took Melody shopping for a few last-minute Christmas gifts that I needed for my family, and Winnie went home to write for a while.

I'd left the house while she and Melody were eating dinner, which was torture because they were laughing and having a great time. Winnie had made spaghetti and meatballs that smelled fucking fantastic.

I didn't want to leave them.

But the thought terrified me enough to get my ass out the door.

And now I was currently sitting across the table from Samantha Moth. A woman I'd gone out with a few times.

Scratch that.

A woman I'd hooked up with a few times over the years.

Typically after far too much alcohol had been consumed.

I'd never taken her out on an official date, because she'd had no interest in that in the past.

Tonight, I'd insisted. I declined to meet her at her house and insisted that we start with dinner.

Try to do things the right way.

"So what's with the formalities tonight? I figured we'd just meet at my place. Drink far too many bottles of wine. Knock boots and chase our release a couple times, and then you'd make up an excuse about having an allergic reaction to the grapes in the wine and call a car to take you home." She shrugged as she cut into her steak.

"I just thought it might be nice to actually have a good meal and talk," I said, regretting my decision to do so, because this was awkward as hell so far.

Turned out we had nothing in common, outside of being two lonely people who occasionally needed sex.

I'd learned that she despised children and wondered why anyone would choose to have a child in this day and age.

I'd reminded her that I was a single dad and loved my daughter more than anything, to which she rolled her eyes and said that we should change the topic.

I'd inquired about her family, only to learn that she'd sued her parents over an inheritance disagreement and had no contact with them. Her grandparents had passed away, and she hadn't spoken to anyone in her family in years.

"All right. What else can we talk about? Seems like we've hit some big topics already," she said.

I gave her a look, because maybe she should try coming up with something, seeing as I'd struck out twice already.

"Please tell me you aren't one of those holiday guys who puts up a Christmas tree and wraps presents in paper covered in photos of a weird man in a red suit who pretends to bring children presents all over the world. As if any man could do that all in one night," she said with a loud laugh. "It's ridiculous that people buy into this shit."

My God. I'd had a fling with the Grinch, and I hadn't even realized it.

"I am that guy. I even sprinkle glitter and oats out in the snow with my daughter, to attract Santa's reindeer to our home." I shrugged.

"Why would a reindeer eat glitter?" she asked, her brows cinched together with concern, as if I'd lost my mind.

"Well, they don't. It's just supposed to be a beacon of light that the reindeer follow to your home. I grew up doing it, and I have continued doing it for my little girl."

"I think it's really stupid, Archer." She held her wine glass up for our waiter to refill. "And I think it's actually irresponsible to teach your daughter some bullshit beliefs that a man in a ridiculous suit is going to ride a reindeer to her house and bring her presents. In fact, if I ever meet Melanie, I'm going to do the right thing and tell her the truth." She pursed her lips together as her blue eyes locked with mine.

Note to self: This woman is never to come within a hundred feet of my daughter.

"Her name is Melody, and I promise you that you will not be

meeting her." In fact, I would be okay if I never saw this woman again.

"I'm fine with that." She winked at the waiter after he'd given her a very healthy pour. "The last kid I met was a menace. He actually burped in my face. He behaved like an animal. It was shameful."

"How old was he?"

"I don't know? Six months? And he couldn't do shit. He just sort of sat there, staring at me with judgy eyes." She took a long sip from her glass. "It was my coworker's son, and I wanted to call that kid's ass out."

"He's a baby." I shook my head with disbelief. "How would one call out a baby?"

"I don't know, but I was ready to give Sterling a piece of my mind. That kid belched in my face and then just stared at me, before his eyes watered, and his parents celebrated the fact that he was taking a shit." She downed the rest of the red wine. "It's appalling the way parents praise their children for the most minor achievements."

At the moment, I would much prefer to be in the company of a baby taking a shit over being tortured by this conversation.

"Have we ever had an actual conversation?" I asked as I cut another bite of my lobster tail and popped it in my mouth.

"No. And I actually preferred it. I think you mentioned having a kid, but I thought it was just a trick to get the hell out of my house."

"It wasn't a trick." I reached for my phone and was disappointed that there were no messages from Winnie.

Samantha was busy flirting with the waiter as she asked for another glass of wine and inquired about the tattoo on his forearm, and I sent a quick text to check on Melody.

That's my story, and I'm sticking with it.

Me: *Hey. How are the Christmas cookies coming along?*

Winnie: *Amazing.*

Winnie: *<screenshot of a picture of Melody holding a bag of red icing and smiling at the camera>*

Me: *Looks like fun.*

Winnie: *How's your date going? If you want to stay the night, I can sleep in the guest room in the main house.*

She'd asked if I had a date, and I didn't lie about it. I thought it would be good for her to know that I was going on a date, so it wouldn't be weird between us.

But now she was encouraging me to spend the night out?

For fuck's sake. I get it. You don't give a shit what I do. But no need to push me into bed with a woman I can barely stand.

Me: *No need. I won't be home late.*

Winnie: *Don't rush on our account.*

Me: *Thank you. Also, Bridger might stop by to drop off his gifts for Emilia because he wants to hide them at the house so she doesn't see them.*

Winnie: *Yes. He already came by with his friend Brenner.*

Me: *Yes. Brenner Layton is Bridger's executive assistant. He's a great guy.*

Winnie: *Oh, that's good to know. He hung out for a while and asked me if I'd want to go to dinner tomorrow night.*

Scratch that. Brenner Layton was no longer a great guy. How dare that fucker hit on my nanny.

Me: *Sounds like fun.*

I seethed as I looked up to see my date writing her phone number on a cocktail napkin for the waiter.

This night just keeps getting better.

Winnie: *Are you okay with me having the night off tomorrow?*

Me: *Of course. Go have a great time. You deserve it.*

I set my phone down as anger radiated from me.

"Hey, dude. As soon as you're done exchanging numbers with my date, how about you bring me the bill," I hissed.

But I didn't give a shit about what Samantha did.

I was only focused on the fact that my nanny was going out with Brenner Layton.

I quickly shot a text to my cousin.

Me: *Why the fuck did you allow Brenner to ask out my nanny?*

Bridger: *Why are you so pissed? <winky face emoji>*

Me: *Fuck you. She's off limits.*

Bridger: *She's a grown-ass woman. If you like her, ask her out.*

Me: *She's too young for him.*

Bridger: *He's the same age as you and he has no problem with her age.*

Me: *Fuck you for bringing him over to my house.*

Bridger: *Is someone jealous?*

Me: *<middle finger emoji>*

Bridger: *I knew you liked her.*

He was right. I fucking liked her.

I just couldn't do anything about it.

14

Winnie

"Thanks for making time for me, Winnie. It was lovely to spend time with you," Brenner said as he pulled into the driveway at Archer's house.

"You too." I unbuckled my seat belt and smiled at him. "And I hope you have a wonderful holiday."

"Thanks." He got out of the car and came around to open my door. Brenner was a complete gentleman, and though there hadn't been a spark or a romantic connection, I definitely felt like he'd be a great friend. I stepped out of the car and walked toward the exterior door to my place, because it was late, and I didn't want to wake Archer and Melody by going through the house.

Though I doubted Archer was asleep.

He'd texted no less than a dozen times during my dinner with

Brenner with random questions.

Where had I put the Scotch tape, because he was wrapping presents.

I reminded him that it was exactly where he always kept it, in the kitchen junk drawer.

Had I seen the holiday gift wrap that he'd purchased yesterday in case I had more gifts to wrap.

I'd responded that we'd already discussed that this morning, and I thanked him again.

Did I like the new brand of mint chip ice cream he'd picked up for me.

Again, I responded that I loved it, and we'd also already discussed that this morning as well.

He'd shoveled the walk, so not to worry when I got home, because it should be clear.

I thanked him.

It was ridiculous, really, and it made no sense.

He was either a controlling boss who really wanted me to be aware of what was going on at the house while I was gone, or he didn't like the idea of me being out with Brenner Layton.

Brenner placed the palm of his hand on my lower back and guided me toward the door. But before we could make it past the front entrance to the side, the door to the main house swung open.

"Oh, hey," Archer said, standing in the doorway. "I thought I saw lights in the driveway and wanted to make sure you got home safely with the crazy weather conditions."

Brenner chuckled under his breath as I glanced around. It wasn't snowing. It was cold, but still a very calm evening as far as the weather went.

"The roads are fine."

"Oh, I thought a storm was rolling in," Archer said, crossing his arms over his chest as he glanced up at the sky as if he were checking for a storm. "Anyway, I was waiting up to discuss your travel plans for tomorrow. There's a few things I wanted to go over with you, if you have a moment."

Brenner covered his laugh with a cough this time.

"I'll be right in, Archie," I said with a sigh.

He nodded and stepped back, closing the door a bit, but leaving it cracked open for me.

"Listen, I sense a little something here, and I certainly don't want to step on any toes." Brenner smirked. "Archer is a great guy, and I got the feeling he wasn't happy about me taking you to dinner when I picked you up earlier."

"Ahh… you mean when he was playing with his power tools in the garage for absolutely no reason at all?" I laughed, because Archer had acted odd as hell when Brenner showed up at the front door.

He was the one who had been avoiding me.

He'd gone on a date last night, and I hadn't acted irrationally.

I worked for the man, for God's sake.

He was the one who said that the almost kiss was a mistake.

"Or when he told me about how he has a membership to the gun club and flexed his muscles several times while standing in the doorway, glaring at me?" Brenner pursed his lips.

"There really is nothing going on here." I shrugged. "I mean, he's great, but he's not interested in me that way."

"I don't think that's the case, Winnie. And Bridger kind of warned me that I was barking up a dangerous tree by asking you out." He chuckled.

"I think Archer is just protective because I work for him."

"Sure he is," he said with a smile. "How about this… We can

be friends and grab a bite to eat anytime. And you figure out what's going on with that jealous boss of yours in the meantime. I noticed the way your cheeks pinked when he came out to check on you, so I have a feeling there's a little more here than either of you want to admit."

"It doesn't mean anything will come of it. I work for him, and I just got divorced."

"You've been separated from your husband for a year. You deserve to be happy, Winnie." He leaned down and kissed me on the cheek.

"Thanks, Brenner. I had a really nice time." I held up my hand and waved as I walked toward the front door.

I couldn't believe that Archer had waited up for me.

He was by far the most confusing man I'd ever met.

I pushed inside and caught him hurrying down the hall toward the kitchen.

"Nice try. You were totally spying on me."

He turned around, wearing this lazy, sexy smile on his face. "I was just making sure you got home safely. What kind of boss would I be if I didn't check on you?"

"A normal one," I said dryly as I followed him to the kitchen. "I don't think it's common for a boss to check on his employee when she's out on a date. And you texted me an awful lot with ridiculous questions."

"Really?" He gaped at me. "Inquiring about your favorite flavor of popcorn is ridiculous?"

"It's certainly not urgent," I said as I hopped up on the counter. He opened the freezer and pulled out the new tub of mint chip ice cream and shook it in front of me before grabbing two spoons. "Nor is your need to know if I carry pepper spray with me."

"Hey, you can never be too safe." He handed me a spoon. "I'm glad you like this new brand. We did some damage the other night, and they were out of that brand when I stopped at the market."

I dipped my spoon in the green goodness, and my gaze locked with his as I wrapped my lips around the utensil and chuckled. "Ice cream is my weakness."

"Ahh… bows are your superpower, and ice cream is your kryptonite," he said, reaching around my head and tugging gently on the red bow tied around the elastic.

"What's your kryptonite, Archie?"

"I didn't know I had one, but I think I might have been wrong." He moved closer, and his green gaze locked on mine.

"Did you hook up with that woman last night?" I whispered.

"I did not."

"Did you kiss her?" I pressed, because I wanted to know.

"No, but I'm fairly certain the waiter did. I'm not even sure if they waited until I left the restaurant before they started hooking up." He chuckled, his hand moving to my cheek.

"You're joking," I said, shaking my head with disbelief.

"Nope. They had a real connection, and I was too busy texting you the whole time."

"Yet, you've been avoiding me since we almost kissed the other night."

"Correct."

"Why?"

"For starters, I'm too old for you." He ran the tips of his fingers along the edge of my jaw before stepping back and dipping his spoon in the ice cream.

This man is so hot and cold.

"You're so hung up on my age." I rolled my eyes. "Honestly,

I think I'm far more mature than you are."

He swallowed down the bite he'd taken, and his mouth fell open. "Shots fired. How are you more mature than me?"

This man managed to be ridiculously sexy with his mouth hanging open, standing here in a pair of gray joggers and a white tee.

"Well, for starters, you were spying on me when I got home from my date. You didn't see me doing that last night after you went out, did you?"

The corners of his lips turned up, and he sighed. "I'm sorry. Did I interrupt a kiss good night?"

"No. I wasn't going to kiss him either way."

"How come?"

"Because I like him as a friend. I don't have romantic feelings toward him."

He nodded. "Did I make you uncomfortable the other night?"

"No. I wanted you to kiss me."

He narrowed his gaze as he studied me. "Yet you weren't jealous last night when I was out with someone else?"

"I didn't say that," I snorted. "I just wasn't lame enough to spy on you."

"Oh, I'm lame, am I?"

"You're confusing, Archie."

"How so?"

"You're very hot and cold with me, and I can't read you," I admitted.

"You're my daughter's nanny. And the best damn thing to happen to both of us in a very long time," he said. His eyes softened, and I saw all that vulnerability there. "I don't want to fuck that up."

"And kissing me would fuck that up?"

"I don't know, Winnie. I don't really date, and kissing a woman who lives in your home and works for you seems like a bad decision." He stepped closer. "Even if I really want to."

I blew out a breath and put my hands on his chest, pushing him back the slightest bit before jumping off the counter. I set my spoon in the sink and replaced the lid on the ice cream before setting it back in the freezer.

And then I turned to face him. "Listen, you need not worry. I wanted to kiss you the other night, too, but I don't want to kiss you tonight, Archie."

He looked surprised by my words, and I moved past him, heading for the door to my bedroom.

"You've lost interest that quickly, huh?" His voice was laced with humor, but I could hear the vulnerability.

I turned around and shrugged. "It's not about losing interest; it's about knowing my worth. And I don't want to kiss a man who isn't sure about me. Even if it's the first man in a very long time that I've wanted to kiss."

He nodded. "I'm sorry for being hot and cold with you. I don't want to mess this up."

"Neither do I." I forced a smile.

"All right. So, we're friends?" he asked.

"Of course we are."

He chuckled. "And not the kind of friends who kiss."

"Nope. The next man I agree to kiss is going to have zero doubts when he looks at me. When I left my miserable marriage, I made a promise to myself not to settle for anything less than that."

"Nor should you." There was a tortured look in his eyes.

But it wasn't my job to convince Archer Chadwick that I was worth the risk.

It had taken me a long time to find my worth again.

And I meant it when I said I wouldn't settle for anything less.

Even if I was desperate to kiss my sexy-as-sin boss.

• • •

"Merry Christmas, Winnie girl." My father was wearing the same Santa hat that he'd been wearing every year for as long as I could remember.

"Thanks, Dad." I chuckled as I unwrapped my gift and gasped. "What did you do?"

"I think you're due for a new laptop, aren't you?" he asked.

I'd had the same laptop for several years, and I was definitely in need of a new one.

"This is amazing. And way too much." I leaned forward and wrapped my arms around his neck. "Thank you so much."

"You deserve everything, sweetheart." He smiled.

"And so do you." I stood and walked to my room, the one I'd grown up in. We'd lived in this little two-bedroom house right down the street from my father's mechanic shop my entire life. I leaned forward, pressing my hands on the top of the package as I pushed the large gift out to him, and his eyes widened.

"And what did you do?" He chuckled as he tore the paper off and unveiled his new Craftsman rolling tool chest. "Wow. This is amazing."

"Apparently it holds hundreds of pounds of tools."

"It sure does." He leaned forward and kissed the top of my hair. "Thank you very much. But you should be saving your money."

"I'm doing pretty good now that I don't have someone emptying the bank account anytime there's something in it," I said as my phone vibrated, and I saw an incoming FaceTime call from Archer.

My father glanced over and chuckled. "Your boss sure calls you a lot."

I moved to my feet. "I promised Melody we could FaceTime this morning so she could show me her gifts."

My father was right. Archer and I talked several times a day. Sometimes about Melody.

Sometimes just about life.

About the weather, our families, friends, work, books, movies—we talked about everything.

He nodded and waved me off as he tore open the box to start building his tool chest.

"Merry Christmas!" I smiled as they came into focus on my phone screen.

"Winnie! I misses you!"

"I misses you, too, sweet pea."

"Merry Christmas, Winnie," Archer said, his hair disheveled, as a sexy grin spread across his handsome face.

"What time are you guys heading over to your aunt and uncle's house?"

"In an hour. We're just talking about how much we miss your pancakes," he said.

"Oh yeah?" I walked into my bedroom and closed the door. "I miss you guys, too."

I really did. I was surprised at how much I missed them, when I'd only been gone for a few days.

After spending years in a relationship with Jaden, I'd felt nothing but relief after I left.

And a few days away from Archer and Melody had been much more difficult than I'd imagined.

And I couldn't wait to get back home.

Home.

Rosewood River felt like home.

Archer and Melody felt like home, too.

15

Archer

I'd spoken to Winnie multiple times a day while she was gone. I was shocked at how much I'd missed her. How she'd become a part of our family structure in such a short time.

She'd moved in less than two months ago.

But I supposed having someone in your life day in and day out—she was here in the mornings and at night—could cause you to grow attached to them.

Who knew.

She'd become someone I trusted and depended on where my daughter was concerned.

Hell, she'd become someone I trusted and depended on personally as well.

I'd missed her in a way I hadn't expected, and she'd only

been gone for a few days.

I knew this wasn't good, wasn't smart—but I didn't know how to stop it.

And don't even get me started on how many times I'd gotten off to this woman in the shower every damn day. It was the one guilty pleasure I'd allowed myself.

To give in to my desires from afar.

Sure, it was a little fucked up, but it was a hell of a lot better than acting on it.

"Winnie, I can't believe you got me the best gifts ever," Melody gushed.

We'd agreed that we'd celebrate Christmas when she got home. And my daughter had been so excited to open the final gifts under the tree that Winnie didn't even get to go to her room and relax after we'd picked her up from the airport, because we jumped right into gift-opening.

"You like them?" she asked.

"You know how much I love to draw," Melody said, holding up the wood case with hundreds of colored pencils and the large drawing notebook she'd gotten her. "And I can't wait to make lots of friendship bracelets together."

She'd gotten Melody way too much.

A bracelet-making kit, the drawing pencils and paper, and she still had two more packages to open.

"Open this one next," Winnie said, handing my daughter the large box.

Melody tore the paper off and gasped when she lifted the lid to the box and saw the pink cowboy boots. "Winnie! You gots me the pink boots I love."

How the hell didn't I know she loved pink cowboy boots?

"I did. I remembered that day we saw them at the store, and I couldn't wait to get them for you." She pushed one more package in front of her. "And this is the last one."

Melody opened the box to find a matching cowboy hat, and when she squealed with excitement and flung herself at Winnie, I was fairly certain I saw tears roll down both of their cheeks.

I loved how much this woman adored my daughter.

It was genuine and real and rare.

Melody ran off to her room to check herself out in the mirror with her new boots and hat on, and Winnie turned and handed me a package.

"I thought we said no gifts for us?"

"It's nothing big. Just a little something to wish you a merry Christmas, Archie." Her cheeks pinked, because she had no idea that I'd also broken the agreement.

"Thank you," I said as I tore the wrapping off the box. When I lifted the top and set it aside, I took out the gorgeous frame with a collage of five photos in it. The one in the center was me lifting Melody above my head as we both laughed. It was the first day that it had snowed in Rosewood River, and we'd all three gone out to play in the snow. The next one was of Melody dressed as a reindeer for the holiday program. The third one was of Melody at her riding lesson up on her horse, Biffle, and she was clearly smiling at Winnie with her hand up. The last two photos nearly took my breath away, because they were so unexpected. One was of me sitting with my daughter on my lap reading her a book, and she was looking up at me with so much wonder. And the last one was of the night we put the Christmas tree up, and I was bent down handing Melody an ornament, and she was smiling at me with her hand on my cheek.

Moments you don't realize are even happening.

She'd captured them.

She was always taking photos with her phone or her Polaroid camera.

"You could also be a photographer if you decide on a career change," I said, staring down at the photos. "You're so talented."

"I'm not the reason those photos are so special."

"Thank you. I love these." I cleared my throat, surprised how emotional I felt after looking at them.

"Daddy, can we give Winnie her present now?" Melody asked as she came bounding down the hallway in her hat and boots.

"Hey, I thought we said no gifts," Winnie said, frowning at me.

"Are you seriously going to pull the no-gifts rule out when you just gave me a gift?"

"Fine." She chewed her bottom lip.

Fuck. She was cute as hell.

Sexy and sweet and brilliant, all at the same time.

"Come on, Winnie," Melody said, reaching for her hand.

"Oh, we're going to the gift? The gift is not in here?" she asked, her brows cinched together.

"We're going to the gift," I said, leading her down the hall.

I'd worked hard on this room while she was gone, and I couldn't wait to show her.

Winnie deserved a real office. She wrote a lot, and she should have her own space to work.

There was a bow on the bedroom door across from where my gym was, and she turned to look at me. "This is the guest room."

"Not any-mores," Melody sang out as she pushed the door open.

I'd found a vintage printer's desk at the antique store in town, and I immediately thought of Winnie. She was an old soul, and she enjoyed the story behind things, such as furniture and art and other unique pieces. She was always asking questions when we walked through town, about where things originated, and how they'd come about.

"Daddy and me painted the walls your favorite color, safe green." My daughter clapped her hands together.

"Sage green," I said, shoving my hands in my pockets because Winnie had yet to speak. Maybe this was too much.

What was I thinking?

It had started as just adding a desk to the guest room, and then I'd spoken to Emilia, who'd helped come up with a plan to transform the space for Winnie.

Emilia had talked to the girls, who'd framed a few of their favorite quotes from Winnie's books and placed them on a chair in the corner.

She glanced up at the antique crystal chandelier hanging in the center of the room.

"Uh, Emilia said the light was a big part of setting the mood for your workspace," I said.

She turned to look at me, and I startled when I saw two tears rolling down her cheeks. "I can't believe you did this for me."

"I can't believe all that you've done for Melody. For us. This is just our little way of thanking you."

"Winnie, are those sad tears or happy tears?" Melody asked, her brows cinched together with concern.

"Definitely happy tears, sweet pea." She sniffed a few times and swiped at her face. "This is the nicest thing anyone has ever done for me."

She continued moving in a circle, taking it all in.

"How about you go grab Winnie some tissues," I said to my daughter.

The minute Melody was gone, Winnie moved toward me.

She placed a hand on each side of my face, pushed up on her tiptoes, and kissed me. I didn't hold back. I tangled my hand in her hair and tilted her head to the side. Needing more.

Needing everything.

Her lips parted the slightest bit as my tongue slipped inside and tangled with hers.

I wanted to kiss every inch of her.

But she pulled back, cheeks pink and lips plump.

And she smiled. Eyes tender and full of emotion.

"I know that wasn't smart, and I know it can't go anywhere, but I needed to do that. Just one time, okay?"

I was still processing her words when Melody came running in the room with a box of tissues.

"Thank you," Winnie said to my daughter, and then her gaze locked with mine. "Truly, this means the world to me."

"You're going to write all the books in here." Melody danced around the room, and Winnie smiled up at me.

"Yes. This is officially the romance room. And there is definitely a story behind this desk."

I chuckled, still a little stunned that she'd kissed me. "I knew you'd want to know the story behind it, and it came with a little explanation about the history of the piece. I tucked it in the top drawer."

She sighed as her gaze locked with mine. "You're full of surprises, Archer Chadwick."

"So are you." I winked at her.

"I'm hungry, Daddy," Melody said, and Winnie quickly pulled her gaze from mine.

"Hey, how about we do breakfast for dinner?" Winnie said, scooping Melody into her arms. "I know you've been missing my pancakes, and I can make some bacon and eggs, too."

"Yes! I loves the breakfast at dinner time, right, Daddy?"

"Right."

I'd just kissed my nanny.

I'd kissed Winnie.

And I'd fucking liked it. Liked it more than I'd ever liked kissing anyone.

"Relax, Archie. We'll eat some pancakes and it'll all be fine." Winnie chuckled and glanced over her shoulder at me, as if she knew I was having a mild freak-out. And then she walked toward the kitchen.

"Yeah. It's pancakes, Daddy. Winnie's pancakes!" My daughter's head fell back in a fit of giggles as Winnie set her down on the floor in the kitchen.

But I knew the fucking truth.

This was so much more than pancakes.

16

Winnie

I'd finished unpacking my suitcase, tied my hair in a bun on top of my head, and slipped into a hot bath.

I still couldn't believe Archer had made me an office in his home.

And not just any office, but the most beautiful writing space I could have dreamed of.

He'd acknowledged how important my career was to me and created a place for me to sit down and write.

Talk about the ultimate act of service.

So, I'd briefly lost my mind and kissed him.

The truth was, I'd wanted to kiss him for weeks. And nothing about this kiss felt like settling.

At the end of the day, it didn't matter if it didn't go anywhere.

Couldn't it just be a kiss?

Didn't people do that all the time?

It was difficult for me to navigate this type of thing, because I'd only ever been with one man.

I'd only had sex with one man.

And up until today, I'd only ever kissed one man.

But this was what people my age were supposed to do.

I didn't need to overthink it.

And Archer was clearly doing that for both of us. He'd barely spoken during dinner, not that it had been noticeable, because Melody had caught me up on everything that I'd missed over the last four days.

My phone vibrated on the little bench beside the tub, and I reached for it.

Archie: *I just got Melody bathed and in bed. Should we talk?*

Me: *What would you like to talk about, Archie? <lips emoji>*

I chuckled, because it was kind of adorable that he was freaking out.

Archie: *Don't be a smartass, Winnie. We should talk about what happened.*

Me: *Did you like it?*

Archie: *Of course I did. Should we talk in person? Do you want to meet in the kitchen?*

Me: *I'm in the tub.*

Archie: *Fuck me. You can't say things like that.*

Me: *I can't tell you that I'm bathing?*

Archie: *You can't tell me you're naked.*

Me: *Should I bathe in a swimsuit? <laughing face emoji>*

Archie: *Winnie.*

Me: *Archie.*

Archie: *Fine, we can text while you soak naked in hot water. <blowing smoke emoji>*

Me: *Okay. Let's hear it. It was a huge mistake. It shouldn't have happened. It can't happen again.*

Archie: *Is that what you think, or is that you speaking for me?*

Me: *That's me speaking for you. <laughing face emoji>*

Me: *Listen. I acted on impulse. I wanted to kiss you and I'm fairly certain you wanted to kiss me.*

Archie: *We've established that. But we've also discussed why it shouldn't happen. Do you remember that?*

Me: *Because I wouldn't kiss someone who wasn't sure that they should kiss me. We had the discussion last week, and I remember it clearly. I'm younger than you, so my memory is much stronger. <winky face emoji>*

Archie: *Such a smartass. My point is, those issues are still there. Nothing has changed. But I'm not going to deny that I wanted to kiss you. My hesitation has nothing to do with how badly I want you, Winnie.*

My heart raced at his words. Because I wanted him, too. I wanted him more than I'd ever wanted anyone or anything.

Me: *Listen, I don't have any expectations. I got divorced six months ago. I'm not looking for anything. But it's been a long time since I actually wanted to kiss someone, so I don't regret it. I liked it, and it's the first time in a very long time that I felt something like that, if that makes sense.*

Archie: *Something like what?*

Me: *That I felt wanted. Desired. And I reciprocated those feelings. Maybe that's what I need right now. It doesn't have to be a big thing. You made it clear that you don't date, and I'm not looking for a relationship. So maybe you're just my boss who's also my friend, and we just kiss sometimes. Is that a thing?*

Archie: *Do you want it to be a thing?*

Me: *Do you?*

Archie: *I do, but I know I shouldn't.*

Me: *Why? It's just a kiss, Archie.*

Archie: *I don't want to fuck things up, Winnie. You've been the best thing to happen to Melody, and to me, in a very long time. I'm not used to feeling this way.*

Me: *What way?*

Archie: *This way. Wanting you. Thinking about you when you aren't around. Thinking about you when you are around.*

Me: *I'm getting out of the tub. I want to kiss you right now. Are you okay with that?*

Archie: *I'm waiting outside your door.*

Holy shit. I jumped out of the bathtub, quickly dried off, and slipped into my robe, then glanced in the mirror and tugged my hair out of the elastic before slipping my bow into the pocket of my robe.

I'd definitely need my superpowers right now.

I pulled the door open, and he was standing there, leaning against the wall.

"Hey," I whispered.

"Hey." He snaked an arm around my waist and tugged me closer. I saw zero hesitation in his eyes as he dipped down and his mouth crashed into mine.

It was different this time.

Frantic and needy.

His hands came around my backside and lifted me off the floor as my legs wrapped around his waist. He stepped into my room and pressed me up against the wall, our lips never losing contact.

Had I ever been kissed like this?

No. Definitely not.

His tongue swirled with mine, and I rocked against him when I felt his hard length grow between my legs. My robe had opened, and I was bare beneath it, just the layer of cotton from his sweatpants between us.

My God, I was so turned on.

My fingers tangled in his hair as I shamelessly slid up and down his erection. Chasing pleasure I hadn't felt in years.

And he kissed me relentlessly. His tongue slid in and out as my body burned with desire.

We just stayed right there making out for the longest time as I ground up against him, my body moving of its own volition.

I was panting as a groan escaped my lips.

He nipped at my bottom lip.

"Take what you need," his deep voice commanded as he guided my hips up and down. "Come for me, Winnie."

My head fell back against the wall, and white lights exploded behind my eyes as I shattered.

He claimed my mouth again as I rocked against him and rode out every last bit of pleasure.

Once my hips had stopped moving, he pulled back to look at me. The corners of his lips turned up in the sexiest way, and it took all I had not to tug his mouth back down to mine.

"That wasn't embarrassing at all," I whispered.

"That was fucking beautiful." His green gaze looked at me with complete adoration, and my chest squeezed.

I slid down his body and adjusted my robe. "Well, it was a bit more than a kiss."

"It was," he said as he stood with his back to the wall, watching me.

My gaze moved to the erection that was currently tenting his joggers. "Should we do something about that?"

He laughed. "No. I'll take care of it."

"You'll 'take care of it'?" I smirked.

"Yes, Winnie. I'm a man raising a little girl on my own. I don't get out a lot, so I'm quite well versed in taking care of my needs."

I bit my bottom lip, and I didn't know what to say, but I didn't want this night to end. "Do you want a cup of tea?"

He chuckled. "A cup of tea?"

"Yes. I'm not sleepy, so I thought we could just—hang out?"

He smiled and gave me a little nod. "How about you start the tea, and I'll grab a shower, because I can't sit and talk to you when I'm hard as steel, not that I haven't done it many times before."

"You sure you don't want me to give you a hand?" I chuckled.

"Don't tempt me. I'll meet you in the kitchen in five minutes."

"Ohhh… it's that quick, huh?" I teased as I walked behind him.

He startled me when he turned abruptly, pinning me to the wall with a mischievous grin on his face as he leaned down and spoke against my ear. "I'd force myself to take my time if I were buried inside you. But if I'm just thinking about you, I can pretty much come on command."

I could barely catch my breath as I stared at him, and he leaned down and gave me a chaste kiss. "See you soon."

I heated water in the kettle, my body still on a high after the pre-tea orgasm. I poured the water into our mugs to steep, and Archer stayed true to his word and returned in just a few minutes, looking relaxed with his wet hair and handsome face. He'd changed into navy joggers and a white tee.

We settled on the couch, where we shared stories about our childhoods and our families.

"That must have been so fun growing up with all of your cousins, too. Living on the same property the way you did."

"It was the best," he said as he set his mug down on the coffee table. "How about you. Did you like being an only child?"

"I mean, I would have loved to have siblings, but with my dad raising me on his own, it was always just me and him against the world, you know?"

"Yeah. And do you talk to your mom?" he asked.

"No. She left and never looked back. That's what made things so complicated with Jaden." I let out a deep breath. "He had this great family, and his mom and I were so close. But I couldn't stay in a relationship with a man just because I loved his mother, you know?"

"I get it, but it's no way to live. And you weren't happy for a while?"

"I wasn't even excited on my wedding day. I felt like such a cliché getting married at twenty-one when I was still in college. But he was so lost during that time, and he was adamant about either getting married or breaking up. I was young and not as confident as I am now, I guess, so I went along with it."

"Life is all about the journey. We learn from the things we do, and we can't turn back time, so you take your experiences and the knowledge you have from them, and you move forward." He traced his fingers along the palm of my hand.

"How about you? Did it take you a long time to get over Melody's mom?" I asked.

"In some ways, yes, and in other ways, no. I loved her, and that part was difficult. But from the moment she left, I was thrust into this new life raising a tiny human, so I didn't have a lot of time to wallow or feel sorry for myself. But I do think it's probably made me cautious about relationships with women, not to mention I'm raising a child on my own, so it changes things."

"And you're fine raising Melody on your own now?" I pressed. "You like keeping your relationships casual?"

"Being Melody's dad is the best thing I've ever done. But it's a lot of work, and I'm committed to it. And I wouldn't just bring someone into her life unless I was certain about it. So my life works the way it is, at least for now."

I nodded. "You two have a good thing going."

"Yeah, she's the best." He cleared his throat. "And if you wake up tomorrow morning and you feel like we crossed a line, just know that you are calling the shots. So if this was a one-and-done, you just send me a text, and I won't push you, Winnie."

"I will not wake up and feel that way, but thanks for saying that. It was—a first for me," I whispered.

His face paled. "What was a first?"

I chuckled. "Relax. Obviously, I've made out with a man before. I just meant that the ending was a first."

He leaned closer, his fingers finding my chin as he tipped my face up to look at him. "You've never come before?"

"Not with a man," I said, feeling my cheeks heat. "I say that like I've been with a lot of men. I've only been with Jaden, and it wasn't great. It was fast and one-sided. That's probably why I started writing romance, because I craved something more."

His gaze softened. "It should never be one-sided. You take whatever you need from me, Winnie."

"I might take you up on that." I waggled my brows. I fought the urge to crawl onto his lap and kiss him again. I needed to be cautious, though, because Archer Chadwick was the kind of man you wouldn't want to kiss just once.

I knew that deep in my soul.

I stood up abruptly. "Okay, I should probably get some sleep. Thanks for—the midnight kiss and orgasm."

He laughed. "Anytime. I'll see you in the morning."

"Sweet dreams, Archie," I said as I walked toward my room.

And when I got to the door and stepped inside, I turned around to find his eyes still on me.

I held his stare for a few beats before closing the door.

I was in so much trouble.

17
Archer

Sunday dinner at my aunt and uncle's house was something we'd been doing since I was a kid.

My parents lived next door to my aunt Ellie and uncle Keaton, in the home I'd grown up in.

We were all eating dinner around the big farm table, and I glanced over at Winnie, who'd quickly become a member of the family. Everyone adored her.

Me included.

We'd made out like teenagers last night, and there hadn't been any awkwardness this morning.

I'd gotten off to thoughts of her in the shower again, because having Winnie rub up against me while my mouth claimed hers was the hottest thing I'd ever experienced.

"You okay, honey?" my mom asked, looking at me with concern from across the table, and I realized everyone was staring at me.

Meanwhile, I was thinking about my nanny dry-humping me while I was sitting at Sunday dinner.

"Yeah, yeah, yeah, of course. What did I miss?" I shrugged.

Bridger laughed. "The entire conversation."

"Sorry, I've got a big meeting tomorrow morning, and Melody is back to school, so I just have a lot on my mind." I glanced over at Winnie, who appeared to buy it, as did most of my family.

But Bridger raised his eyebrows as if he knew exactly what I was thinking about. And when I looked over at my brother, Axel, he also had a goofy grin on his face.

"Anyway," Lulu said, "I was just about to read this week's 'Taylor Tea.'"

"I love when she reads it in that mischievous voice," Emelia said.

"The Taylor Tea" had already written about my new nanny moving to town, and they'd spoken about me like some pathetic man who needed assistance in order to survive daily life. Luckily, they hadn't brought it up again for the last few weeks.

"Go ahead, Lu." Henley took a sip of her wine.

"'Hey there, Roses, I hope you all had a wonderful holiday. Things have been busy in Rosewood River, so buckle up because the tea is boiling hot today,'" she said, looking up and waggling her brows.

"What does that even mean? Isn't tea always hot?" Bridger grumped.

"No. I drink iced tea," Emilia said with a laugh before encouraging Lulu to continue.

"'Word on Main Street is that our favorite mailman may

be delivering mail from the doghouse for a while, because he was seen canoodling with a tourist who was not his baby mama. Looks like his lady might be sending him a big fat goodbye letter and overnighting it to the dog £, where the man should stay.'" Lulu laughed. "I mean, they really call people out, don't they?"

"I feel bad for Cara," Emilia said, empathy painted all over her face.

"Cara Carmichael egged your flower shop," Bridger hissed. "We caught her on camera."

"And that was because you told her that I write 'The Taylor Tea,' remember?" She chuckled and kissed his cheek. "I can still feel bad for her that her man has a wandering eye."

"Agreed. Continue," Eloise said.

"'In other breaking news, our favorite single daddy has been moping around town because his nanny isn't around to take care of him. But apparently she arrived back in town, and we expect our favorite Daddy O to be all smiles again.'" Lulu paused, her mouth hanging open as she glanced at me.

"'Daddy O'? What is that about? And I was hardly moping around town—that's ridiculous," I said.

Everyone laughed, of course, because my family found the whole thing to be hilarious.

"I actually think you were mopey for a few days." Bridger shrugged as he reached for another dinner roll.

"You're always mopey, so who are you to judge?" I snipped.

"Takes one to know one. And I'm not the topic of conversation, Daddy O."

I rolled my eyes. "Can we be done with this ridiculous column, please?"

Winnie's gaze found mine, and she smiled.

Great, now she'd think I was a stalker.

I did miss her when she was gone, but I was hardly moping around.

"We can absolutely be done with the column, honey," my mother said, tossing me a wink.

"How's the book coming along, Winnie?" Aunt Ellie asked.

"Really good. I'm at around seventy-five percent of the way."

"It's so good. She's letting us read it as she finishes each chapter," Emilia said.

"Yes, we're so lucky to be reading while she's writing it." Eloise beamed at Winnie, and I laughed.

"Did you always know you wanted to be a writer?" my father asked.

"I've always loved to write. I used to write all kinds of stories when I was a little girl." Winnie smiled at the memory.

"And me and my Winnie write stories together all the time now," Melody said. "Sometimes we make up stories when we go on walks. Because life is a big story, right, Winnie?"

"It sure is." Winnie leaned over and cut Melody's chicken into smaller bites. She did things like that all the time. As if she just knew what she needed and when she needed it.

"So Winnie, I heard you went on a date with my man Brenner Layton right before Christmas," Bridger said, glancing over at me, and my hand fisted beneath the table.

"We just went to dinner. He's a nice guy."

"Brenner's the best." Axel dabbed at his mouth with his napkin. "He's been great, finding help for my business and screening candidates. He's a cool dude."

"He's not that cool." The words slipped from my mouth before I could stop them, and everyone gaped at me. Aside from Bridger, who was all smiles. "I just mean that he wears suits when he's here in town, so he stands out like a sore thumb."

"I wear suits," Bridger said.

"And you're also not cool." I smirked.

"Hmm… you always liked Brenner. Is this a recent change of heart?" he pressed, and I could tell he was enjoying himself.

"Nope. I've never thought he was cool."

"Brenner? Come on, dude. He's a fabulous dresser, and he's like the Ray Donovan of the business world," Rafe said with a laugh. "Anything Bridger throws at him, he can fix. Hell, if I were a woman, I'd date him. You should give him a chance, Winnie. I mean, if you aren't interested in anyone else."

He glanced over at me, as did Easton, Clark, Axel, and that dickhead Bridger, who'd started this.

They were all in on it.

Trying to make me jealous.

I rolled my eyes. "This is like an episode of *The Bachelor.* I don't think Winnie needs you to fix her up with anyone."

"I'm actually enjoying being single right now," she said. "But Brenner and I can definitely be friends. He's a really nice guy. I'm just not looking for a boyfriend."

Mic drop.

I shot them all a look.

Suck it, bitches.

"Yeah, play the field, girl. You're young and beautiful and talented. You don't need to be strapped down with some guy," Lulu said, and Rafe gaped at her.

"What?" he grumped.

"Not everyone is like you, baby," she said, patting his cheek. "Power to the woman."

I laughed, and Rafe glared at me.

We finished dinner and cleared the table, and Bridger texted in the group chat for us to meet out by the firepit.

Melody and Winnie were helping my aunt Ellie get the s'mores ready, and all the girls were in the kitchen, talking and laughing.

I zipped my coat up and walked out back, where Bridger had started a fire.

"What the hell is wrong with you guys?" I hissed once we were far enough away from the house that I knew no one could hear us. "Why the fuck are you pushing Brenner Layton on my nanny?"

"Because we know you like her," Rafe snipped, and Clark burst out in laughter.

"I mean, this was Bridger's strategy to get you to admit it, and personally, I didn't think it was our best option." Easton shrugged.

"You're taking advice from a man who bought his woman a toilet as an apology gift?"

"Don't you dare shit on that toilet." Bridger got the flame going on the fire, and we all settled on the Adirondack chairs surrounding it.

"Aren't you supposed to shit on the toilet?" Axel said with a smirk.

"My point is, this guy doesn't know what he's talking about." I gave Bridger the finger. "But I do enjoy the toilet, so thank you."

He'd gifted me the world's best toilet, and even though he was on my shit list, I still appreciated it.

Pun intended.

"Dude," Bridger said as he took the seat across from me.

"Yes?"

"I'm trying to help you."

"By setting up my nanny with everyone you know?"

"It was one person, and your reaction is very telling. For the record, I didn't know he was going to ask her out. He did it on his own without giving me a heads-up. I would have discouraged it. But he told me she wasn't into him because she's into you." He popped the top of his beer. "And he said that you made it very obvious that you're into her. So stop fucking around and do something about it."

"How, pray tell, did I make it obvious? I did no such thing." I crossed my arms over my chest. I was frustrated with the whole situation. And I didn't need input from my family. I was a grown-ass man.

"I heard you pulled a gun," Clark said with a laugh.

"I heard that you twirled a large knife in front of Brenner." Easton looked at me.

"The fuck are you guys talking about?"

"So maybe I made the story a little more exciting," Bridger said with a smirk. "But he did say that you mentioned guns and the gym, and maybe talked about sharpening your knives?"

"You crazy bastard. I did not." I had to chuckle. "Maybe I discussed the gun club and flexed my muscles a few times. But I'm just being protective."

"I love you, brother, but this isn't you being protective," Axel said. "And it's been a long time since I've seen you actually happy to be around someone other than Melody. Don't run from that."

"I'm not running from anything. I'm trying to do the right thing."

"Don't overthink it," Clark said.

"That's a luxury that I don't have. Fuck. I have to overthink everything." I looked them each in the eyes before continuing. "I have a child to think about. I can't just act on whims. Not to mention, Winnie is a decade younger than me, and she just got out of a relationship with a complete douchebag. She's young. I'm sure she wants a family and things people her age want. I have my family with Melody, and I can't fuck things up with a nanny my daughter is crazy about."

"Your life is not over just because you're a father," Easton said.

I rubbed my face. "I'm not saying it's over. But I can't be irresponsible. I can't just do whatever the fuck it is that I want to do."

"You're a good dad, Archer." Axel blew out a breath. "But you also deserve to be happy."

"I am happy. I have everything I need. I don't need to complicate it." I shrugged. "I shouldn't have been an asshole about Brenner taking her out. In fact, you should encourage him to ask her out again. I'll get my head on straight."

I'd been a complete asshole.

I knew better, and I'd done it anyway.

She deserved better.

18

Winnie

Archer had been very distant since our make-out session a few days ago. Ever since we'd gone to his aunt and uncle's house for Sunday dinner, his texts were short and there was zero flirtation, and our conversations were strictly about Melody.

Today was New Year's Eve. Archer's mom and dad were going to have Melody spend the night, as Bridger and Emilia were having a New Year's party at their house, and Archer thought it would be fun for me to go as well.

But he'd just announced that he was no longer going to the party over dinner.

I was trying not to show my disappointment.

I couldn't get that kiss out of my mind.

"I'm not going to Mimi and Pops's house for a sleepover?" Melody asked as she munched on the homemade pizza I'd made.

Archer groaned after taking a bite. "Wow. This is the best pizza I've ever had."

"Thanks," I said, considering that was the most he'd spoken to me in a few days.

He turned his attention to Melody. "Nope. I'm staying home with my girl so we can ring in the New Year together."

"I can stay home if you'd like to go to the party," I said, since I'd never planned on going—he was the one to insist on it before I'd even left to go back home for the holidays. This was coming out of left field. "I don't mind at all."

"No. My parents offered as well. I'm the one who canceled."

So his parents hadn't changed their minds; it was all Archer.

He didn't want to go.

It wasn't like I hung all over the guy. I hadn't brought up what happened between us, nor had I expected it to happen again.

It was a fabulous freaking kiss.

I didn't expect anything from him.

But it was hard not to feel like I was the reason he wasn't going. What kind of nanny was I if the dad I worked for couldn't go out because he didn't want to be around me?

"All right." I stood and cleared my plate. "If you change your mind, I'm happy to stay home."

"No. You should go, Winnie. There's going to be a lot of people there, and it would be good for you to meet people your age now that you live here."

People my age?

His obsession with my age was bordering on annoying.

"I've made plenty of friends since I moved here, so you don't need to worry about me. I'm doing just fine." I blew out a breath before stopping to kiss Melody on the cheek. “Happy New Year, sweet pea.”

“Happy New Year, my Winnie.” She smiled up at me, and there was a little smear of pizza sauce on her cheek. “And it’s Winnie’s birthday in February, right?”

“It is?”

“Yes, Archie. Imagine that. I’ll be twenty-five years old in February. Hopefully I can meet people my age after my birthday.” I chuckled.

He sighed as he studied me for a few beats. “Brenner will be there tonight.”

“Yes. He told me that he was going. I’m looking forward to seeing him.” Brenner and I were friends, but I wasn’t going to lie: I didn’t mind that it seemed to get under Archer’s skin.

“Good. I was unfair about him. He’s a good guy.”

“Ahh… he’s not too old for me anymore?”

“Not my place to tell you who to date. I apologize for putting my nose where it doesn’t belong,” he said, but his smile looked forced.

He was clearly done with all the flirty banter.

It stung, but I schooled my features to appear unaffected.

I’d just gotten out of the worst relationship one could have, and I was supposed to be enjoying being single.

This should not hurt my feelings.

“No worries. I’m going to go get ready. Happy New Year.” I turned quickly and made my way to my room.

I’d picked up a fun dress to wear tonight with the gift card my aunt and uncle had gotten me for Christmas.

I spent the next hour shaking off the sullen feeling that had engulfed me after Archer had basically insisted that I go to this party and find a man.

I get it. You don't like me that way.

Maybe it was the fact that I'd literally humped the man like a horny teenager at the height of her sexuality.

He'd probably been horrified.

I picked up my phone and pulled up my playlist. I quickly found my favorite T-Swift song and was soon singing along with "Shake It Off" while I put on my makeup.

I went for a smoky eye and a red lip, which I never did. I curled my hair and left it down tonight. I wore my gold bow earrings that my father had gotten me for my college graduation.

After slipping into my new formfitting black sequined dress and adding my black strappy stilettos, I glanced in the mirror.

I hadn't dressed up in such a long time.

I felt good.

I pushed away the nerves fluttering in my stomach, as I wouldn't know a lot of the people who would be there tonight, but I was determined to have a good time.

I'd made good progress on my book this week, and the new office had proven to be the dreamiest workspace. I'd effectively blocked Jaden, who seemed like he might actually leave me alone this time.

I made my way through the door to the house to get my dress coat out of the front closet. I stored some things in the house, since the closet in my room was fairly small. But yes, a part of me probably wanted Archer to see me in this dress.

I'd bought it thinking he'd be at this party tonight.

Hell, I'd bought it with him in mind.

My heels tapped against his wood floors, and I saw his head turn to look at me out of my peripheral vision.

I made it to the closet and pulled out my black dress coat, and Melody let a loud gasp escape.

"My Winnie looks like a real live princess," she shouted across the room as I slipped my coat on.

"Thank you, sweet pea."

Archer was on his feet, moving toward me. "It's snowing out there. Are you driving?"

Bridger and Emilia lived less than two blocks away.

"No, because I'm sure I'll have a few cocktails tonight. So I'm going to walk."

"You can't walk in this weather." He gaped at me, and then his eyes scanned the length of my body down to my four-inch heels. "You're walking in those shoes?"

"Well, I hadn't thought about the shoes. I guess I'll wear my boots and carry my heels in a bag." I chuckled as I leaned down to unstrap my shoes.

"Absolutely not."

"Excuse me?"

"You're not walking in this weather, not to mention it's not safe to walk alone at night." He was already slipping on his cowboy boots. "Grab your coat, angel face."

"Yes!" Melody punched her fist toward the ceiling.

"This is Rosewood River. I'm from Chicago. I am not afraid to walk alone here." I laughed and shook my head with disbelief. "Archie, I've been taking care of myself for a very long time."

"I'm sure you have. But the tourists are out, and you don't need to take care of yourself when you've got me to drive you." He paused for a second. "How about you don't argue, and you let me win this one."

I nodded. "Fine. I'll take the ride and save my feet."

Melody ran off to get her cowboy boots, and Archer turned to look at me. "You look beautiful, Winnie."

"Thank you." I could feel my cheeks heat. What was it about this man that just made me so reactive? "I'm sorry you aren't coming to the party. It's going to be lots of fun."

"I think a night in watching *Frozen* for the hundredth time sounds far more appealing than cocktails and music and grown-up conversation."

My gaze locked with his until Melody came bustling down the hallway. "I'm ready."

The three of us piled into Archer's truck, and a part of me just wanted to stay home. I'd grown so comfortable with them. But he didn't want me here tonight, and he'd practically insisted I go out and meet people.

Archer's Bluetooth announced an incoming call from his mother, and he answered.

"Hey, Mama, what's going on?"

"Where are you?" she asked.

"Melody and I are dropping Winnie off at Bridger and Emilia's."

"Hi, Isabelle," I called out, because I loved Archer's mother. She was sweet and funny and very warm.

"Hey, sweetheart. You go and have some fun tonight."

"I will. Thank you."

"I was calling to see if you and Melody want to drop by," Isabelle said. "I baked a couple pies, and they're still warm. I've got ice cream and whipped cream, too."

"Yes, please!" Melody shouted from the back seat, and I chuckled as we pulled into Bridger's driveway.

"All right. We'll come by after we leave here. See you soon." He ended the call and turned to look at me. "Call me if you need a ride home."

"Really? You think I'm going to have you bring Melody out

in the cold after she's gone to bed?" I asked. "I'll be fine. You need not worry. Have a good night."

"Yeah, you too."

There was something unreadable in his gaze.

But Archer Chadwick was going to give me whiplash if I tried to figure out what was going through that head of his.

He'd made it clear that he wasn't interested in me. I didn't need to be told again.

"Bye, my Winnie!"

I opened the back door and kissed her cheek. "I'll see you in the morning. Sweet dreams. And eat some pie for me."

She was still giggling when I shut the door as a car pulled into the driveway. I turned around as Brenner Layton stepped out of his fancy black Mercedes.

"Hey, Winnie. Happy New Year. I'm glad you came." He offered me an elbow, and I slipped my hand through it to help me keep my balance on the slick pavement.

I glanced back to see Archer watching us, and I quickly looked away.

This was what he'd insisted I do tonight. If he didn't like it, he'd need to figure it out all on his own.

Once we stepped inside, it was party time. Emilia had decorated the place like nothing I'd ever seen.

They had an enormous black-and-gold balloon arch that must have stood thirteen feet high. White roses with large gold bows were wrapped around the vases on every surface in their home. There were crowns and horns and all sorts of fun New Year's things. Lulu and Henley rushed over to me when Brenner helped me slip my coat off.

"Look at you!" Lulu said as she wrapped her arms around me. "And you don't look too shabby yourself, Brenner."

"Thank you. But it's hard to look good next to this one," he chuckled as he flicked his thumb in my direction.

Henley hugged me, and Emilia, Eloise, and Wren hurried over to join us.

"And that's my cue to go find a drink. Come find me in a little bit," Brenner said as he winked at me.

"He's definitely into you," Emilia said.

"But she's not feeling it," Lulu said. "I know when a woman is into a man. I've got my PhD in reading the vibes between people."

Henley laughed. "You do have a gift for reading a room."

"So, is she vibing with anyone here?" Wren asked.

"Too soon to tell."

"Well, Clark invited a few players from the team, and I'd love to introduce you." Eloise wiggled her eyebrows at me, and I chuckled.

"Sure."

We started walking toward the crowded great room, and Lulu put her arm around my shoulder and leaned in close to my ear. "They have no idea that you've already got your sights set on someone."

"I do?" I wasn't sure what she was referring to.

"Let's just say, you're writing a single-dad romance, but I think you might be living one, too." The corners of her lips turned up.

"Nope. Because in romance books, the hero and the heroine *both* have to be interested in one another. And that is definitely not the case here. He practically shoved me out the door and told me to meet some people my own age." I rolled my eyes.

"Welcome to the Chadwick men. They don't ever take the

easy path." She gave me a little squeeze when the girls stopped to get us all flutes of champagne from one of the waiters they'd hired for the event. "But good things are always worth the wait, Winnie."

I'd waited a long time for something good to come along.

But a part of me wondered if real romance would only ever live on the pages of my books for me.

Not everyone was destined for happily ever after.

19

Archer

My mother had of course convinced Melody to stay at her house, luring her with pies and crafts, and she tried to convince me to go to Bridger and Emilia's party.

I couldn't explain to anyone the panic I was feeling.

The fact that I'd gotten off to Winnie in the shower daily for the last week.

The fact that I'd made out with my nanny, my too-young-for-me nanny, and couldn't stop thinking about her.

The last thing I needed to do was be at a New Year's party with endless alcohol and a woman I was dangerously attracted to.

Melody was thriving. We'd found someone who'd completely stepped up to the plate. My daughter depended on her.

I depended on her.

I warmed up the pizza she'd made us and watched some UFC fights, glancing down at my phone to check the time repeatedly.

Maybe she wouldn't even come home tonight.

She was young and single, after all.

Maybe she'd go home with Brenner.

It wasn't my business.

"Fuck," I groaned, because the thought made me physically ill.

My phone vibrated, and I picked it up to see a text from Winnie.

Winnie: *Happy New Year, Archie!*

Me: *Happy New Year. Are you having a good time?*

Winnie: *Yes, it's a great party. You should have come. I'm probably going to suffer tomorrow because I've had more lemon drops than I can count.*

Me: *I'm glad you're having fun. You've earned it.*

Winnie: *What are you doing?*

Me: *I'm enjoying your pizza and a little UFC, so I'm doing just fine.*

Winnie: *Is Melody asleep?*

Me: *My mom convinced her to stay the night with them when we stopped by.*

Winnie: *So why didn't you come?*

Me: *Just needed a night in.*

She didn't respond. She'd looked wounded earlier when I'd

changed the plan to go. And fuck, when she'd walked out in that tiny black dress, I knew I'd made the right decision.

A little space would do us both some good.

Me: *Do you have a ride home?*

Winnie: *Are you worried about me, Archie?*

Me: *Of course.*

My phone rang, and I saw her name flash across the screen.

"Stop worrying. I'm a grown-ass wooooo…" Her words were slurring, and I immediately sat forward. "Womaaannn? Woman? Is that a word, or did I just make that up."

She laughed hysterically, and I heard Eloise's voice next.

"Yes. You're a woman!" Eloise shouted.

"Put Eloise on the phone, please," I commanded.

"Archie wants to talk to you," Winnie said, and now she'd stopped laughing and sounded hurt.

"Hey, Archer, happy New Year," Eloise said, and her words also sounded slightly slurred.

It was New Year's Eve. I shouldn't have been surprised.

"Hi, happy New Year. Winnie sounds like she's had a lot to drink, and I want to make sure that she has a ride home?" I rubbed the back of my neck.

"Well, there's a few guys from the team here that would love to give her a ride home. She's a real hit with these guys," Eloise said over hysterical laughter.

I was not laughing.

"Tell him to stop worrying. I'm walking home," Winnie called out in the background.

"A beautiful woman shouldn't be walking home alone. I'll give you a ride." I heard a voice that sounded a lot like Wizz, a professional hockey player for the Lions, the team my cousin

Clark played for.

"Tell her to stay put. I'm coming to pick her up," I snipped before ending the call and slipping on my shoes and coat.

I wasn't going to let her walk home, nor was I going to let some dude who was used to women falling at his feet give her a ride home when she was intoxicated.

It was the right thing to do.

I drove the short distance to my cousin's house and jogged inside.

"Look who decided to show up," Bridger said, a goofy smile on his face as he took a pull from his beer bottle.

"Winnie shouldn't be walking home by herself," I grumped.

"I don't think anyone was going to let that happen. She has plenty of offers for rides home."

I looked over to see several hockey players standing around Winnie as she told them all an animated story. I then watched as Winnie, Wren, Henley, Emilia, and Eloise lifted shot glasses off the bar and chanted something about boozy book clubs and tipped their heads back.

"I wasn't going to let some drunk asshole take advantage of her. She's my goddamn nanny. I'm not allowing that on my watch."

"'Drunk asshole'? Brenner is like a family member to me, and those hockey players are tight with Clark. No one was going to take advantage of her, Archie. Why not just admit why you're here?" he said with a smirk.

"I just told you why I'm here." My gaze locked with Winnie's across the room, and she smiled.

"Archie! You came," she shouted across the room.

"That's what she said," Rafe said as he walked over, and we all laughed.

Winnie came running toward me, lost her footing, and nearly fell before I caught her and pulled her against me.

"Are you all right?" I asked as she tucked her hair behind her ears and smiled up at me.

"I'm great." She sighed, and her cheeks were flushed. "Maybe a little queasy."

"Yeah? You want me to take you home?" I asked.

"That would be great. I just need to say good night to everyone." She moved around the room, swaying a bit as she did, and it took all I had not to step in and carry her out of here. But she was busy hugging everyone goodbye, and I didn't miss the way every single dude in the room was watching her.

"We missed you." Rafe clapped me on the shoulder.

"Yeah, I just chilled tonight."

"And where the hell have you been?" Bridger asked Rafe, a suspicious look on his face.

"I was in your bathroom, you know, the one off your bedroom, having a moment with your toilet. Those chicken wings had a kick to them."

"You fucker. There are three guest bathrooms. Why the fuck did you use our private bathroom?"

"The fancy toilet, you shitburger."

I chuckled, but my eyes never left Winnie, who made her way back to me with her coat in hand. "I'm ready if you are."

"Sounds good." I said goodbye to the few people I passed on my way out of the house, as the party was still going strong, and I paused to help her into her coat. "It's cold as hell out there."

"You do know I'm from Chicago, right? I could have easily walked home." Her words were slurring more than ever now. I buttoned the top button on her coat, and she reached in her pocket for her pink beanie and pulled it over her head. Damn, she was cute.

"I think the walk to my truck is going to be challenging enough," I said with a laugh as I offered her my elbow.

"I'm fine. You're being ridiculous," she said as she walked right out the door in her high heels, then spun to look at me, all while completely losing her balance.

For fuck's sake.

I lunged forward, trying to break her fall as she took us both down into the pile of snow beside the walkway.

She was on her back, and my hands sank into the snow as I tried to keep my weight from falling on top of her.

"Hey, Archie," she said, a goofy smile on her face.

"Hey. Are you all right?"

"Never better." She sighed as I stood, and I reached for her hand. Once I'd pulled her upright, she started to slide again, and I'd had enough. I scooped one hand beneath her knees and lifted her off the ground, cradling her like a baby.

"How about you let me get you to the truck in one piece."

"Wow. I'm getting the royal treatment. You're such a gentleman," she said as her cheek rested against my chest.

I opened the passenger door and set her on the seat before pulling the seat belt across her body and snapping it in.

I jogged around the truck and moved inside before turning on the engine and cranking the heat.

"You doing okay?" I asked.

"Yeah. I had a lot of fun," she said. "Thanks for picking me up. You really didn't need to come out in the cold to get me, though. I could have gotten a ride."

"I didn't mind at all." It was the truth.

"You're a confusing man, Archer Chadwick."

"Am I?"

"Yes. You really are," she said, and it was clear she was drunk.

I pulled into the garage and came around to the passenger door, where I unbuckled her before pulling her into my arms again.

"I can walk. I'm fine."

She wasn't fine.

"Just let me help you, okay?" I said with a laugh. I moved inside, headed straight for her room. I carried her to her bed and set her down.

She pushed her coat off her shoulders and tried to kick off her shoes but made no progress whatsoever.

Drunk Winnie was fucking adorable.

I bent down, pulled her ice-cold foot into my hands, and unbuckled the strap.

"Ahh…" she moaned. "Your hands are so warm."

"This is why you don't walk in weather like this. You would have gotten frostbite." I set the first shoe beside me and reached for her other foot.

"Why were you ignoring me earlier?"

I unbuckled the strap and glanced up at her. I thought about denying it. But I decided not to bullshit her. We could be straight with one another. Besides, she'd probably forget by the morning. "Because I think it's best that I keep my distance."

She sighed. "Because you're embarrassed that I kissed you and then shamelessly chased my pleasure against all your… *hardness*."

I laughed. She was ridiculously cute.

"First of all, you didn't kiss me, I kissed you. Second, I offered up my 'hardness,' also known as my very excited dick that was reacting to you. You weren't in that alone."

"Well, I'm the one who made a fool of myself. And at first you seemed fine, but then you literally avoided me after, so I know you're mortified by what happened." She fell back on the bed.

I moved to sit beside her and pulled her upright in a sitting position. "Don't do that."

"Don't do what?"

"Don't decide things for me, Winnie. 'Mortified' would be the last word I would use to describe how I felt after what happened, unless you're referring to being mortified by my own behavior."

"You offered yourself up to me. You were a perfect gentleman. And you let me grind up all over you like a filthy animal." She tossed her hands in the air dramatically. "That's how you see me now. Like a filthy, horny animal."

I couldn't stop the laughter from coming. "Umm… that's some crazy tequila you had tonight if you think that."

"So, you avoided me because you think I'm amazing?" she asked, oozing sarcasm. "It's probably all the dumb bows I wear. Jaden hated them. He thought they were stupid."

"Winnie." I reached for her chin and turned her face so her gaze locked with mine.

"What?"

"You are so far off base, you aren't even in the ball field."

"'Ball field'? Are you talking dirty to me, Archie?" she chuckled.

If she only knew the filthy thoughts running through my mind every time she was in the room.

There was only one filthy animal here, and it was definitely not Winnie.

20

Winnie

"I'm trying real hard to do the right thing. And trust me when I tell you, it's proving to be the most challenging thing I've ever done."

This man made no sense, and my drunk ass was done with the games.

"Please. Just admit that you don't like me that way. I get it. We kissed, and now it's awkward for you because we work together. But this isn't Wall Street. I'm a part-time nanny. There's no board of directors coming for your ass." I fell back on the bed. I was drunk, and I couldn't look at him without seeing three Archers.

And trust me, one Archer was more than I could handle.

"I'm aware of our professional situation," he said with a smirk. "But it's a hell of a lot more complicated than you just working for me."

"Explain it to me, then." I exhaled sharply. I wanted answers. And I had the liquid courage to ask for them tonight.

"You told me that you weren't willing to settle, and I couldn't agree with you more. And trust me when I tell you, you'd be settling if we let things go any further."

I shot back up to a sitting position. "I meant that I didn't want to kiss a man who didn't want to kiss me. You clearly ran with that one."

His lips turned up in the corners. "What I mean is, we're in very different places, Winnie. You're twenty-four years old."

"Twenty-five in a few weeks." I wriggled my eyebrows. "Why are you so hung up on my age?"

"Well, for starters, I'm a decade older than you. At least for a few more weeks, that is." He sighed. "But it's not even about your age. I have a child. I've got nothing to offer you. You've got your whole life ahead of you. I'm sure you want to get married and have a family and the whole white picket fence bullshit. That's not for me. I'm on a different path."

I gaped at him. "That's what you took from me saying that I wasn't going to settle? For goodness' sake, Archie, that's a lot. For starters, I already got married. I'm ahead of you on that one. And look how that ended for me. So the last thing I'm thinking about is marriage and children and white picket fences. I don't even like front yards with fences. I prefer open spaces."

He chuckled. "You're good for Melody, and you're good for me. And if we let things go further, we would fuck that up."

"Because you think I expect it to lead somewhere?" I shook my head. "From where I'm sitting, you're the one who's going far into the future. I just liked making out with you."

He studied me, a wide grin spreading across his handsome face.

Damn. This man was so freaking gorgeous. The broad shoulders and tousled hair. The emerald green eyes and the peppered scruff around his jaw. He had this masculine scent of amber and cedarwood that made it difficult to think straight when I was around him.

"I liked making out with you, too." He tucked my hair behind my ears. "I just don't want to do anything to mess up what we have, you know? Having you in our home has been really great, Winnie. And if I take things too far, if I hurt you, if I hurt Melody—I'd never forgive myself."

"You put a lot of pressure on yourself. I don't have any expectations, Archie. I've been divorced for seven months. I'm happy to be single. I was in a horrible relationship for a long time. I haven't had sex in two years." I blew out a breath. "Two years. And this"—I motioned between us—"it's the first time I've felt anything. And it feels good to feel something again, you know?"

His gaze softened. "Two years?"

I laughed that that was the one thing he'd focused on. "Yes. We separated a year ago, and that last year of our marriage, we slept in separate rooms. I'm fairly certain he wasn't faithful. He was out all the time. We were both miserable. And I poured myself into my books and my words. I came here for a fresh start. Not to find a husband or have a child. Hell, Melody is the first child I've even been around, and she makes a good argument for children of course, but I'm certainly not thinking about a baby of my own."

"I'm sorry for making assumptions." He looked away before turning his attention back to me. "I didn't expect to be raising a child on my own, but I wouldn't change anything. I love my daughter fiercely, and I'm used to being on my own. Sure, I go out occasionally, and I certainly haven't gone two years without having sex, though it's been a while for me as well. But having you in my home, in my life—it's been nice, Winnie. And that's terrifying for a multitude of reasons. And I don't want to do anything to let you down, because I don't have much to give. Not in the traditional sense."

I laughed. And once I started, I couldn't stop.

"Is something funny?"

"Did it ever cross your mind that I don't want anything from you other than your lips on mine, and maybe access to your body," I said with a chuckle, because I couldn't believe how blunt I was being with him. "I mean, I'm grateful for your friendship, too, of course, but you're incredibly sexy, and you make me feel things I haven't felt in years. So I don't have anything to offer you, either, other than my impressive nannying skills and cooking skills, and maybe I could make you feel as good as you make me feel."

I fell back on the bed and covered my face with my hands because I'd really just said it, hadn't I? Obviously my buzz hadn't worn off yet to be able to admit all this. Ugh.

He fell back to lie beside me. "That's a very impressive offer, Winnie."

I rolled on my side. "I can't believe I just said all of that. I clearly feel comfortable with you."

"I mean, it's probably because you find me incredibly sexy." He smirked, and I swatted at his chest.

"Maybe you stop making it into more than it needs to be, Archie. We like hanging out. It doesn't complicate things for me with Melody. And I like our friendship. I've never been so open with someone before."

He ran a thumb over my little gold bow earring. "You should always say what you think."

My stomach started churning, and a wave of nausea hit me out of nowhere.

"Well, I'd like to make out with you again, but I fear the tequila is catching up with me at the moment." I jolted forward, then jumped to my feet and ran to the bathroom. "Good night, Archie. Thanks for everything."

I pushed the door closed as the most overwhelming need to vomit took over my body. I leaned over the toilet and heaved several times, hoping like hell that he'd left my room.

Another couple of heaves, and the door opened.

"Don't come in here. It's a crime scene," I groaned.

A deep chuckle came from behind me as his big hands gathered my hair and he reached for an elastic on the countertop and tied it up on my head. "Stop being dramatic. We're friends, right? This is what friends do when one friend drinks a ridiculous amount of tequila."

I flushed the toilet just as he handed me a wet washcloth, and I wiped my mouth with it and sat so that my back was leaning against the wall.

He sat beside me and wrapped an arm around me so that my head could rest on his chest.

"Don't say that word. I'm never drinking again."

He handed me a Gatorade, and I looked up at him with confusion. "Do you have magic powers, Archie?"

He chuckled. "Nope. When I heard the first heave, I went to grab you a Gatorade from the kitchen."

"Thank you. I'm sorry I can't make out with you now." I peeked up at him, my eyes heavy.

He snorted as he moved to his feet, taking me with him.

He carried me to bed and found a tee in my top drawer and handed it to me. "I'll turn around while you put that on."

"Always the gentleman."

"You're drunk, Winnie. Put the shirt on," he said as he showed me his back.

I unzipped my dress and let it fall to the floor before slipping the tee over my head. "I'm dressed, but I want you to know I usually engage in a very detailed skin care regimen, but I don't feel like tonight is the night for that."

"I agree."

"I need to brush my teeth." I sighed as he turned around and lifted the comforter for me to slip in. "Get in bed. You can do all of that in the morning."

"So bossy," I chuckled as I moved beneath the comforter.

And then he did the most surprising thing of all.

He turned off the lights, kicked off his shoes, and slid into bed beside me.

"What are you doing, Archie?" I said, my voice coming out hoarse.

I was a weird mix of exhausted, drunk, and emotionally charged because I was so happy that he was in here with me.

"I'm going to stay with you in case you get sick during the night."

"You can't stay away, can you?" I whispered.

"That's not untrue. Go to sleep, Winnie."

I rolled onto my side so I was facing him, and I tucked my head beneath his neck. "Sorry for the vomit breath."

He chuckled before kissing the top of my head.

And I listened to the sound of his heart beating, and sleep finally took me.

• • •

The sun poked through the opening of the curtains, and I squinted as a loud pounding sounded in my head.

It was as if a mariachi band had started playing in my bedroom.

"What is that noise?" I groaned as I looked up to see Archer Chadwick sitting on my bed, fully clothed, sipping a cup of coffee.

"Morning, sunshine. I can assure you, it's a very quiet morning. What you're hearing is the aftermath of a world-class hangover."

"Why do you look so happy about it?" I sat forward, covering my mouth as the memory of vomiting in front of Archer came back to me. I hurried off the bed and rushed to the bathroom to brush my teeth.

"Listen, dragon breath, there's no judgment," he said with a laugh from the bedroom.

I quickly brushed my teeth. My hair was a disaster, so I ran a brush through it, then pulled it into an elastic and tied a little bow around it, because I'd need those superpowers today for sure. I walked back to the bedroom.

"I assure you, my dragon breath is gone."

"Replaced with a bow," he said, glancing at the back of my head as I slipped beneath the comforter.

"Correct. I'm sorry you had to sleep in here all night. I would have been fine. I just can't hold my liquor because I don't drink very often." I shrugged.

"Maybe I wanted to stay." He set his coffee down and pointed to the nightstand beside me. "That's a fresh Gatorade. You should drink it."

I reached for the blue drink, unscrewed the cap, and took a

sip, then replayed our conversation from last night.

Oh. My. Gosh.

Did it ever cross your mind that I don't want anything from you other than your lips on mine, and maybe access to your body.

I set the drink down on the nightstand and slid under the covers, pulling the comforter over my head because the embarrassment was real.

"Winnie?" His deep voice was too damn sexy.

"Yep."

"Why are you under the covers?"

"Because of the things I said to you. I'm going to need a minute to process."

Loud laughter filled the space around me, and then the comforter lifted briefly as he slipped beneath it beside me. "You mean about wanting to use my body and finding me ridiculously sexy?"

"Please, stop," I groaned.

"I find you ridiculously sexy, too," he whispered against my ear, nipping at the sensitive skin and making me yelp.

I pushed the comforter back, and we both sat up. "You don't have to say that to make me feel better. Can we just pretend that last night never happened?"

"Nope. I'm glad last night happened. Let's talk about it now that you're sober."

Oh, my.

This I was not expecting.

I tightened my bow and turned to look at him. "Okay. Let's talk about it."

21

Archer

This woman was so far under my skin, I couldn't see straight. I was done fighting it. She'd made some fair points last night, and if that was truly how she felt today, now that she was sober, then I was open to discussing it.

"Do you remember the conversation from last night?" I asked.

"The one where I made a fool of myself? Yep. It's playing on repeat in my head at the moment." Her cheeks flushed pink, and she wouldn't look at me.

"Winnie," I said, reaching beneath her chin to turn her face to look at mine. "What you said was very honest, and I appreciate it. I should have talked to you, but I chose to avoid you to try to make it easier. I'm glad you called me out for it."

"I guess we know who the mature one is, huh?" She chuckled as a wide grin spread across her gorgeous face. "Listen, I stand by what I said, Archer. I like you. But I'm not looking for anything more than you are. It can be something we just keep between us, and if we kiss again, great. If we like it, great. If it leads to doing more than kissing, and we're both feeling it, great. It doesn't have to mean everything. I've tried that path, and it didn't work out so well for me."

"I get that. I just didn't want to do anything to risk destroying this," I said, motioning between us. "You've been really good for Melody and for me. And I like having you in my life. I just don't want to disappoint you."

I cleared my throat, because that was a lot.

Her gaze softened. "You have no idea how high my threshold for disappointment is."

I had to laugh. "That doesn't sound good."

"I won't be disappointed, Archie. We've literally talked about what we don't want and what we do want more than I ever discussed my needs with the man I dated for years and then married. I promise, you need not worry."

Her words struck me, and I felt my chest tightening.

Because Winnie was pure goodness. I'd recognized it pretty quickly upon meeting her.

She deserved to have her needs met.

She deserved to be heard and respected and loved.

And it bothered me that I couldn't give her everything she wanted, but I could sure as hell give her more than she was asking for.

That much I knew.

"How about this," I said, reaching for her hand. "We already spend a lot of time together, and we continue doing that, but when we're alone, we do whatever you want to do."

"And what do you want to do, Archie?" she asked as she moved closer. She climbed on my lap as I wrapped my arms around her.

"Right now, I want to do this," I whispered before turning her in my arms and kissing her. Her fingers moved to my hair as my hands slipped beneath her loose tee and stroked the soft skin of her back.

We sat there making out like teenagers once again, and my dick raged against my joggers.

I could kiss this woman for hours and never tire of it.

Her lips were soft, and she made these little noises that turned me the hell on.

Had I ever wanted anyone the way I wanted her?

My phone rang from the nightstand, startling us both. I pulled back, and her eyes were wild with need, lips plump from where I'd kissed her.

My gaze locked with hers as my phone rang a second time.

"Get it. That might be your mom," she said, but she didn't slide off my lap, and I loved it.

I reached for my phone and kissed her hair before answering. "Good morning."

"Daddy, why didn't you pick up the first time?" Melody asked.

"Hey, angel face. Sorry about that. I couldn't get to the phone quick enough," I said.

"Mimi is making pancakes, and we want you and my Winnie to come eat breakfast with us."

I looked down at the gorgeous woman sitting on my lap. She nodded, then hopped off the bed and moved to the closet to grab some clothes.

"Sure. We'll be there soon," I said. "Love you."

"Love you, Daddy."

I ended the call as Winnie hurried to the bathroom. I moved to my feet before quickly getting dressed. I walked that way and noticed that she hadn't closed the door. She pulled a sweater over her head as she turned to look at me. She'd already slipped into a pair of faded jeans.

Her eyes moved down to where my dick was still straining against the gray fabric of my joggers.

I cleared my throat and shrugged. "Can't really help it."

"I know we need to go, but how about we make a deal to meet up later tonight?" She raised her brows. "Finish what we started."

"I'm just getting started, Winnie," I said as I moved closer and my large hand covered the side of her face.

Her chest was rising and falling. "Me too."

"All right. Until later," I said. I leaned down and kissed her once more before I took her hand and led her out of her bedroom. We both pulled our jackets on and were soon out the door.

"I like our new normal," she said once we were in the truck.

"Our new normal?"

"Yeah. We act completely normal around everyone else, and then we have this secret of our own when we're alone."

I laughed. "I like our new normal, too."

I just hoped like hell I wasn't fucking things up.

Once we arrived at my parents' place, Winnie and I acted like we always did. There was no touching, no heated glances. Melody talked up a storm about her night and showed off the painting she'd made, and I could tell Winnie was completely entranced with my daughter.

"Stop it!" she gasped at the painting. "I love this."

"That's you and me and Daddy," Melody said. "We're making snow angels like we did last week. Even though Daddy's looked like a big blob."

My parents both laughed, and I rolled my eyes.

"Hey. I'm bigger than you, and you didn't give me much space between you two."

"Don't worry, Daddy, I gave you a good snow angel in my painting."

I looked down at the piece of construction paper and smiled. She loved to paint and to draw.

"It's perfect."

"So, did you end up going to the party?" my mother pressed.

"No. I went and picked up Winnie because she was insisting on walking home." I had another bite of red velvet pancakes and groaned. "These are so damn good."

"Oh, you owe me a dollar, Daddy. Mimi and I also made a swears jar. If you say a bad word, you've gots to give me a dollar. Right, Mimi? Right, Pops?" My daughter hopped down and hurried to the counter, then brought back a large glass jar that read SWEAR JAR COLLECTION.

"I think it's more than fair," my father said.

"Says the man who curses on the daily." I laughed.

"Not around my granddaughter. Do you see a dollar in the jar, Archer?"

I pushed my plate away, as I'd eaten far too much. I reached in my pocket, pulled out a dollar, and dropped it in the jar. "First dollar."

"Uncle Bridger is going to owe me the most, I thinks," Melody said, giggling.

"If I were a betting man, I'd say you're probably going to collect the most from him."

"Winnie never says the swears," my daughter said, beaming up at the woman holding her.

"Well, some of us are just a bit more mature than others." She smirked, and my parents seemed to think her remark was hilarious.

"Fine. You're more mature than I am," I said, winking at her.

"Clearly." My mother looked between us. "I've always been more mature than Dad. I think women just get it, you know?"

"Totally," Winnie said.

"Am I a woman, too?" Melody asked, tipping her head back and looking up at Winnie like she held the moon in her hands.

I realized in that moment that we both looked at her that way.

It took everything I had not to pull them both onto my lap.

"You're a perfect little girl right now," Winnie said. "But someday you'll be a woman. And honestly, you might be more mature than your daddy and your uncles already."

"Hey," I said over my laughter.

"I can't argue that," my father said.

"Is no one on my side here?" I threw my hands in the air, unable to hide the big smile on my face.

"I think your daddy should have to help me with the dishes, since he already put a dollar in the jar." My mother stood.

"I can help," Winnie said.

"Nope. You just relax, sweetheart." Mom winked.

"I don't know why I have to pay a dollar *and* do the dishes," I grumped as I stacked the plates and followed my mother into the kitchen.

She was still laughing as I set the pile in the sink.

"Don't be a baby. You wash and I'll load."

"All right."

"I'm taking my pops and my Winnie out to the tree swing," my daughter called out, and I heard the back door close behind them.

"She's good for you, you know?" my mother said.

"She's great. She's really good for Melody."

"I agree. But I see as much of a difference in you as I see in Melody."

I rolled my eyes. *Here we go.*

My mother was always playing matchmaker. She'd put expectations on our sort-of-relationship if she knew what was going on, and that would not be good.

We'd already agreed that it wasn't going anywhere. We were just having some fun. Involving other people would only complicate matters.

"She makes my life easier, that's a given."

"I've never seen you smile or laugh so much, either. You're more relaxed around her. And I see the way she looks at you. The way you look at her."

"Now you're just romanticizing things." I handed her the last plate. "She works for me. She's too young for me."

She shrugged. "You do know that I'm eleven years younger than your father. Don't judge someone by their age."

Like she said, my father was more than a decade older than my mother, but he didn't have a child when they'd met. They'd wanted the same things. To build a family together. It made a difference.

I dried off my hands and turned to face my mother. "She's newly divorced, and she wants to be single. And I'm in the same boat. I'm not looking to expand my family."

"And why not?" she pressed.

"Because I can't risk that with Melody. I can't bring someone into her life who might leave in the end. With me and Melody, there's no risk of anyone hurting her." I was surprised by my own words. I hadn't realized how deep that need to protect my daughter ran.

"Are you worried about Melody or yourself being hurt?" She held her hands up when I started to argue. "I'm just saying, you stepped up to the plate for Melody. And I've seen your guard come up over the last five years, and I get it. But not everyone is going to leave, Archer. Look at you. You chose to stay."

"Winnie's young, Mom. She deserves a family of her own. But we're friends, and I'm happy I hired her. She's been great to Melody, and she's become a good friend to me. So how about you don't make it weird for anyone, huh?" I held my arms out, and she stepped into my embrace.

"I just love you, and I want you to be happy."

"I'm happy, Mama. You don't need to worry about me."

I glanced out the back window and saw Melody and Winnie on the tire swing in the snowy yard, my father pushing both of them. Their heads fell back in laughter, which made my chest squeeze.

My mother was right about one thing.

Winnie was good for both of us.

22

Winnie

I'd just come out to the kitchen to make breakfast and pack up Melody's lunch when she came around the corner, crying frantically.

It was early. She wasn't usually up just yet.

"Winnie! Daddy's hurt and he's calling for you. He needs help, I thinks. He needs help!" Melody had tears running down her cheeks, and I dropped the pan I'd been holding in my hand on the counter and started running after her.

"Where is he?"

"He fell in his bathroom," she croaked.

We both turned into his bedroom. I raced for the door and pushed it open, with Melody right beside me.

There stood a naked Archer Chadwick in all his glory as he

stepped out of the shower.

Dripping wet as he wrapped a towel around his waist.

I clapped a hand over Melody's eyes as I stared at him.

We'd made out more times than I could count now. But we'd never taken things further. I'd never seen the man naked. Sure, I'd ground up against him enough times to know that he was large and thick, but I'd never seen it in all its glory.

And oh my… this was the kind of body that could inspire an entire romance book.

He was the book boyfriend dreams were made of.

Chiseled and hard and built.

A little trail of dark hair led down to his well-endowed package, which appeared to be more than happy to see me.

"Holy shit," he said at the sight of us. He tied off his towel at his waist before crossing his arms over his chest. "What the hell is going on?"

"Two dollars, Daddy," Melody said as I took my hand from her eyes now that he was covered.

"Um, I'm, er, I'm so sorry. Melody said you were hurt, and that you'd called for me." I shook my head as I backed up to leave the bathroom.

"Hurt? What are you talking about, angel face?" He held on to the towel at his waist and bent down to meet her eyes as he took in her tear-streaked cheeks. He used the pads of his thumbs to wipe away the wetness. "I'm fine, baby girl. I was taking a shower."

"I woke up early and came in your room and I heard you crying in the shower, Daddy."

"What?" he asked with confusion as he stroked her hair to comfort her. "I wasn't crying, honey."

"You were making crying noises, like, 'Uhhh, uhhh, uhh,

ohhhh,'" she said, mimicking the noise, and my eyes nearly popped out of my head as the realization of what she was saying hit me. Archer closed his eyes for a few beats as if he'd just put it together, too, and then he stood.

"I think I was reacting to the water being a little too hot this morning." He cleared his throat. "I promise you, I'm fine."

"And then you made this crying sound for Winnie. You called out for her. I thought you needed Winnie to help you?"

Oh. My. Gosh.

He turned to look at me as he scrubbed a hand down his face. "I might have been calling out for Winnie to turn the hot water down in the garage. I'm sorry about that, sweetheart."

My gaze locked with his, and he had this goofy grin on his face that basically said: *Busted.*

"It's okay, Daddy. Sorry we saw you a little bit naked."

"That's okay. It happens." He blew out a breath, and I glanced in the mirror to see my cheeks were bright pink. "How about you go brush your teeth, and I'll be in to help you get dressed in a few minutes."

"Okay!" And just like that, Melody skipped out of the bathroom. Kids were so resilient, and it always surprised me how quickly she bounced back from things.

"I'm so sorry for barging in here," I said, trying my best not to burst out in hysterical laughter.

"Are you, though?" he asked with a smirk. "I guess you caught me. Thinking about things that I shouldn't be thinking about."

"You're not the only one, Archie," I chuckled. I walked out of the bathroom while still facing him. "Thanks for that morning show. You gave me plenty of inspiration to write today."

"Yeah? You like what you see, Winnie?"

"I really do," I said, just as he shocked the shit out of me by tugging his towel free and letting it fall to the ground.

I couldn't breathe. I was stunned speechless.

"Daddy! Which shirt do you like better?" Melody called out from behind me as she came running back in the room, and Archer jolted for his towel, hitting his head on the counter in the process.

"Fuck."

"Another dollar for the jar, Daddy." Melody came to a stop beside me as he tucked the towel back in place and rubbed his hand over the big red spot on his forehead.

"I'll get Melody dressed and start breakfast. You just—take care of business, Archie."

Melody jogged back to her room, and I followed as Archer grumped under his breath, "I already took care of business."

Melody hopped up on her bed as I opened her closet door and pulled out her jeans with little flowers embroidered on them, a white tee, and her pink hoodie. "How about this with your pink cowboy boots?"

"Yes!" She pumped her fist. "Can you do the two buns on my head with the bows today?"

"Of course. I love that style on you because you're so cute," I said as she raised her arms over her head and I pulled off her jammies and got her dressed. Baths were nightly occurrences, so getting her ready for school in the morning was super easy.

We moved to her en suite bathroom so she could brush her teeth before I sat her up on the counter and did her hair.

"Pink, white, or red bows?" I asked, holding up the options in my hand.

"Can we do one pink and one red?"

"Absolutely, I love that idea."

"Who used to do your hair when you were a little girl?" she asked, and I glanced up to meet her gaze in the mirror.

"Well, my dad tried, but he wasn't real good at that. He's great with cars, but not so much with hair." I chuckled at the memory.

"Yeppers. Daddy is good with his works but not so much with hair, either." She smiled, and it reached her chocolate brown eyes.

"I taught myself pretty early on how to do it. But honestly, I would just wear a ponytail most days and tie a ribbon around it. I learned the fancy stuff later." I picked up the hair spray and sprayed it over her head to keep things in place.

Archer didn't know much about hair products, so I'd taken him shopping one day. We'd picked up some good detangler and conditioner for her hair, some light hair spray, and more bows.

A girl could never have too many bows.

"I'm glad I have you to do this with me. Mrs. Dowden didn't know how to do hair, and I like that you and me both wear pretty bows together."

"I like it, too." I kissed her cheek. She smelled like her peach-strawberry lotion, and I just breathed in all that sweetness.

"Should we go make breakfast?" I asked her as I helped her off the counter.

"Yes. Can we make heart pancakes and bacon?"

"Sure, that sounds perfect." I took her hand and led her down the hallway toward the kitchen.

Melody loved to set the table, so I whipped up the batter as she did that. But all I could think of was a naked Archer Chadwick.

The man was chiseled perfection.

I wanted to take things further with him, but I was afraid to at the same time.

I'd only been with one man in my life.

And it hadn't been great, to say the least.

I wanted to keep things casual, and a part of me wondered if sex would complicate things.

Making out was one thing. Sex was another.

We'd talked about it. Hell, we talked about everything.

Archer Chadwick was my boss, but he'd also become my friend.

A really good friend.

He listened and encouraged me with my writing.

He was the best kisser I'd ever met as well, so I had no doubt he'd be a great lover.

The kind of lover I wrote about in the pages of my books.

"That smells good," he said, startling me from my thoughts as he brushed up against me where I stood at the stove. His breath tickled my ear as he leaned in close to me.

I glanced over my shoulder to see Melody coloring at the table. Archer moved to pour himself a cup of coffee as I plated the food.

"Pancakes and bacon. The breakfast of champions," I said as I set our plates down at the table.

Archer set three glasses down with a pitcher of fresh orange juice.

There was a drawing on the table and a card with my name on it.

"What's this?" I asked as we all took our seats.

"You're finishing your book today, right?"

"Yes. Hopefully I can wrap it up today."

"You've got this. You've got five thousand words left, and you get to write your two favorite words after that." He winked.

My chest squeezed at his words. This man listened to me.

He really listened.

He cheered me on and encouraged me, which meant more than I could ever put into words.

"What are your two favorite words?" Melody asked as she cinched her brows together and looked at me.

"'The end.'" I chuckled. "They are the best words, because it means you finished another book."

"I want to write books like Winnie someday," Melody said.

"I think she's a good person to look up to. And if you work hard, you can do it, too. Because we see how hard Winnie works, right?"

This man had a way of stealing my breath.

He validated my career, took note of the work that went into it, and celebrated my milestones.

"Winnie's the hardest worker," she said over a mouthful of pancakes, and I chuckled. "Do you want to have babies, Winnie?"

My eyes widened.

I'd quickly learned that kids just said whatever came to mind. They didn't overthink. If they had a question, they asked it.

But this one had come out of left field.

"Hmmmm… I don't actually know." I shrugged, because it was the truth at the moment. "I've always wanted a big family. But things haven't worked out for me so far, so I'm not sure it will happen. But yes, I would like to be a mother."

Jaden and I had plans to have a baby after I graduated from college, but then he couldn't find a job, or at least not a job that he felt was up to his standards.

His words, not mine.

We were dependent on my income, so we postponed those plans.

And I was grateful that it hadn't worked out, because being tied to that man for the rest of my life would have been horrible. Not to mention the fact that he was far too selfish to be a parent.

"I wish I could be a baby again and you could be my mama," Melody said, and I noted the way Archer's hand froze with the strip of bacon between his fingers.

My chest tightened at her words.

"I'm glad I met you now," I said, clearing my throat. The lump forming there was so thick it made it difficult to speak. "It wouldn't be possible to love you more than I do right now."

"I love you, my Winnie." She smiled, and I reached for her hand and squeezed it.

I loved this girl big, and I'd only known her for three months.

Archer's eyes met mine, and he didn't say anything.

But I saw the panic there.

We were all getting too close, which I knew terrified him.

I forced a smile, and he gave me the slightest nod.

Things were getting complicated.

And I knew Archer Chadwick didn't like complicated.

23

Archer

Me: *Happy Birthday and Happy Valentine's Day! I think it's very fitting that a romance author has her birthday on Valentine's Day.*

Winnie: *Thanks, Archie. I agree. And thank you for the pastry you left on my desk. You even tied a bow around it. Nice touch.*

Me: *Seems wrong for you to be working on your birthday.*

Winnie: *I'm almost done for the day.*

Me: *How's the read-through going?*

Winnie: *Really good. I've only got a few days left. How is work today?*

Me: *Slow.*

Winnie and I had fallen into a routine. We were together every day with Melody. We'd have breakfast, and she'd head into her office to work, and I'd take my daughter to school. And then she'd pick Melody up and take her to her activities. We'd all three have dinner together, and after I put my daughter to bed, Winnie and I would make out like horny teenagers.

Things had grown more heated, and I'd spent most of my nights going to sleep rock hard.

But we both seemed determined to keep things casual; anything more than that scared the shit out of me.

I'd grown dependent on Winnie. I looked forward to seeing her first thing in the morning.

I liked that she was the last person I spoke to before I went to bed.

I wanted her in my bed.

I wanted all of her, and I felt like a selfish prick for wanting that.

Winnie: *Want to come home?*

Me: *Do you want me to come home?*

Winnie: *I do.*

Me: *On my way.*

Hell, I'd do anything she asked. We just got along. Winnie Smith had somehow become my best friend over the last few months.

My best friend who I was painfully attracted to.

"Hey, Lucy," I said as I pulled my coat on. "I'm heading out early. I've got some errands to run."

"All right, boss. I'll see you later. Tell Winnie I hope she has the best birthday," she called after me, because everyone here adored her. She baked treats for my office once a week, and she'd stop by and see everyone.

Lucy had found out her pen name, and now she was reading her books as well.

"Will do." I held a hand over my head, anxious to get home.

I missed this woman when I wasn't with her.

The lines were graying, but I just didn't give a shit about fighting it anymore.

I stopped by Emilia's flower shop and grabbed Winnie a bouquet of pink roses, because I knew they were her favorite, and then I drove the short distance home and pulled into the garage.

When I stepped in the house, I called out her name, and I chuckled when I saw the swear jar on the counter. I could see the twenty-dollar bill through the glass that my cousin Bridger had tossed in there when he'd said "shit" three times the other night when he and Emilia had stopped by.

He'd decided to prepay in advance, as he knew he'd go through his twenty bucks fairly quickly.

"Hey," she said as she came around the corner. She was wearing a pink sweater with red hearts on it and a pair of baggy jeans. The front of her hair was pulled away from her face, and I noticed that the bow I'd wrapped around her pastry this morning was tied in her hair. "I'm glad you're here."

"Yeah? Me too." I moved toward her. "Happy birthday. Melody made me promise not to give you your gift until dinner tonight."

I wanted to say "Happy Valentine's Day," but my nerves got the best of me. Winnie was the woman in my life, but nobody knew it. Nobody but she and I. But I felt like I should be buying her flowers for Valentine's Day, so that's what these were.

"These are gorgeous. Thank you. You did not need to do that. Nor did you need to get me a gift."

"Of course we did. It's your big day."

"That's true, and you said I should always voice what I want, right?" she asked as she took the flowers from me and grabbed a vase from the cabinet and filled it with water.

"Yes. Absolutely. What's going on?" I leaned over the kitchen island as she placed the stems in the water.

"Well, remember I said that it had been a while since I'd had sex?" She set the vase down and looked me right in the eyes. Her golden honey-brown gaze locked with mine.

"Yes." I adjusted myself because just the mention of it had me getting hard.

Who was I kidding? Every time I was with her, I was hard as steel.

"Well, today is officially two years. Two years since I've had sex." She moved around the counter, closer to me, and crossed her arms over her chest. "I know you don't want to cross certain lines, but I do, Archer. I don't want to hold back any more. And it doesn't have to mean anything. It can just be sex, if that's what we need it to be."

She'd barely finished the sentence before I rushed her.

I'd been waiting for her to say the words.

I fucking wanted this woman in a way I couldn't explain.

My mouth was on hers, and I lifted her off the ground, her legs wrapping around my waist.

I was a man unhinged now.

I carried her down the hall, our lips never losing contact, as I kicked the door closed behind me. I pressed her against the door before letting her feet drop to the ground.

I pulled my mouth from hers, kissing my way down her neck before dropping to my knees. She wasn't wearing shoes, and I looked up at her as I unbuttoned her jeans and pulled down the zipper. I slid the denim down her legs, and she lifted each foot for me to pull them free. I reached for the band of her pink lace panties, glancing up at her. Her breaths were coming fast now, and she nodded.

"I need to fucking taste you. I think about it every goddamn day," I hissed.

"Tell me, Archer. Stop holding back and tell me what you want."

"I want this. I want you. I want to bury myself inside you. I want to taste you. I want to fuck you in every room in this house. I want to make you cry out my name so many times that you don't think of another man. That's what I want."

"Me too," she said, her words breathy. "Please don't make me wait another minute."

I tore the band of her lace panties because I didn't even have the patience to wait to pull them down her legs.

I pressed my face between the apex of her thighs, breathing her in. "Spread those pretty thighs for me, beautiful. I want you to come on my lips before you come on my cock."

She gasped at my words and spread her legs as I reached for one foot and placed it over my shoulder. I licked her from one end to the other, dragging my tongue slowly through her slit and groaning at how good she tasted.

Teasing her over and over as she ground up against my face.

I fucking loved the sounds she made when she was turned on. Little moans and groans, letting me know how much she wanted me.

I reached for her other foot and pulled it over my other shoulder as my tongue slipped inside her, and her legs squeezed around the side of my face.

"Archer. Oh my. I, please," she panted. "Please don't stop."

Not a fucking chance I'd stop.

I slid my tongue in and out of her heat as her hands tugged at my hair and she bucked against me.

Over and over.

Faster.

I couldn't get enough.

"Archer, please. Please. Please," she begged.

I pulled back just long enough to slip in a finger. I couldn't get over how tight she was. I slipped in another, and she gasped.

Leaning forward, I sealed my lips over her clit.

Sucking and licking as I fucked her with my fingers.

Her head fell back against the door, thighs tightening around me as she gasped and panted, and I felt it when it happened.

She shattered as my name left her lips with a cry.

And I stayed right there as she rode out every last bit of pleasure.

I pulled back to look up at her, her eyes sated, lips parted as her breathing started to slow.

"Hey," she said as I slipped her legs off my shoulders and set her feet on the ground.

"Hi." I smirked and stood up. I towered over her. "You're so fucking sweet, Winnie. I knew you would be."

"Thank you," she whispered, and I startled when I saw a tear moving down her face. I wiped it away with my thumb.

"You okay?"

She nodded. "Do you know that I've never done that? Jaden wasn't a fan of it."

"Of oral sex?" I asked, my gaze searching hers.

"Well, no, he liked receiving. He didn't like giving it. He thought it was tedious."

"You were married to a real selfish fuck, weren't you?" I said, stroking her cheek.

She nodded. "I can't argue with that."

"Was that too much?"

Her lips turned up in the corners, and she shook her head. "No. It wasn't enough. It was amazing. And I really want to return the favor."

Her hand came down between us, and she stroked me over my jeans.

"You don't need to return the favor. I fucking love making you feel good."

"And I love making you feel good, and I've yet to get to do that." She turned me so that my back was against the wall, and she dropped to her knees.

I nearly came at the sight of her down on her knees, looking up at me with those golden honey eyes as she licked her lips.

She reached for the button of my jeans, tugged the zipper down, and pushed the denim along with my briefs to the floor in one quick movement.

My dick sprang free, and to say that he was delighted about this turn of events would be an understatement.

I was rock hard, and her eyes widened as she took me in.

She wrapped her hand around my cock and stroked a few times as I sucked in a breath.

And then she leaned forward as her lips wrapped around me.

Holy fucking shit.

Her mouth was wet and warm, and she took me deep, gliding her lips back and forth over my shaft.

Her tongue swirled around my dick at the same time, and the sensation was so overwhelming, I had to close my eyes to keep from coming immediately.

My fingers tangled in her hair as I tugged and pulled while she sucked me harder and deeper.

My tip hit the back of her throat, and she just continued bringing me right to the edge as I pumped into her, over and over.

"Fuck, baby. I'm going to come," I grunted as I tugged at her hair in warning for her to pull back.

But she surprised me when she stayed right there, taking me even deeper.

I thrust once more before coming so hard that my vision blurred.

Again and again.

I unloaded into her mouth, and she stayed right there.

I stroked her hair as my movements slowed, and she pulled back, making a little popping sound as she wiped her mouth with the back of her hand.

The move so sexy, my dick threatened to go hard again.

"Wow. That was—" I shrugged because there were no words. "Come here."

I tugged her up on her feet and kissed her hard. My hand moved between us, stroking her with my fingers before I pulled back.

"You're soaked. You liked that."

"I like making you feel good," she said, her voice just above a whisper.

I slipped my fingers in my mouth and groaned. "So sweet, Winnie."

My phone rang from where it sat in the pocket of my jeans in a slump at my ankles.

"Definitely not taking that call," I said as I leaned down to kick off my boots and jeans.

"You should check just to make sure it's not Melody. Remember she had a tummy ache this morning, but then she said she was fine after she ate?"

I nodded. This woman was so thoughtful it was hard to wrap my head around it.

"Rosewood River Elementary School" flashed across my screen.

Fuck.

"I need to take this."

"Of course," she insisted.

I had a feeling our little afternoon booty call was about to come to an end.

24

Winnie

I listened as he spoke, and it was obvious that something was wrong. I gathered my clothes and hurried out of his room and down the hallway to my room. I grabbed some clean panties and quickly got dressed. I was stepping back into the main house just as Archer was coming out of his room, fully dressed.

"What's going on?" I asked. I saw the concerned look on his face.

"They said Melody got into an altercation, and I need to come pick her up."

"An altercation? What the hell does that mean?" I grabbed my purse. "I'm coming with you."

He didn't fight me, and we hustled out to his truck and drove the short distance to the school.

"I'm sorry for—you know, cutting things off so abruptly," he said as he stared ahead at the road, his hands gripping the steering wheel so hard that his knuckles were white.

"Don't apologize. Melody is your daughter. I would be appalled if you weren't rushing to the school. And you made me the second contact number at the school, so I would have gotten the call next, and we'd be exactly where we are now."

He nodded as he pulled into the parking lot in front of the school, then put the truck in park. We walked briskly toward the entrance and into the front office before we were ushered into the principal's office.

"Hey, Archer." The man extended his arm, and they shook hands.

"Theo, good to see you. Winnie, this is Principal Carver. We grew up together," Archer said, but his voice was strained. "What's going on. Where is my daughter?"

"Everything's okay. Just wanted to bring you in here first to tell you what happened. She's lying down in the nurse's office." He motioned for us to take the seats across from him. "Melody got into an argument with Justine Schwartz, and it got physical."

"Who got physical? Melody?"

"Justine did, and then Melody acted in self-defense after some words were exchanged about the Valentine treats." Principal Carver leaned back in his chair with his arms crossed over his chest.

"I made cupcakes for the Valentine's Day party. Was that not allowed? I had approved it with Mrs. Groucher ahead of time."

"No, no, there wasn't an issue with the cupcakes. Apparently, Justine made a comment that the cupcakes weren't made by a real mommy because Melody doesn't have a real mommy. And she told the other kids they shouldn't eat the cupcakes." He shook his head with disbelief. "I'm telling you, kids can be cruel, even at a young age."

"So Justine said the cupcakes weren't made by a real mommy and they shouldn't eat them? And then what happened?" Archer asked, his hands clasped together, the veins in his neck strained.

"It happened out on the playground, and several kids shared that Justine was taunting Melody about it. Following her around and making fun of her. From what I've gathered, Melody said that the cupcakes were made with love and that she loves Winnie, and it just escalated. Justine said something that really upset her." He cleared his throat.

"What did she say?"

"According to Melody and a few of the other kids, Justine said that Melody's mom didn't want her, and that's why she left, and that that makes Melody unlovable." He blew out a breath. "Justine then grabbed Melody and pinned her to the wall and said it again, and Melody shoved her back. Justine has been sent home for the day."

I gasped at his words, fighting back the urge to cry on behalf of the sweetest girl I'd ever met being mistreated like that.

"And my daughter is being sent home for defending herself when she was treated cruelly and then pinned to a wall?" Archer hissed, pushing to his feet and running a hand through his hair. "This is fucking insane."

"Archer, relax," Principal Carver said as he got to his feet. "I called you to pick up Melody because she's upset. Obviously, she's not being suspended. I just assumed you would want to take her home because she's been crying pretty hard, but we got her calmed down. I just don't think she's up for being back in class."

Arhcer nodded. "Sorry. I just, I can't stand the idea of someone saying something so cruel to her. Words are terrible weapons, and I don't want her to ever feel like she's unlovable. That little girl could not be more loved."

"I can promise you that your daughter feels loved. She's got a huge family who adore her, and it shows. But yes, words hurt, and Justine was cruel. She's got her own issues going on, and it appears she's lashing out."

"All right. Can you take us to see Melody, please?" Archer said, and I moved to stand, anxious to check on her as well.

"Of course. Follow me."

Once we left his office, we made our way to Nurse Lindstrom's office. Melody was sitting up drinking an apple juice, and her gaze met mine. Her eyes were puffy, and when she turned to look at her father, her bottom lip started trembling.

Nurse Lindstrom took the juice from her as Archer reached for his daughter.

"I'm sorry, Daddy," she croaked. "She wouldn't let me go, and I pushed her because she was hurting me."

"You have nothing to be sorry for, angel face." He wrapped her in a hug, and I swear my chest squeezed so tight it was painful. "If someone is hurting you, you need to take care of yourself. You aren't in trouble. I'm very proud of you. And you're Daddy's forever Valentine, remember? So how about we take you home early."

"Okay, Daddy," she whimpered, and then she looked up at me and reached for me. "Can I give my Winnie a hug, too?"

"Always," he said, and I scooped her right up and hugged her extra tight.

"You're okay, sweet pea," I whispered into her hair.

She placed a hand on my cheek as her bottom lip trembled. "I don't care what my friend Justine says, you feel like a real mommy."

I wasn't sure what caught me off guard more.

The fact that she was referring to me as a mommy, or the fact that she'd just called Justine her friend after the girl had treated her so poorly.

Archer glanced over at me as he pulled the door open, and I slipped her into her car seat and buckled her up.

I closed the door, and he paused as he glanced over at his daughter through the window. "Who the fuck says that? What is wrong with that girl, and why would Melody call her a friend after what she said?" He kept his voice low as he ran a hand through his hair.

"Because you raised her to be a forgiving, loving, amazing little girl," I said, placing my hand in his to try to comfort him. "She doesn't have an unkind bone in her body, so she doesn't even know how to respond to someone treating her this way."

He lifted my hand and kissed it.

"Thank you for saying that. Thank you for being here. Thank you for loving my little girl," he said, leaning down close to my ear. "And I didn't get a chance to thank you earlier, but thank you for the world's best blow job."

I chuckled. "It was a long time coming. Pun intended." I winked at him.

I hopped in the car and buckled up as the three of us drove home.

My heart was heavy for Melody, and I wanted to do whatever we could to turn this day around for her.

But for the first time in a very long time, I felt a sense of contentment wash over me.

As if I was exactly where I was supposed to be.

As if I'd found everything I needed, when I didn't even know I was looking for it.

25

Archer

I held my little girl a little longer tonight. She'd been quiet at dinner, even though she'd tried to rally for Winnie's birthday, and Melody had always loved Valentine's Day. But the hurtful words that Justine had said to her today had definitely taken the wind from her sails.

I'd talked to her about it, and she'd listened and nodded, but I knew that she was wounded, and it fucking killed me.

"I'm glad you came in here for bath time, too, Winnie. Bath time is my favorite. Tonight, we don't have to wash my hair, right, Daddy?" Melody said. That little twang in her voice was like a straight shot to my heart. She was pure sweetness.

"Right, angel face. Last night we washed your hair, so tonight we're just washing your body."

"Bath time is my favorite time of day, too," Winnie said as she held up the body wash. Melody held her hand out for a few pumps. Winnie and I were both down on the floor beside the tub, as my daughter had asked us both to be in here tonight.

She'd had her feelings hurt real bad, and it wasn't familiar to her. So she was working through it.

I was just pissed off, and tempted to give Justine's mother, Sarah Lynn, a piece of my mind, but Winnie talked me out of it.

She thought I should sleep on it, and see how I felt tomorrow.

As a parent, we're prepared for how challenging the newborn stage is. The sleepless nights, the diapers, the feedings, all of it. Everyone talks about the difficulties that you will face.

We're even prepared for the commitment that comes with parenting—the time, the financial expectations, all the safety issues that you need to be aware of. Again, it's discussed all the time.

But no one tells you how to prepare for this kind of stuff. For seeing your child get hurt. For how deeply you feel that pain and desperately want to take it from them.

So I forced myself to remain calm and talk her through it. To just love her the best way I could and hope that it was enough.

"Me and you's love bows and bubble baths," Melody sang out, and then she chuckled.

"We sure do, those are two of my favorite things, but you know what else I love?" Winnie asked as she handed my little girl a washcloth to wipe away the water that had splashed her face.

"What?"

"You." She smiled at my daughter. "I love you so much,

Melody. And when your daddy hired me, I admitted I hadn't been around kids much, so I was a little nervous. But once I met you, I knew I was lucky because you're the most lovable girl in the whole wide world."

Melody blinked a couple of times. "You and me don't have mamas, but we're still lovable."

"Absolutely we are." Winnie sighed. "Having a mama doesn't make you lovable—it's what's inside your heart that makes you lovable. And you, Melody Chadwick, have the best heart I've ever seen."

"I like your heart, too, Winnie." Melody's bottom lip started to quiver. "I felt real sad today when Justine said those things to me, because I do sometimes wish you were my real mama."

My fucking chest tightened so much, I was doing my best not to show my discomfort. Seeing my little girl in pain did crazy shit to me.

"I'm your *real Winnie*, and I think what we have is even better than if I'd met you as a baby."

"You do?" Melody asked.

"I do. Because we both found each other when we needed the other most."

Fuck me.

These two owned me right now.

I glanced over at Winnie, but she was focused on my daughter. On healing her pain. On making her feel better and taking away that hurt.

"I'm happy about that." Melody smiled and then raised her arms over her head. "I'm ready to get out and have the sweetest dreams."

I stood and scooped her out of the water before wrapping her in a towel, and Winnie left to go get her jammies.

The next hour was spent getting her ready for bed, and then Winnie read her three books tonight. We both kissed her good night, and I pulled the door closed behind me, leaving it open just a crack so I could hear her if she called for me.

Winnie walked toward the kitchen, and I grabbed her hand, stopping her at the end of the hallway and pressing her against the wall. "I'm sorry for fucking up your birthday."

She shook her head, brows cinched together with confusion. "Archie, I love that little girl of yours. And I love the way that you love her. I couldn't care less about my birthday, and you guys did too much anyway. The cake. The gorgeous monogrammed journal, the flowers, the delicious dinner, which you wouldn't even let me help clean up."

"I'm glad you enjoyed it, but I know that I was distracted. I hate seeing that sadness in her eyes," I admitted. "You just somehow know all the right things to say."

She chuckled as her hand reached up to stroke the side of my face. "Trust me. I'd like to throttle Justine for what she said, but I tamper it down, because Melody doesn't need to see anger right now. She just needs comfort and love."

"And what do you need, Winnie?" I stepped closer, tucking the hair behind her ear.

"I'm pretty content at the moment." She smirked. "You rocked my world earlier, so you left me with plenty to think about."

"We could finish what we started," I whispered, feeling bad at the way things had turned this afternoon.

She shook her head. "Today is not the day for that. I know you're upset about what happened, and you don't need to worry about me. There's no rush here. This was actually the best birthday I've had in a very long time."

"Yeah? Which part? The cake? The presents? Or was it when you came on my lips?" I whispered against her ear.

Her cheeks flamed pink, and she smiled. "All of it."

"Good. What would you like to do for the rest of your birthday?"

"How about we watch a movie? I have a feeling Melody may wake up a few times tonight. When I used to get upset as a kid, I'd never sleep well after."

I leaned down and picked her up, then cradled her in my arms and carried her to the couch before settling her on my lap. "I hate even thinking about you being upset."

"It didn't happen often. I had an amazing father, just like Melody does. It makes a difference." She snuggled against my chest, and I reached for the remote.

I let her choose the movie, since it was her special day, and seeing as it was Valentine's Day, we had an endless rom-com selection to choose from.

This was nice. We just sat there cuddling on the couch. She didn't expect anything from me after the day I'd had, yet I wanted to do everything for her.

I got up and made us some popcorn, and we laughed and talked and enjoyed the movie. She fell asleep with her head on my lap during the last half hour of the movie, and I carried her to her room. She gave me a kiss good night before going to her bathroom to get ready for bed.

"Good night, Archie. Thanks for making today so special."

"Night, Winnie."

I made my way to my room, but I knew it was time to step up my game.

This wasn't casual anymore. At least not for me.

I picked up my phone and texted in the group chat.

Me: *I know it's late. Is anyone up?*

Rafe: *I'm on the shitter. My ass is on fire from the lobster bisque Lulu and I had tonight to celebrate Valentine's Day.*

Bridger: *Use the turbo on the toilet, and flush that shit out of your system.*

Easton: *Perhaps you should start tracking what you eat. You are clearly intolerant to many things.*

Bridger: *I find him intolerable, so it makes sense.*

Rafe: *<middle finger emoji>*

Clark: *Agreed. You can't spend your life squeezing your ass cheeks together and running to a shitter.*

Axel: *Little Mills just woke me up to go take yet another piss, because she has the world's smallest bladder.*

My brother and Wren had gotten a puppy a few months back, and he loved to tell us how many times a night he woke up with Millie.

Rafe: *Two little wieners in one house is a lot to handle.*

Axel: *Hey. They didn't call me Well Hung Chadwick on the football team for no reason.*

Me: *I do not remember that being your handle.*

Easton: *Wait. Why were you asking if we were up, Archie?*

Bridger: *Do you have the shits, too?*

Rafe: *At least he has the good toilet if he does.*

Clark: *Tell us what's going on.*

Axel: *Is Melody okay?*

I'd filled them all in earlier about what had happened at school this afternoon, and they'd all texted separately and checked in several times.

Me: *She seems to be doing okay.*

Bridger: *Do not make me go down to the school and supervise my girl.*

Rafe: *What are you going to do? Buy the little bully a shitter?*

Bridger: *<middle finger emoji>*

Axel: *What's going on, brother?*

Archer: *It's nothing bad. I just need some advice.*

Easton: *I love giving advice.*

Clark: *Let's hear it.*

Me: *I like my nanny.*

Bridger: *<head exploding emoji>*

Bridger: *You don't say?*

Bridger: *I told you that you liked her, you fucker.*

Rafe: *Aren't you supposed to be the man of few words?*

Easton: *By like her, do you mean… you're happy to have her working for you? Or you like her. <winky face emoji>*

Bridger: *Do you think he'd send us a text on Valentine's Day when it's almost midnight if he wanted to tell us he was happy he hired her? Wake the fuck up, dumbass.*

Easton: *Tone down the tude, dickfuck.*

Rafe: *Motherfucker. You're giving me an upset stomach. I can't handle tension right now.*

Clark: *Dude. You were born with the shits.*

Clark: *Archie, I'm happy for you. Winnie's great. I think we already knew you liked her, though.*

Bridger: *Ya think? Why does nobody listen to me?*

Rafe: *Because you're mean.*

Axel: *And angry.*

Easton: *Kind of terrifying.*

Clark: *Moody as shit, too.*

Archer: *I just thought you were wrong. But I don't disagree anymore.*

Axel: *Did something happen.*

Bridger: *Yeah, he just decided in the middle of the night that he likes his nanny. Of course something fucking happened. Nobody comes in the group chat asking for advice before something happens.*

Rafe: *I came in the group chat and asked if you thought I was lactose intolerant last year, and that was before I shit my pants in the parking lot of the Honey Biscuit Café.*

Clark: *Can we please focus. What happened, Archie.*

Archer: *I'm not here to discuss what happened. I just want to know what to do now. I want to take her out on a date, but we sort of live together. So it feels weird. And what the fuck do we tell Melody? And I don't even know if she wants to date me.*

Easton: *You don't sort of live together. You actually live together.*

Rafe: *Always the lawyer. <eyeroll emoji> Of course she wants to date you. You're Archie fucking Chadwick. The best dude I know.*

Bridger: *Wow. Tell us how you really feel. <middle finger emoji>*

Easton: *Pickleball is starting up again next week. You could ask her to play on the Chad-Six. That's a good icebreaker.*

Rafe: *She could happily sub for me. I'm over pickleball.*

Easton: *Fuck you, and your irritable bowels.*

Clark: *Forget about pickleball. Ask her out. She likes you. You don't have to tell Melody anything. You can say she's your friend.*

Axel: *Agreed. And Melody loves her.*

Archer: *Exactly. So what happens when it blows up in my face, and it's awkward.*

Rafe: *I don't like the negative attitude, Archie.*

Easton: *You just both need to agree that no matter what happens, it doesn't affect your work relationship.*

Clark: *Didn't your work relationship become an issue for you and Henley when you were first together?*

Easton: *Glass fucking houses. You're dating and living with your team physical therapist.*

Bridger: *And, she's your coach's daughter. <laughing face emoji>*

Clark: *And… it all worked out. BOOM, BITCHES!*

Archer: *But what if it doesn't? What if I fuck this up and Winnie ends up hating me and Melody loses her nanny, who she adores.*

Axel: *You won't fuck anything up. You've spent months together, and you clearly like one another. Why do you expect the worst?*

Archer: *She works for me. She's a decade younger than me. She lives in my home. She's recently divorced and wants to be single.*

Bridger: *Shit. Who brought the dark cloud to the party. <laughing face emoji>*

Axel: *Stop overthinking it. You deserve this.*

Easton: *Sometimes you've got to take a fucking risk.*

Rafe: *Let's go, Archie!*

Clark: *Fuck, yeah!*

Axel: *Let's do this!*

Archer: *I just wanted some advice. I wasn't looking to get pumped up.*

But either way, I was pumped up.

I was going to officially ask my nanny to date me.

26

Winnie

I sent my book off to my editor and blew out a breath. I did it. Another book in the books. Pun intended.

I sat back and thought about how crazy the last twenty-four hours had been.

An absolute roller coaster.

Things had escalated with Archer and me, and it wasn't just the physical stuff. Yes, I'd been all in yesterday, and if that phone call hadn't come through, I'm fairly certain we would have had sex.

And I was completely on board with that.

It didn't even scare me.

But it was the emotional connection that was so surprising. We talked about everything. I loved the way he was with his daughter. The way he cared so deeply.

Archer Chadwick was everything I never knew I needed.

At a time in my life when I'd made a conscious decision not to need or want anyone.

Melody had seemed back to normal this morning, and I'd told Archer that I wanted to tag along to drop her off at school today. He didn't argue or tell me it wasn't necessary. He'd just smiled and nodded.

But I knew it would comfort both of them if I was there.

Justine hadn't been at school when we dropped Melody off, and Mrs. Groucher hugged Melody so tight that it made my heart squeeze.

I'd grown fond of the grumpy woman over the last few months. I'd surmised that being a school teacher was not an easy job, and most people didn't understand that and judged unfairly, me included. But I got this woman now, and I'd learned that kindness could go a long way.

She'd softened somewhere along the way, and my guess was that she couldn't deny how sweet Melody was, so she'd just accepted it.

Archer seemed a little off this morning. He'd been quieter than usual, and he seemed uncomfortable around me when he dropped me off at home on his way to work.

I wasn't going to read into it.

A lot had happened, and maybe he was just processing everything.

My phone rang, and I saw that it was my agent, Laney.

"Hey, I just sent the book to you and Daisy," I told her.

Daisy was the editor I worked with at my publisher.

"Yes. I just got it. I can't wait to dive in," she said. "But I wanted to call you to talk to you because I just hung up the phone with Daisy, and they want to send you on a tour for *Whisper Sweet Nothings*."

They'd discussed doing a book tour later in the series, but I hadn't expected it to be so soon.

"Really? So the tour would be for the April release?" I asked, and my heart raced in my chest, because that was only two months away.

"Yes. Every retailer has picked it up, and I think this one's going to put you on the map. Really make a name for yourself. I'm guessing you can retire from your nanny gig after this release." She chuckled.

I cleared my throat. "Okay. I'll have to talk to Archer and make sure he can work with my schedule. How long will I be gone?"

"We're planning on a five-stop book tour, so you'll be gone for a week," she said, and I could hear the excitement in her voice.

I should've been excited.

This was everything I'd wanted.

Everything I'd worked for.

It was all happening. My books were taking off. My career was going in the direction that I'd only dreamed of.

"Oh wow. That sounds great. I just need to make sure that Archer can cover everything on his own with Melody while I'm gone," I repeated, because they were all that I was thinking about at the moment. I'd made a commitment to them, and I wouldn't leave them high and dry.

"All right. I'll have the team send over an itinerary, and we'll start getting your travel planned in the next week or so. But you may want to give him notice soon about an early retirement." She chuckled again. "In all seriousness, Winnie, I think you're going to get very busy here after this release. I think this series is about to explode."

"Okay, yes. This is amazing." Of course it was amazing.

Get on board, Winnie.

"I'll be in touch after I go through these edits. Talk soon."

"Sounds good. Thanks for the good news."

"You got it." She ended the call, and I pulled out my calendar to see what I had scheduled during release week.

Melody had riding lessons and dance class that week. I was sure Isabelle could help get her to her activities. I was just about to text Archer when my phone vibrated.

Archie: *Hey.*

Me: *Hi. How are you?*

Archie: *Good. How are you?*

I chuckled. This was slightly more formal than we normally texted one another.

Me: *I'm good. Are you being weird?*

Archie: *Maybe. I need to ask you something.*

Me: *Okay. Ask away.*

Archie: *Do you want to have dinner with me tonight?*

Me: *Don't we have dinner every night?*

Archie: *Yes.*

Me: *What's going on? You were weird in the car, and now you're being weird again.*

Archie: *Because I had something to ask you in the car and I didn't know how to ask.*

Me: *You wanted to ask me to have dinner with you when we have dinner together every night? I was going to make short ribs tonight. Does that work?*

Archie: *Winnie.*

Me: *Archie.*

Archie: *I don't want you to make short ribs.*

Me: *Okayyyyy. I could make chicken?*

My phone rang, and his name flashed across the screen.

"Hello?" I chuckled.

"Hi." He cleared his throat. "I don't want you to cook dinner for me. I want to take you to dinner."

I paused on my way to the kitchen. "Me, you, and Melody?"

"Fuck. I'm not good at this." Goodness, was that a nervous catch in his voice?

"Not good at what?" I asked, my heart racing so fast I could hear it in my ears.

"I'm trying to ask you on a date. And clearly, I'm failing." He laughed. "I would like to have dinner. Just you and me."

"I thought you didn't do that?"

"I don't."

"But you want to do it with me, Archie?"

"I definitely want to do it with you, Winnie."

Now it was my turn to laugh. "You're ridiculous."

"Listen, I know you're not looking for anything serious, but…" He groaned. "I really do suck at this."

"You're doing great. Continue, please."

"I know you're not looking for anything serious, and I know I said that I wasn't looking for anything serious. But I don't know, Win, I feel like maybe we found something special when we weren't looking."

Swoon.

Serious swoon.

"You aren't speaking. Uh, was that too much?" he asked.

"Not at all. I was swooning." I chuckled and added, "I think we found something special, too. And I didn't know how to bring it up. It's probably weird because I live in your home, and obviously I don't want to complicate things with Melody."

"We're on the same page. But I think she knows we're friends, and we don't need to say more than that. My mom asked if she could have Winnie for a sleepover tonight. I thought maybe I could take you out for dinner. Just you and me."

"You and me, Archie. I can get on board with that."

"Yeah? All right. It's a date, beautiful." Even the way this man spoke was sexy. "Did you finish the read-through?"

"I did. I just sent it off to my editor."

"That's amazing. Congrats. We've got something special to celebrate tonight."

"Thank you." I dropped to sit on the couch and sighed. "I'll see you tonight."

"Yes, you will."

We ended the call, and I couldn't help but smile.

Life was good.

When was the last time I'd thought life was good?

It had been a while.

I stood and headed to the hall closet to grab my coat, as there was still a chill in the air.

I decided to take a walk downtown to look for something to wear tonight and pop in to see my aunt and uncle.

"There's my favorite girl," Uncle Oscar said as he wrapped me up in a hug.

"Hi. Did you have a nice anniversary yesterday? And I know you spoiled Aunt Edith for her birthday." I smiled at him.

"Of course I did. We had a great night. Ate too much, but that's par for the course." He chuckled.

"Good. And it's pretty slow today, huh?"

"It is. What if I join you for a muffin and some coffee?"

"I'd love that," I said.

"Did you send the book off to Laney?" he asked.

"I did. I sent it before I came here." I slipped into the booth, and he took the seat across from me.

"It's the best feeling in the world, right?" he asked as Edith came over and gave me a hug before leaving to get us coffee and muffins.

"It really is. And they want to send me on a book tour in April for the *Whisper Sweet Nothings* release."

"You don't sound thrilled."

"No, I'm excited about it. I just need to make sure I can get things covered with Melody." I thanked my aunt when she dropped off our drinks and wrapped my hands around the warm mug.

"It'll be good for you to go out and meet readers," he said. My uncle was the one who inspired me to write my first book. He'd had a very successful career as an author of thrillers under the pen name James Covington, which he'd retired from over a decade ago.

"Says the man who never toured or did interviews." I chuckled. He'd kept his identity very private.

"The landscape of the industry has changed, so you've got to change with the times." He took a sip of his coffee. "That's when I walked away. I didn't want to do all that social media stuff, nor do I care for interviews. But you're young, and you're much more social than I am."

"You had an impressive career," I said. "And you know you're still my favorite author."

He'd hit the *New York Times* and *USA Today* bestseller lists multiple times. He'd actually had a brilliant career, and most people who knew him here in Rosewood River had no idea that he'd been a big deal in the publishing world back in the day. His books still sold well, and his royalties were pretty sweet; my aunt and uncle lived very comfortably. Their little café barely stayed profitable, but for them it was more about being involved in the community.

"And you're my favorite author, aside from the sexy stuff. But Aunt Edith likes those parts, so who am I to say."

"Okay, good to know."

"I like seeing how happy you are being here," my uncle said. "You're away from that toxic ex of yours, and you seem to be spending a lot of time with Archer and Melody." He gave me a mischievous grin.

"I'm the nanny, so obviously we spend time together."

"That little girl is the sweetest thing I've ever seen, aside from you." He smiled as his gaze locked with mine. "And I see the way that man looks at you, and I just want to make sure that you know that it's okay to be happy again. You spent a lot of years being unhappy, and I know you came here to throw yourself into work and be on your own, but sometimes things happen for a reason. Don't fight it."

"Are you seriously giving me dating advice?"

"I wish I'd given you dating advice before you married that scoundrel."

"Yeah, me too. But it's all part of learning and growing, right?"

"Yes, but sometimes when you get out of something bad, it makes you feel like you need to protect yourself. And the truth is—when you get out of something bad, you should start looking for something good."

"We're going deep this morning, huh?" I chuckled.

"I just love you, sugar bear. I want you to have everything that you deserve."

"Thank you. I'm glad we got to catch up this morning. I'm going to head over to the Vintage Rose to say hi to Emilia, and then I'm going to pop into Strawberry Fields and find something cute to wear on my date tonight." We both moved to our feet.

"Your date, huh?"

"Yep. I'm having dinner with a real handsome single dad." I waggled my brows. "See, you don't need to worry so much. I promise I'm doing just fine."

He whistled, which made me laugh, and I hugged both my aunt and uncle goodbye and promised to come see them over the weekend.

And I couldn't wipe the smile from my face because I was having dinner with a man I was crazy about tonight.

And I was fairly certain that he was crazy about me, too.

And I hadn't felt that kind of excitement in a very long time.

27

Archer

I was relieved that Melody had had a good day at school, and I reminded her that she could talk to me if anything was bothering her.

She was very excited to go to my parents' house, as they were going to watch a movie and do some baking.

"Thanks again," I said to my mom as I kissed her cheek. Melody had just run out the back door with my father to check out the chicken coop.

"So, you didn't tell me what you were up to. And obviously Winnie is up to something if she isn't staying with Melody." She gave me a smirk.

I groaned. "You can't help yourself, can you?"

"Not really. Just give me something."

"Winnie and I are grabbing dinner tonight." I crossed my arms over my chest. "We don't want to make it a big deal, because we both want to be cautious with Melody. This could go nowhere, and I don't want to make it confusing for her."

"I think you probably already know that it's not going nowhere, or you wouldn't be taking this risk." My mother put her hand on my shoulder. "You can be a fabulous dad and have a life of your own, Archer."

Until recently, I'd never understood why my family pushed this narrative that I didn't have a life of my own. Being around Winnie made me want things that I didn't think I wanted.

A relationship. A connection. A partner.

Maybe I'd been guarded because of the way things had ended with Scarlet.

I hadn't realized it before now. I'd thought this was just my new normal, but in hindsight, I'd closed myself off to any sort of connection with women. I'd kept things very surface level.

Light conversation. Good sex. No strings.

And now, that wasn't enough.

Not with Winnie.

She was different.

But it still didn't need to get complicated. We were just going to see where things went.

"I know. And thank you. I appreciate it." I kissed her cheek. "Love you. Call me if you need anything."

"We won't need anything. Go have a good time," she said as I held my hand over my head and waved as I walked out the door.

I was back home in no time. Winnie was standing in the kitchen, and I came to a stop. She wore a black off-the-shoulder sweater and dark jeans, paired with a pair of black heeled boots.

Her hair was pulled back in a knot at the nape of her neck

with a black silky ribbon tied around it.

I had thoughts about what I wanted to do with that ribbon later.

She glanced over her shoulder and smiled. "Hey, you're back."

"Yeah." I shoved my hands in my pockets. "And you look—stunning."

A wide smile spread across her face as her eyes scanned me from head to toe.

"Thank you. You look great, too."

I reached for her coat that was lying on the chair and held it up for her. "Come on, let's go grab dinner. If we stay here any longer, I'm going to peel those jeans off of you and bury my face between your thighs."

"Ahh… bringing the dirty talk tonight?"

I chuckled as we stepped outside, and I helped her into the truck. I drove us to Rosewood's, which was the best steakhouse in town.

We were taken to a private area in the back, as I'd requested.

Winnie ordered a glass of wine, and I stuck with soda water, as I wanted a clear head tonight. We made small talk about our days before placing our orders. She told me about the book tour her publisher was planning, and she appeared nervous about telling me.

"Of course we'll manage," I told her. "Mom will be delighted to cover for a few days. This is huge. I'm happy for you. Don't worry about things here at all."

She blew out a breath. "I just don't want you to think I'm shirking on my responsibilities."

"Winnie, your career is taking off. This is a good thing. I'm happy for you."

It was also a good reminder not to get ahead of ourselves. Winnie's future was unknown at this point. Things were happening for her, and I was happy for her.

But I could be happy and cautious at the same time.

"Yeah. I'm excited. Thanks for understanding," she said.

"So, what's behind the title, *Whisper Sweet Nothings*?"

"Well, the definition is the exchange of affections by lovers," she said as she reached for her wine glass, with this sexy-as-sin smirk.

"And the characters exchange a lot of affection, huh?"

"Not in the beginning. It takes them some time."

"And how about you? Are you affectionate in your relationships?"

She sighed. "I've told you that I've only had one relationship, which is sort of embarrassing for my age. But Jaden was not affectionate, nor encouraging. So I guess I like to write about it because I probably longed for it for years."

"Again, the man sounds like a real tool."

"Yeah. How about you? I know how affectionate you are with your daughter. And the way you are with me is definitely affectionate." She chuckled as her cheeks flamed pink. "Is that the norm for you in relationships?"

"I honestly don't know. I was definitely affectionate with Scarlet, though that wasn't really her thing. And after she left, I only dated casually, so there hasn't been a lot of—" I paused. "Hmm… what's the word I'm looking for."

"'Wooing'?" she purred.

I leaned forward and ran my finger over the back of her hand. "I'd enjoy wooing you, Winnie."

"I can get on board with that." Her tongue swiped out along her bottom lip.

"Tell me what you want?" I asked, keeping my voice low.

"I'd like to see where this goes. No expectations, but no more holding back."

"I'm down for that, too. What does that look like to you?" I'd need her to tell me what she wanted.

"So, we've done the friends with some benefits thing." She wiggled her eyebrows. "So what if we add more benefits and stop holding back there, and up the stakes on the friendship by going on dates sometimes? Is that too much for you, Archie?"

I laughed. "It's definitely not too much for me. It's what I want, too."

"I like you, Archer Chadwick." She blew out a breath and reached for her wine glass.

"I like you too," I said.

I like you so fucking much it's fucking with my head.

"Then we're on the same page." I nodded as our server took away our salad plates and set down our entrées. She'd ordered a steak and I'd decided on the lobster, and we said we'd share both entrées.

Which was exactly what we did.

We laughed and we talked, and when I asked if she wanted dessert, she shook her head no as her cheeks flushed. "I'm ready to get home."

Check, please.

I handed my credit card to our server and quickly signed the check, my gaze never leaving hers.

I reached for her hand and helped her into her coat, and once she was in the truck, I leaned over and buckled her seat belt, and her fingers grazed along my forearm. I leaned over and kissed her, and her hands moved to my hair, tugging me close. A gust of wind blew by. I had the door open and was standing in the parking lot.

"Take me home, Archie. No more waiting."

I closed the door and then made my way around the truck, moving quickly as I got myself buckled. My hand found hers between the seats, and she smiled up at me.

When I pulled into the garage, I lost all my patience.

How long had I wanted this woman?

I hurried around to the passenger door and reached for her, pulling her over my shoulder, fireman-style.

A fit of giggles escaped her, and she smacked me on the ass. "You do know that I can walk, right?"

"Maybe this is part of those extra benefits we're tossing in." I chuckled as I walked straight to my bedroom and set her down on the bed. I shoved my jacket off my shoulders and crouched in front of her, then pulled her boots off one at a time before setting them on the floor. "I'm going to take my time with you tonight, Winnie."

"I'm counting on it." Her words were breathy as she pushed her coat off her shoulders, and I tossed it on the chair beside my bed.

I peeled her jeans down her legs, admiring the pretty lavender lace panties she was wearing. I ran the tips of my fingers up her thighs and over the lace fabric, and she shivered.

She sat forward and I pulled the sweater over her head, sucking in a breath as I took in her matching strapless bra. "Do you how many times I've thought about these tits of yours? How long I've wanted to see them. Lick and taste and suck them until you beg me to fuck you."

I reached behind her and unsnapped her bra, which fell beside her on the mattress.

And holy shit.

Her tits were works of art.

Perfect handfuls, with little pink nipples that were calling me. Her chest was rising and falling rapidly as my mouth came down over each hard peak.

My tongue flicked and twirled around her nipple, and I covered her breast with my mouth and sucked as she gasped. I took turns, moving from one breast to the next.

Her hands were in my hair as she squirmed beneath me.

Needy and desperate and so ready.

"Archer, please don't make me wait any longer. I need you now," she said, her voice gruff and laced with desire.

I pulled back, then tore my sweater over my head and kicked off my boots as she sat forward and tugged my jeans and briefs down.

My cock sprang free, and I stepped out of the denim and the briefs and moved to my nightstand to grab a condom.

"I want to do it," she whispered as she pushed to her knees and held out her hand.

She was wearing nothing but her lacy lavender thong, and I could stare at this woman all day. I stepped closer, handing her the foil packet.

Her fingers trembled as she tore the top off, and then she looked up at me with those big golden honey-brown eyes before looking back at my dick and rolling on the condom as if she were performing surgery.

"If this is too much, you just say the word," I said, reaching for her chin and tipping her face up to meet her gaze.

"It's not too much at all," she whispered as she finished rolling on the condom. "I'm just not sure how this is going to work."

I studied her.

"How this is going to work? You've done this before, right?"

I chuckled, but part of me was alarmed by the question.

"Yes. But let's just say, I've been with one person, and he didn't look like—you." She glanced at my erection and then back up at me.

I laughed. "You're going to set the pace, beautiful."

I moved onto the bed, lay on my back, and quickly adjusted her above me, with my tip settling at her entrance as if he'd waited a lifetime to be here.

"Okay," she said.

I reached up and tugged her face toward me so that I could kiss her.

I felt her body relax the minute my mouth covered hers.

And then she slowly took me in.

Inch by glorious fucking inch.

I sucked in a breath as she moved.

She pulled back, letting out a long breath as her hands found the tops of my thighs, and she arched her back as she continued to move down my shaft.

So fucking tight.

Nothing had ever felt better.

"Take your time, beautiful," I said, my hands covering her breasts.

Her tongue swiped out along her bottom lip, and she shifted until she'd taken me in.

All of me.

I stayed perfectly still, forcing myself not to take control.

And then she looked down at me, her gaze locking with mine and her lips parting the slightest bit as she rocked back and started moving.

Slowly at first.

My hands moved to her hips, gliding her up and down my

erection as we found our rhythm.

Our breaths the only audible sound in the room.

The moonlight peeking through the crack in the curtains formed a halo around her as her hair tumbled down her back and she rode my cock like she was born to do it.

So fucking perfect.

Our bodies were covered in a layer of sweat as we moved faster.

"Archer," she moaned, and I knew she was close.

I moved my hand to her clit, applying the slightest bit of pressure, and she gasped as her entire body started to shake and she tightened around me as she shattered.

It was the most beautiful thing I'd ever seen.

I was in awe of the woman.

I drove into her one more time as I followed her into pure ecstasy.

Bright lights exploded behind my eyes as waves of pleasure ripped through me, and a guttural sound escaped my mouth.

We rode out every last bit of pleasure.

My gaze locked with hers, and it felt like the earth had shifted beneath us.

And I'd never get enough of this woman.

28

Winnie

The sun coming through the opening in the curtains had me stretching my arms over my head as I glanced around the room.

I was in Archer's bed, and the spot beside me was empty now.

I lifted the comforter and noted that I was still naked. Not surprising, seeing as we'd had sex three times.

Three times.

In one night.

Definitely a first for me.

But the more surprising part was that the thin black ribbon that had been tied around the chignon at the nape of my neck was currently tied around my hips with a little bow, like it was a present.

I chuckled just as Archer came strolling into the room with two cups of coffee.

"Good morning, beautiful." He smiled as he set one mug on the nightstand on my side of the bed, then moved to the other side of the bed and slid in beside me.

"Good morning. Why is there a bow tied around my hips?"

"Because your pussy is magnificent, and clearly it's your other superpower, so it should be rewarded with a bow." He smirked.

I sat up, taking the blanket with me and tucking it beneath my arms to keep it in place.

"You're ridiculous," I chuckled. "But my body is on a high, so I'm in no position to complain."

"Good. That was the plan." He winked as I reached for my mug and took a sip.

"Yep. It's good to know that the sex I've been writing about in the pages of my books really does exist. This was actually the best kind of research."

Who knew?

Certainly not me.

He glanced over at me, a sexy grin spread across his handsome face. "Good to know. But it's not always like that."

"So I'm not the only one who hasn't had good sex?"

"I've had plenty of good sex, but it didn't compare to what that was last night. That was—different." His tongue swiped along his bottom lip as his gaze locked with mine.

"Different in a good way, right?" I set my mug down and turned to face him.

He tugged the blanket from my hand, and it pooled around my waist. He set his mug on the nightstand beside him.

"Don't hide yourself. Not from me. I've spent months wondering what was beneath your clothing, and it's even better than what I imagined." He traced his fingers over my breasts, moving from one to the other, as shivers ran down my arms.

This man touched me in a way that I'd never been touched.

Made me feel things that I'd never felt.

"Fine. Answer the question."

"I've never had sex like that with anyone, Winnie. It was fucking fantastic."

"What was different?" I pressed, because I loved how open we were with one another.

He tugged me close to him and wrapped his arms around me as his fingers traced along the bow he'd tied around me.

"For me, I think it has a lot to do with our connection. I don't know. Ever since Melody was born, I've kept my relationships very casual. I've been open with the women I've been with, and it's not like I'm out there hooking up with women every weekend. I don't get out that often." He chuckled. "So it's been good, but nothing like last night."

"So your last serious relationship was with Scarlet?"

"Correct."

"Do you think you closed yourself off to anything other than casual just because of Melody, or do you think you were protecting yourself after she left?" I tipped my head back to look at him, and he arched one eyebrow, clearly surprised by my question.

"Are you a therapist now, Winnie?"

"Just a romance author who loves to deep-dive into people's backstories." I leaned up to look at him as I chewed my bottom lip. I wondered if my questions were pushing things too far.

Jaden was always annoyed by questions. In all honesty, he was kind of annoyed by conversation in general.

It had a lot to do with me pouring my feelings into the pages of my books.

My marriage had been a very lonely place for me these last few years.

As if he could read my mind, Archer's hand moved to the side of my face. His thumb stroked my cheek. "Hey, you can ask me anything you want. You can also tell me anything you want to tell me as well. I love that you care so much."

"Thank you," I said, my voice quiet now.

"I think maybe it was a mix of both. But I've always been a man who trusts my gut. And my gut has been pointing me to you for a while now." He tucked the hair behind my ear. "But yes, I think I was being cautious because I want to protect my daughter, but I'm sure I want to protect myself a bit, too."

"And you don't feel like you need to protect yourself from me?" I asked with a grin.

"Oddly, no. I don't. And what about you? I know you had a plan to be single. But if we're going to continue this whole friends-who-date-with-all-the-benefits thing, that might make things complicated for you."

"Well, I made that whole decision before I knew that book boyfriends really exist." I laughed. "I'm happy to secretly date you, Archer Chadwick."

"I don't think we have to keep it a complete secret. I think we need to be cautious with Melody, but I don't think that means no one else can know."

"What are you saying, Archie? Do you want to date me for real?"

"Are we in high school? Oh wait, you weren't there that long ago, were you?"

"I'm twenty-five years old now. And you're thirty-four. Hardly too old to date. And I swear you have the penis of a teenage boy. It's very eager and easily impressed," I said over a fit of giggles as he flipped me on my back and hovered above me.

"Only for you, Winnie," he said. "But I kind of want to fire you now."

My eyes bulged. "Why would you fire me?"

"Because how does this work? We're going to actually date one another, and you live in my casita and cook dinner for us and do Melody's laundry—it feels barbaric."

Loud laughter bellowed from me. "You actually don't ask me to do anything outside of caring for Melody. I added in a lot of things because I like to do them. And let's face it, your eggs are terrible. I wouldn't be eating at all if you were doing the cooking."

He nipped at my earlobe, and I squealed.

"I don't want it to be weird. I'd like to see where this can go."

"Then don't make it weird," I said. "And you're not firing me. I'll file a complaint with the HR department."

He snorted. "Fine. You can keep making us delicious meals whenever you want."

"Thanks, boss."

"'Boss,' huh? I'll show you just how bossy I can be," he said as he leaned down and kissed me.

And I couldn't get enough of this man.

• • •

"Okay, this is by far your best book yet. The acts of service this man does for her. I can't even handle it," Emilia said. We were having our boozy book brunch at the Honey Biscuit Café, and we were discussing my book, of all things.

"Agreed. I stayed up all night and finished it." Eloise reached for her mimosa.

"Girl, I don't know where you come up with this stuff, but it's so addicting," Lulu added. She broke a piece of her muffin off and popped it in her mouth.

"And you even had them riding horses in this one." Wren wiggled her brows.

"That horse wasn't the only thing she was riding," Lulu said as the table erupted in laughter.

"Seriously, how lucky are we that we get to hang out with our favorite author all the time?" Henley leaned her head on my shoulder.

"Thank you. I feel like the lucky one. I appreciate you all reading this new one early for me." I tried not to get emotional, because finishing a book and handing it over was a very vulnerable feeling.

"We love you," Lulu said, "but are we all going to ignore the elephant in the room?"

"Are we talking about Josh Black, who keeps staring over here?" Henley asked before taking another sip of her mimosa.

"Nooooo. He's a whole other issue. I'm talking about 'The Taylor Tea.' Has no one read it this morning?"

Everyone shook their heads no.

"It just came out this morning. I don't usually even hear about it until Sunday dinner," Emilia said.

"Same," Wren and Eloise said at the same time.

"Seriously? I wake up on Saturday mornings and I pull it right up. It's brilliant." Lulu turned her attention to me. "And this morning's article was very captivating."

"Did my pen name get exposed?" I whispered, because the way she was looking at me made it clear that it was about me.

"Ummm… no. But you've been holding out on us, you dirty

little bird." She wagged her finger at me.

"Ahh… I do have something to share, but now I want to know what the article said before I come clean."

"Let's hear it, Lu," Henley said as I reached for my mimosa.

Lulu read in her most dramatic voice, per usual, as we all listened with rapt attention. She went through the usual tidbits about local things that were going on, and then her voice grew more playful.

"'Our favorite single daddy seems to be swooning over his lovely nanny. Word on Main Street is that there's a lot more going on here than the usual childcare duties. Many have noticed the time they spend together, and heads up, Roses, these two lovebirds have been caught out alone… Can't imagine the job requirements include a romantic dinner for two at our favorite steakhouse, where they left hand in hand. Seems like they're awfully cozy these days, and our favorite bachelor might be off the market.'"

All five of them turned to look at me, all gaping aside from Lulu, who just had a wicked grin on her face.

"So, there's been some changes on the home front," I said with a laugh.

"I knew it," Emilia and Wren said at the same time.

"I suspected it, too." Henley pulled me in for a hug.

"Really? Of course you did. We all did!" Lulu tossed her hands in the air. "You've clearly been picturing one another naked for weeks at Sunday dinner. I know that look, and you've both had it bad."

I had to laugh. "I do have it bad for that man."

"Awww… I love this so much," Eloise said as she squeezed my hand. "You both deserve to be happy. You've been through it, and so has he."

"Yeah. I love when good things happen to good people." Emilia raised her mimosa and motioned for us to all do the same.

"Cheers to finding your own real-life book boyfriend," Henley said as we all clinked glasses.

"I'm so happy for you both," Wren gushed. "Axel and I were saying how much happier Archer has seemed these last few months, and that's all because of you. I think you really complete both him and Melody in a way."

"She was the missing piece." Emilia smiled, her eyes wet with emotion.

"Well, they complete me, too. It sounds so corny, but it's true. I didn't know what I was missing in my life before coming here. I just wanted a fresh start, you know? I'd been unhappy for a long time. In my job, in my relationship—and it's easy to settle and just try your best not to rock the boat, and I'm embarrassed to admit that I did that for a long time."

"I relate to this so much," Wren said, a genuine smile spread across her face and her eyes crinkled in the corners. "I think we can stay stuck for a long time because change is… uncomfortable. But when you take that leap, it's so freeing."

"It is. And coming here has just been filled with so many unexpected surprises that I didn't see coming," I said.

"I'm so happy you're here," Lulu said. "You make boozy book brunch even better. And we get the perks of reading all your books early," she added with a laugh.

Aunt Edith walked over with fresh mimosas and set them down.

"I wanted to ask you a favor, while your uncle is in the back eating far too many blueberry pancakes," she said, leaning over the table as she faced me.

"Of course. Anything."

"Well, the man is driving me crazy because he has basically confiscated my laptop because his keeps freezing up and is having all sorts of issues. I've tried to get him to go into the city and have it looked at, but you know how stubborn that man can be," she said, and we all chuckled.

"Do you want me to take him into the city?" I asked.

"No. He won't do it. And we aren't tech savvy, but I thought maybe you could look at it and see if you could fix it? It could be something simple. He likes to get on there and write poetry just to keep his writer brain sharp. But now he's on my computer every night instead, which means I don't have one to use now."

"I'd be happy to look at it. And Archer is pretty good with that stuff, too." I smiled up at her.

"Bridger could check it out if you can't figure it out," Emilia said as she reached for her glass.

Bridger was a billionaire IT guy, so if Archer and I couldn't figure it out, we'd definitely ask him.

"Ahh… that would be great." Edith sighed. "Don't tell him I said anything, because he won't want to bother you with it. I'll drop it by your place later today."

"You've got it. My lips are sealed, and I'll try to get that fixed so you can have your laptop back."

"Thanks, doll," she said as she walked off.

"Ummm… Oscar writes poetry?" Lulu gaped at me.

"He does. He's actually the reason that I got into writing." I leaned in, keeping my voice low. "Oscar was a famous author back in the day. Have I not told you this?"

"Oscar Smith was an author?" Wren asked, her brows cinched together as if this was the most puzzling thing she'd ever heard. "I'm surprised 'The Taylor Tea' hasn't vetted this out."

"Right? Probably because he doesn't talk about it, but he was pretty famous. He wrote fifty-seven books before retiring over a decade ago. His pen name was James Covington. He wrote thrillers, and he had a huge following."

"Shut up!" Eloise gasped before her hands moved to cover her mouth, which was now hanging open. "Oscar is James Covington. I've read everything he's ever written. He's brilliant. I literally binged his books within a couple of months when I was in college."

"I'm shook." Emilia's eyes were wide. "I've also read everything he's written. How is this not known?"

"He's pretty private about it, but it's not like it's a secret, really. They moved full-time to Rosewood River after he retired and opened the café, and he just left that life behind him. But he's always encouraged me to write, and he's been my biggest cheerleader."

"Clearly 'The Taylor Tea' is for amateurs. We've got two big-time authors living in our small town, and the people here are completely unaware."

"Well, some things are meant to stay private," Henley said with a chuckle. "But I'm glad we know this little secret because I will be diving into those books right away."

Eloise told her where to start on his backlist, and they all agreed to keep his past career a secret.

I was grateful that I'd found such amazing friends in these women.

They felt like family.

And this town felt like home.

29
Archer

We'd dropped Melody off at my parents' house because my cousin Emerson and her husband Nash were in town with my nephew Cutler. Melody and Cutler were close, and my dad and my uncle Keaton were taking the kids riding today.

"You sure you're up for this?" I asked. I glanced over at Winnie in the passenger seat as we pulled into the parking lot at the Rosewood River Country Club.

The sun was shining today, though there was still a chill in the air.

"I thought this was just practice?" she asked.

"It is. But you haven't seen Easton on a pickleball court."

"I've heard he's—intense."

I climbed out of the truck and came around to open her door, then pulled her up against me and kissed her hard.

"That's an understatement," I said before reaching for her hand and leading her inside.

We'd stopped hiding our relationship for all intents and purposes. I kissed her in public. Held her hand. Kept her close.

We were only cautious when we were with Melody, because we didn't want to confuse her.

"So what is this? A tryout?" she said with a laugh.

"Well, he wants you to sub for Henley this week, and then he announced a practice out of nowhere. My guess is that he's going to see how well you play." I pulled the door open, placing my hand on her lower back as I led her inside.

"I used to play back at home with some friends, but I'm certainly not a pro." She blew out a breath, and I could tell she was nervous.

"Don't even worry about it. It's supposed to be fun. He takes it too far, and we just ignore him." I laughed as we walked through the clubhouse and back outside toward the courts.

Winnie looked cute as hell in her white-and-green tennis skirt and matching jacket. Her hair was tied up in a ponytail with a matching bow.

Not everyone was here today, because it was tough enough to get everyone to show up for regular games.

But Easton had insisted we come out and have a practice, and I knew it was because he wanted to see if Winnie could actually play. He'd said that Henley had a big caseload coming up at work, and she wasn't going to be playing as much.

"Hey, thanks for coming out today. Welcome to the Chad-Six," Easton said as Winnie gave him a quick hug. Rafe and Bridger walked over, and neither looked happy about being there.

"Where is everyone?" I asked.

"It's just the four of you playing, and I'm going to observe," Easton said.

"You know you're a prick, right?" Bridger said, his tone completely flat.

"So I've been told." Easton smirked.

"Is this because I said Lulu isn't going to be playing as much this coming season?" Rafe grumped. "I would also like to play less."

"You joined the Chad-Six and you made a commitment. Chadwicks don't just quit."

"Is it quitting when you've played for years and you just don't feel like playing anymore because your brother is an actual psychopath when it comes to pickleball?"

"Lulu isn't playing anymore, either?" I asked. The girls loved to play, so it surprised me that neither of them were joining in this season.

"Yep. She's got a busy travel schedule coming up," he said, but he looked away when he said it, so something was clearly up.

"I, um, I've played a couple of times, but not competitively or anything," Winnie said, and Bridger cinched his brows together.

"See what you're doing? You've got everyone stressed out, dickfucker. How about you just let people play." Bridger glared at Easton before turning and tossing a wink at Winnie.

"That's what I'm doing. So how about you just go play, and I'll chill out here." Easton moved to sit at the tables beside the courts.

"Great. Order me a piña colada and some nachos," Rafe called out before jogging down to the courts.

"And we wonder why you always have a stomachache," I said.

"Yeah, Lu's got me eating real healthy at home, so I can splurge a little when I'm out." He gave us a look to make sure we were in place before serving.

And the next forty-five minutes were a little bit shocking.

I shouldn't have been surprised because everything Winnie did, she did well.

But she was good. Damn good.

And nobody held back once they realized what a good player she was.

In fact, she kind of kicked our asses, though she seemed clueless that she was a strong player.

Easton was clapping his hands together when we stepped off the courts.

"We've got ourselves a ringer, boys." He gave me a questioning look as if I'd known and kept it a secret.

"I didn't know she could play like that," I said with a laugh before wrapping an arm over her shoulder and kissing her hair.

"Thanks. It's been a while since I've played, but I've always loved it. And come on." She gave me a sexy look. "Who doesn't love a good pickleball outfit?"

Everyone laughed as we chatted for a little bit, and we all shared Rafe's nachos before getting ready to leave.

"Hey, B," I said, turning to Bridger. "I need a favor."

"Shoot," he said as he walked out to his car with us. Rafe and Easton had stayed back, since they were deep in conversation when we left.

"Edith asked Winnie to see if she could fix Oscar's laptop, and we have it at the house. I've tried rebooting it a few times, but it's frozen, and even with a hard reboot, it's not doing anything. I thought maybe you could take a look at it?"

"Yeah. No problem." He shrugged. "I can follow you to your place now. Emilia is working late, so I've got some time."

"Thanks," Winnie and I said at the same time.

We made the short drive home and walked inside. Winnie grabbed us all glasses of sparkling water with limes as we settled around the farmhouse table in the kitchen.

Bridger opened the laptop, and Winnie handed him a piece of paper with the password on it, and he got to work. My cousin was a brilliant man, and he knew his way around a computer.

"I wanted to talk to you anyway, and I thought Winnie could help me with something," he said as he opened the top, hit the power button, and then waited for things to turn on.

"Oh, this sounds exciting." Winnie rubbed her hands together mischievously.

Bridger started typing on the keyboard, some sort of weird gibberish that was way beyond my skill level. A window then popped up, and he continued typing before looking up. "I'm going to ask Emilia to marry me. And we know my track record with gifts isn't the best, so I thought maybe being a romance author, you could help me out."

I filled Winnie in on the fact that Bridger had owed Emilia an apology for accusing her of writing "The Taylor Tea," and he'd sent her a toilet as an apology gift.

She winced. "Oh. That's not really the best way to say 'I'm sorry.'"

"Right. I know that now." He rolled his eyes. "But I'm not really sure what the best way to ask someone to marry you is. She's a sentimental lady. I want it to be special."

"Well, the fact that you're asking and you're thinking about it is already the best start." Winnie smiled.

I glanced over to see that Bridger had already gotten further along than I had on the laptop because it wasn't frozen any longer.

"He's got a shit ton of stuff on here, and I'm guessing he's maxed on storage. Let me see if I can move things around a little.

He should start saving things on the cloud."

"Oh, that's what I do," Winnie said. "Can we get that set up for him, and I'll put it on my account? He'll never know how to do that on his own."

"Sure, I can get that set up for him."

"So, when do you want to propose?" Winnie asked.

"Yesterday." Bridger laughed. "I've been ready to marry her for a while now. But I know this is an important part of it for her, and I don't want to fuck it up."

"Yeah, it'll be something she remembers forever," she said. "What are her favorite things?"

"Decorating. Books. Flowers. And me." He continued typing on the keyboard like he was writing a novel.

"Okay, that's easy enough." She laughed. "What about making a backdrop out of book pages that we string between the trees in your backyard. You've already got the perfect setting out there. And on the backdrop, you could have large letters that say 'Marry Me.' You could have floral arrangements sitting in large baskets all around it, and you can have candles and lights if you do it in the evening."

He looked up at her. "I like this. How do I make a backdrop out of book pages?"

"I can make it for you," Winnie said. "I'm sure the girls would help me."

"And I'll order a bunch of flowers. But how the hell am I going to get this set up without her seeing it?"

"With help," I said, shaking my head with a laugh. "We get the girls to take her out during the day, and we'll help you set it up, and then you can meet her for dinner, and we'll get the candles and lights ready before you get home."

He nodded. "This could work."

"It'll work. And she's going to love it," I said.

"I can be hiding before the proposal and then come out and take photos for you during the proposal. She'll want to have keepsakes from this special day."

"Oh. I wouldn't have thought of that, but you're probably right. Thank you. Can we pull it together by next weekend? I'm sick of waiting."

Loud laughter bellowed from me. "Patience has never been your strength."

"Agreed." He stared at the screen as he typed some more on the keyboard. "I'm going to clean this up and organize it a bit."

"Thank you so much," Winnie said. "And we can absolutely pull this together by next weekend. I'll get to work on the backdrop today. I've got plenty of books I can use to make the backdrop."

"Just let me know the cost for anything you do, and I'll get the flowers ordered today as well."

"You've still got all those lights from Easton and Henley's wedding wrapped around all your trees, and we can all help you set up lanterns with candles in the yard around the backdrop as well."

"All right. We'll do it next weekend. Saturday night." His fingers froze on the keyboard. "What the fuck."

"What's going on? Did it freeze again?" Winnie asked, scooting closer to Bridger so she could glance at the screen from where she sat between us. "What is this? His poetry?"

"This isn't fucking poetry," Bridger hissed, turning the screen so both of us could see it.

The laptop had a file named "The Taylor Tea," with endless docs inside labeled by date, which appeared to be weekly.

"Oh my gosh," Winnie whispered as she leaned over and

opened one of the docs. And then another. And another. "Uncle Oscar is the author of 'The Taylor Tea'?"

"Fucking Oscar. I should have known. The dude is the pulse of this town. He's at that restaurant every damn day, just listening to all the conversations." Bridger threw his hands in the air. "And it's been a fucking dude the whole time? I thought it was a woman writing that bullshit."

"I mean, the guy is a *New York Times* bestselling author. He knows how to tell a story." I had to laugh, still stunned by the revelation.

Winnie's eyes were wet with emotion as she looked between us. "I think he misses writing, but he doesn't want to write books anymore. He found an outlet that makes him happy. And he never wanted anyone to know who he was even when he was a famous author. His anonymity was so important to him, so I'm guessing this was a way to have an outlet without anyone knowing it was him."

"So he just gets to spread gossip about all of us, and we're supposed to keep it a secret? Why would we protect him for calling everyone out?" Bridger was on his feet now, pacing in little circles in front of the table.

"Listen, I'm not going to tell you what to do. I know you hate that column, but from my perspective, it's done good things for this town," Winnie said as she sniffed a few times, her eyes were wet with emotion. "It's something most locals look forward to every week. I mean, your family reads it every Sunday at dinner together. Lulu wakes up and can't wait to pull it up."

"Why are you upset, beautiful?" I asked her, pulling her close to me and wrapping my arms around her.

"I think it's just the fact that I know he's missing something that he loved so much, and he's found an outlet for it, mixed with the guilt that I asked for help fixing his laptop and just exposed his secret. One he probably loves, because the man loves a little drama, and he's created it in this small town where people are always talking about it and waiting for Saturday to roll in. And now I just ruined it for him."

I glanced up at Bridger, who blew out a strained breath and crossed his arms. "Didn't he just write about you two? Was that not offensive to you? The man was talking about your personal life."

I laughed. "He said that Winnie and I were seen together often, and that we'd gone out to dinner and left hand in hand. Anyone could have said that because it was true. I wasn't offended by it. Hell, I want everyone to know I'm crazy about my nanny."

She smiled up at me. "I didn't care, either. And the girls were excited about us, so his column made it easy to fill them in on what was happening."

Bridger pulled out the chair and sat back down.

"And what about exposing Emerson's wedding disaster and Rafe shopping for an engagement ring for Lulu?" He waited for a response.

"If you recall, there was an apology the following Saturday about Rafe shopping for a ring, and it stated that he'd thought the proposal had already happened because he heard Rafe and Lulu talking about wedding plans. And Emerson's wedding..." I paused and ran a hand through my hair. My cousin Emerson, who was now married to the love of her life, Nash, had been dating Collin Waterstone, and they were all set to be married when she found out he was having an affair with her maid of honor, Farah. It was the biggest news in Rosewood River at the time, and "The Taylor Tea" did not hold back.

"Dude, everyone in this town was invited to that wedding. It wasn't like they didn't know it was called off. And those articles were all defending Emerson and calling out Collin and Farah, not by name, of course, but everyone knew who he was talking about. And Emerson moved to Magnolia Falls and found Nash and Cutler, so it all worked out. 'The Taylor Tea' did not cause her wedding to explode—it just reported on it."

"Fuck. I hate small-town gossip," he grumped.

"It's going to happen whether that column is there or not. Hell, Emerson told me she reads it every Saturday, and she doesn't even live here," I said with a laugh.

He glanced over at Winnie. "Let me guess, you don't want me to expose him."

"I'm not going to ask you to do that," she said as she blew out a breath.

"Look at me, Winnie," he said as he stared at her. "Is that what you want? You want me to keep it a secret?"

"I want my uncle to be happy. He's a really good man, Bridger. He's the reason that I was able to start this new life, and he encouraged me to write when no one thought I should, outside of him and my father." She shrugged. "So, if it were up to me, I would just pretend I never saw this."

"Well, you make my cousin very happy. You make my niece Melody very happy. Hell, you make my future wife very happy with the books you write. You're part of this family now, Winnie. So if that's what you want, that's what you'll fucking get. Even if I hate that fucking column."

My eyes nearly bulged out of my head. "Who the fuck are you, and what have you done with my broody cousin?"

"Hey, what can I say. I have a good woman keeping me in check and a therapist who reminds me to stop and think before I react." He shrugged. Bridger had been seeing his therapist ever since he and Emilia got together because he realized his childhood trauma had caused him to be very guarded. He'd been through some shit, and he'd made huge strides over the last several months. I was proud as hell of him.

Winnie moved forward and wrapped her arms around his neck. "Thank you, Bridger. It means the world to me that you are willing to do this for him."

He hugged her before she slipped back into the seat beside me.

"I'm doing this for you, not for him. So it stays right here, between the three of us." He looked between us.

"Deal," Winnie said, glancing over at me with a big smile on her face.

Damn. She really was part of this family.

I couldn't tell when it had happened, but Winnie Smith was not only a part of this family, but she was also the woman I was crazy about.

She had me thinking about a future that I didn't even know I wanted.

But now I wanted everything.

And that was all because of her.

She wasn't only Melody's Winnie.

She was my Winnie.

She was mine.

30

Winnie

On Sunday morning, I'd sent a text to Eloise, Lulu, Henley, Wren, and Emerson, who was in town for the weekend. I'd told them about the plan for the proposal, and they all met at Archer's house so we could get to work.

"Are you Uncle Archie's girl yet?" Cutler asked as he helped me lay out the book pages. Everyone else sat in the kitchen, cutting out the letters Bridger had requested to say, WILL YOU MARRY ME, ANGEL?

"We're good friends," I said as I glanced over to where Melody was coloring some hearts that she wanted to give to Bridger and Emilia once they got engaged.

His gaze moved to the table where his cousin was sitting and then back to me. "Well, my best friend is also my girl. Her name is Gracie, and I'm going to marry her someday. So you can be Uncle Archie's friend and his girl. And my pops and my mama waited a long time to tell me they were together back then, too."

I chuckled. This kid was so smart. Wise beyond his years. He was barely nine years old and just one of those old souls. The kind of kid everyone wanted to be around. "Thanks, Beefcake. I think Gracie is very lucky to be not only your best friend but also your girl."

"I'm the lucky one," he said as he finished laying out the row of book pages, and he extended his hand so I could pass him another stack. "And my pops says that when you know, you just know."

I moved around, tying the pages together where he'd laid them out with pretty ribbon that I'd picked up at the craft store. We were making good progress in our ginormous backdrop made from book pages. Bridger had ordered a very large floral arch from Emilia's flower shop, and Beatrice, a woman who worked at the Vintage Rose, was arranging everything so that Emilia wouldn't know about it. The backdrop would be surrounded by floral trees and baskets filled with beautiful blooms.

I glanced up when Eloise showed me her letter *M* to demonstrate how she'd covered it in glitter. My favorite thing about this family was the way they all rallied around one another. My father and I had always been that way, but it was just the two of us. This whole family showed up, repeatedly, for each other.

Bridger's words still played in my head.

You're part of this family now, Winnie.

It meant a lot to me that he'd agreed to keep my uncle's secret. I'd returned the computer to Uncle Oscar last night when they'd arrived home from work, and Aunt Edith and I had come up with a plan to say that I'd just stopped by and fixed it easily an hour earlier, adding the extra storage and organizing his files. He looked a little nervous at first, but I acted completely unfazed, and he'd then appeared relieved to have it back.

"Your pops is a smart man," I said as I sat down to start another row.

"And my mama said you write books. I think that's really cool, Winnie."

"I think you're really cool, Beefcake." I chuckled, because his nickname was hilarious.

"Did you always know that you wanted to be a writer?" he asked.

"I always liked writing, but honestly, I don't think I knew that I could be a writer. My father and my uncle both really encouraged me to chase my dreams, and I finally took the leap." I tied off the bow and started cutting new strips. "Do you know what you want to be when you grow up?"

"Well, my mama's a doctor and my pops is a contractor, so in a way they both help people, and I like helping people. And my uncle Hayes built this office space out at his house in his barn, and I was out there all the time watching my pops and my uncle King turn it into this cool space. I even drew an idea for the twins' nursery out there, because Uncle Hayes and Aunt Savvy have twin girls, and they both loved my drawings. So sometimes I think I'd like to draw houses and then build them. So I could do what my pops does, but I'd draw it first."

Wow. Not a lot of nine-year-olds knew what they wanted and had so much passion for it.

"So you'd be an architect? That's so cool."

"Well, I want to take over ROD Construction from my pops and Uncle King someday, because they built it from the ground up. But they don't have an architect, so that would be even better." He winked at me, and I couldn't help but laugh.

This kid had more charm in his pinky finger than most grown men had in their whole bodies.

"I like that you have a plan. I've always been a planner, too."

"You've gotta have a plan if you want to grow up and take care of your girl, right?" He grinned at me. "I've got big plans, Winnie."

"I can see that." I was chuckling just as Emerson walked over.

"This looks great," she said, turning her attention to me. "You are one creative woman. Emilia is going to love this. You've even got my grumpy brother doing romantic gestures now."

I shook my head and smiled. "This was all Bridger's idea. He wants to make it special for her."

"I think she's going to love this. Thanks for stepping up and making this happen so quickly." She bent down and handed me the next ribbon. "And thanks for being so good to Melody and Archer. Melody has always been so full of joy, but it's been a long time since I've seen Archer so happy. He's just lighter now, you know? And that's all you."

My chest squeezed at her words. "Thank you. I'm much lighter since being here, too."

I truly felt that way.

I was crazy about this man in every way. And I adored his little girl.

"Okay, Emilia is texting and wondering where everyone is," Eloise said. "I'm going to go meet her for coffee downtown so she doesn't get suspicious."

Emerson's phone vibrated, and she quickly typed out a message. "Ohhh… she wants to see Cutler, too. I told her we were helping Mom out in the garden, and we'd meet her at the coffee shop in ten minutes."

"Okay, you drive separate, so it doesn't look suspicious." Eloise leaned down and kissed my cheek. "This is going to look so good. Love you, Win."

All of our phones were vibrating with texts from Emilia, and we each came up with an excuse as to why we couldn't meet, hoping she wouldn't find it odd.

But we had more work to do here, and I couldn't wait to get this all set up for her next weekend.

• • •

Melody had gone to sleep about forty minutes ago, and I was folding up the backdrop, which I'd left out for a few hours so the letters we glued on could set. "Hey," Archer said as I placed the backdrop in the office just in case Emilia happened to stop by this week. "I ran you a bath. You need to relax."

Archer and I had a routine now where I'd sleep in his bed and we'd set the alarm for an hour before Melody woke up, and I'd sneak back into my room. We wanted to make sure we handled our relationship right where she was concerned.

"You ran me a bath?" I walked into his arms and hugged him. He was always doing thoughtful things. Putting gas in my car. Leaving treats on my desk when I had big word-count days. Sending sweet texts to encourage me.

"Yeah. Your back must be killing you," he said. "You've been working on that banner all day." He took my hand and led me to his room, closing the door behind him.

"I'm fine. But do you know what I'd love?"

"A glass of wine?" he asked as he reached for the hem of my sweater and tugged it over my head.

"Nope. I'd love if you took a bath with me."

His hand slipped behind my back, and he unsnapped my bra before tossing it on the counter. The comfort I felt with this man was unparalleled.

"You want me to take a bath with you, beautiful?"

"I do. I just want to be close to you right now."

"Done." He leaned down and kissed me.

I tied my hair in a bun on top of my head, and we both finished getting undressed. The bathroom smelled like lavender from the bubble bath he'd poured into the water.

He turned off the faucet and stepped in before dropping down and offering me a hand. I settled between his thighs, my back resting against his chest.

His arms came around me and his nose nuzzled my ear.

"How do you always smell so good?" he asked.

I chuckled. "I guess I take a lot of baths."

He nipped at my ear. "You do. Wait till it warms up, and you can just take a dip in the river, right in the backyard."

A fluttery feeling moved in my stomach at his words. He'd been speaking about the future lately. I liked that he saw me in his future. That he wasn't putting an expiration date on this thing between us.

Because I felt it, too.

I felt it in every inch of my body.

And I didn't want to hold back anymore.

I rolled onto my stomach, which made him bark out a laugh.

"Hey," I whispered.

"Hey, little mermaid girl." He tucked the piece of hair that had broken free from the bun behind my ear as a wide grin spread across his face.

"I need to tell you something," I said.

His brows cinched together, and his smile dropped. "Is something wrong? Are you okay?"

"I'm more than okay."

"All right." His shoulders relaxed a bit. "Tell me what's on your mind."

"I just, well, I wanted you to know that I have these feelings for you. Deep feelings," I said, clearing my throat as the nerves kicked in. I was naked in a tub of water with the most beautiful man I'd ever seen, and I was declaring my feelings in the most vulnerable way possible. "I just feel so much, you know? It's overwhelming sometimes."

My voice started to wobble.

Oh my gosh. This was an epic fail.

His finger moved over my lips to stop me before one large hand covered the side of my face. "I have deep feelings for you, too, Winnie. I didn't see this coming, and I've been trying to control it and slow things down, but I can't. So I understand feeling overwhelmed. But I think it's a good thing, because we both feel it."

I wanted to say it right here.

Right now.

I love you.

But something stopped me from going there.

Maybe it was fear that saying it would scare him off.

Maybe it was fear that it was too soon.

Maybe it was fear of getting my heart broken if he didn't reciprocate those exact feelings.

I wasn't supposed to come here and feel all of these things.

This wasn't the plan.

So we'd leave it at deep feelings for now.

"Love" was just—a complicated word. He and I had both

said it to only one person before now, and both had been failed relationships.

Why curse a good thing?

"I'm glad you feel it, too," I said.

"Me too, beautiful." His gaze locked with mine. "I think it's time that we talk to Melody about it. I don't want you to have to keep sneaking out in the morning. I think it's okay for her to know what's going on."

"The casita is still part of the house," I said with a chuckle.

"It's too far away. I want you in here. In this bathtub. In my bedroom."

I nodded. "I want that, too. But what are we going to tell her?"

That we love each other. That this is the real deal. That we wouldn't be talking to her about it if it wasn't real.

"We're going to tell her that we have—feelings for one another. More than friendship feelings, and we like each other a lot," he said, kissing the tip of my nose. "We'll talk to her tomorrow morning."

I nodded. "Okay. Sounds good."

His Adam's apple bobbed in his throat as he gave me a quizzical look. "Are you sure? Should I say more?"

"No. No, that's perfect." I smiled up at him. "Should we get out of the tub before we start pruning?"

"I have a better idea." His heated gaze found mine.

"Tell me."

"What if we rinse off in the shower, and I fuck you senseless in there."

"Promises, promises," I said while wiggling my brows to shake off my anxiety.

Things were going great. I had nothing to stress about.

He pushed up so fast, I was caught off guard. He stepped out and lifted me easily as my head fell back in a fit of giggles. He carried me to the shower and set me down, then turned on the water and moved me beneath the spray.

I squeezed some body wash in my palm and rubbed my hands together before moving my hands over his chest and down his body. My hand wrapped around his erection, which was rock hard, and I stroked him a few times as he groaned.

"Fuck, Winnie," he said, his voice gruff.

He reached for the body soap and took his time washing me. Covering my breasts with his hands and working his way down my body.

"I want you right now," I whispered.

He nodded and then sighed. "Shit. I need to go get a condom."

I wrapped my hand around his forearm. "I'm on the pill. I've only been with one person, and we always used a condom."

He cinched his brows together, a little wrinkle forming just above his nose, probably finding that odd, seeing as we were married. But he didn't say anything, so I felt the need to explain.

"He was terrified that I would get pregnant, and he didn't want a child until we were older."

"I've never been with anyone without a condom. Obviously Scarlet got pregnant while using a condom because we realized it broke during sex. She wasn't using any other form of birth control at the time." He stared into my eyes.

"So you can be my first and I can be your first," I said as the water sprayed down on my back.

"Are you sure?" He stroked my cheek with his thumb.

"I'm sure."

He moved forward, my back hitting the wall. His gripped my thighs and lifted my feet off the ground as my legs wrapped around his waist.

His tip teased my entrance, and I reached down to find him thick and hard and ready, and then he shifted forward as he filled me. My head fell back at the sensation, and I gasped.

"Yeeesss," I groaned.

"You feel so fucking good, Winnie. So fucking perfect." His voice was pure gravel against my ear.

He pulled back, studying me for a few beats before I leaned down and kissed him.

And he drove in and out of me, over and over.

The water pounded down around us, the shower filling with steam as he fucked me relentlessly.

Nothing had ever felt better.

He pulled back, his mouth losing contact with mine, and I missed him already.

"I want to look at you when you come all over my bare cock."

I nodded as he took his free hand and gathered my wrists and pinned them above my head. And then he thrust forward again.

Over and over.

Harder.

Faster.

My body trembled as he'd bring me just to the edge of ecstasy, and then pull back.

Again and again.

"Archer, please," I pleaded.

His heated gaze found mine as his lips turned up the slightest bit in the corners. He moved his hand between us, knowing just what I needed.

His thumb circled my clit as he drove into me again.

Oh. My. God.

Lights exploded behind my eyelids, and I cried out his name as I went over the edge.

He thrust into me one more time and buried his head in my neck as a guttural sound escaped him.

And he filled me as we both rode out every last bit of pleasure.

I loved this man in a way I never knew was possible.

I may not have been ready to say it, but I felt it.

And I wanted to stay right here forever.

31

Archer

Winnie snuck back to her bedroom an hour ago, and we were going to talk to Melody this morning. It was time.

Things had shifted between Winnie and me, and we couldn't be sneaking around forever.

I wasn't sure what it meant, or where it was going, but I knew it was special and I knew we were both feeling it.

It both excited and terrified me.

This was not something I'd planned for, or expected, but I was going with it.

"Good morning, Daddy," Melody said as she came into my bedroom a little earlier than usual.

"Morning, angel face. How'd you sleep?"

"I slept great. I'm excited about Uncle Bridger posing to Emilia."

I chuckled. "Yes. I'm excited for him to *propose*, too."

"I like weddings, Daddy," she said. She hopped up on my bed as her wild brown hair fell all around her face.

"Yeah? I think they're great, too." I sat up and tucked her hair behind her ear. "I wanted to talk to you about something."

"Are you prosing to my Winnie?" she asked, as if it was no big deal.

"What? No. I'm not proposing to Winnie. But I did want to talk to you about Winnie."

"Okay."

Well, now she had me fumbling over my own thoughts. I thought Winnie and me being together was going to be a big discussion, but she thought I was proposing, so this was not going the way I'd expected.

"I, er, I like Winnie," I said.

"I like my Winnie, too."

"I guess I'm saying that I like Winnie more than a friend." I tucked her hair behind her ears as I looked at her.

"But you don't want to marry Winnie?"

"Well, we aren't talking about marriage." I cleared my throat. "I'm saying that right now, I'd like to date Winnie."

"Oh. I thought you and my Winnie were dating."

"You did?"

"What does 'dating' mean, Daddy?"

"It means that you want to spend time with someone. That you want to be with them all the time."

Her brows cinched together. "You spend lots of time with Winnie, right?"

"I guess I do." I sighed. I clearly sucked at this.

"Hello? Are you guys up?" Winnie called out from the kitchen.

Thank goodness. She'd be better at this than I was.

"Yep. Come on back. We're just talking about you."

"You're talking about me, huh?" Winnie said as she walked in dressed in a pair of gray joggers and a matching sweater. Her hair was in a ponytail, her face free of makeup. She was stunning.

I patted the bed. "Yep. Come on in."

"Daddy's telling me that he likes you, but he doesn't want to marry you." Melody frowned, and my eyes bulged out of my head.

"No. No. No. That's not what I said." I cleared my throat. "I said that I liked you, and Melody asked if I was proposing. And I said no, obviously, but that I'd like to date you. And she doesn't understand what I'm saying."

Winnie didn't appear offended in the slightest. She just chuckled and turned to face Melody. "Tell me what you are confused about."

"Uncle Bridger is prosing to Emilia, but Daddy said he isn't prosing to you. He wants to spend time with you. But I don't know why he's telling me that, 'cause he spends time with you every day." Melody shrugged, giving me this goofy look like I had three heads.

"That does sound very confusing," Winnie said with a smile, and she ran her fingers over Melody's cheek. "So Daddy and I have been friends for a while now, but we realized our feelings are deeper than friendship. We told each other last night that we both have these deeper feelings for one another, and we thought we could start dating, and make it official."

A wide grin spread across Melody's face. "Daddy wants you to be his girlfriend?"

Didn't I say something similar, and I got no reaction?

"Yes. I'd like that," I said, fighting the urge to roll my eyes that nothing I said made sense to my daughter, while everything Winnie said was golden.

"Right. And it just means that we'll continue spending lots of time together, and we won't date anyone else." Winnie smiled.

"But he's not prosing to you?" she asked again.

Since when did she want me to get married so badly?

"No, sweetie. When people decide to date, they spend time together before they do all of that. So we just want to enjoy being together right now. It's a really good thing. And it makes us both happy, but we want to make sure it makes you happy, too."

"I love my daddy, and I love my Winnie, so it makes me very happy that you want to spend time together."

"That's so great, sweet pea. Because we want you to be happy always."

"And Winnie is going to stay in the house sometimes," I said as they both turned to look at me.

"Daddy is so silly today." Melody laughed as she looked at me with that strange look again. "Winnie already lives here, Daddy. Did you forget that?"

Winnie covered her smile with her hand.

I sighed. "I'm clearly not good at this."

"What he meant is that maybe I won't be staying in the casita all the time. I'd stay in the house with you guys, so I might be here in the morning when you wake up."

"Oh, you won't have your own room anymore 'cause you and Daddy want to share a room 'cause you have the deep feels?"

"Yes, that's right. Would that be okay with you?"

"Yes. I like you being closer to my room, too," Melody said before pushing up on her knees and gasping. "Does this mean we'll be a real family? Justine says I don't have a real family because I don't have a real mama. But now I can tell her I do have a real family."

My hands fisted at my side. "Justine is a—"

Winnie's hand moved to my thigh. "Justine is a confused little girl. You've always had a real family. It doesn't take a certain number of parents to make a family. But now, both of our families are growing because we're all going to be together. Does that make sense?"

"But can I tell Justine that you're my family now?"

"There's a lot I'd like to tell Justine," I grumped as I glanced at Winnie, who was giving me that look that meant I should bite my tongue. "However, none of it is her business, really. But you're welcome to tell her whatever you want about our family. We don't have secrets. Winnie and I are dating, and if that's something you want to share with your friends, I would never ask you not to talk about it."

"I like Winnie being in our family, Daddy." My daughter smiled up at me.

I pulled her onto my lap. "I like it, too, angel face. I love you very much, you know that, right?"

"I know that, Daddy." She giggled. "You tell me every day. Lots of times, too."

Winnie sniffed, and I looked up to see her swiping the tear moving down her cheek away.

This had gone well.

At least once she'd come in and helped explain things.

"Okay, who wants to hit the Honey Biscuit Café for pancakes."

"I do!" Melody kissed my cheek, then kissed Winnie's cheek and jumped off the bed. "Will you help me get dressed, Winnie?"

"Of course I will."

Melody ran out of the room, and Winnie moved to her feet. I grabbed her hand. "Will you help me get dressed, Winnie?" My voice was gruff.

She smiled. "That'll have to wait for later. But we've got plenty of time tonight for that."

She gave me a chaste kiss and walked out of the room.

She was right. We had plenty of time.

I hadn't planned on any of this.

But that was not going to stop me from enjoying it.

• • •

Bridger was proposing to Emilia today, and we were all on cloud nine about it. They adored one another, and it was nice to see my grumpy cousin find his happily ever after.

The girls had taken Emilia out shopping, and then Bridger had asked her to meet him for dinner at Rosewood's, while we finished setting up the backyard, grateful that all the snow had melted.

It looked like something out of a magazine. The girls were all talking about how Emilia would appreciate the aesthetic because she was an interior designer.

I didn't know much about that kind of stuff, but it looked great. A giant backdrop made of book pages said Will You Marry Me, Angel?

A large floral arch surrounded the backdrop. Baskets of flowers and oversized wooden lanterns with candles were everywhere, forming almost an aisle leading to the backdrop.

Everyone had just taken off. Wren and Axel had taken Melody home with them, and we said we'd pick her up after Winnie had taken the proposal photos.

Apparently that was a thing.

And my girl loved to capture moments on her camera.

"This looks amazing, right?" Winnie asked.

"It does. I'm really happy for him. For both of them." I glanced down at my phone to see a text from Bridger. "They're here. Where do we go?"

She chuckled. "Let's just come around the corner over here so we stay out of sight. I'll snap some pictures when they're walking in, and then I'll come out and take some photos from beside that bush. You just sort of stay on the side, okay?"

"Got it." I rubbed my hands together as we moved to the side of the house.

Within minutes, the back door opened and we could hear Emilia gasp. I watched my cousin lead her through the yard to where the backdrop was.

"What is this?" Emilia asked with a croak.

"This is me asking you to marry me, angel," he said as he dropped to his knee.

Winnie was already on the move, snapping photos and sliding around the other side of the bush. She was on the ground, and then standing all the way up.

She was determined to catch every angle and every moment.

Emilia had both hands over her face as she cried, and Bridger pulled her hands away. "No crying, baby. I want to look at you when I tell you how much I love you."

Damn. Who knew my cousin was so smooth?

Emilia nodded, sniffing repeatedly, as tears streamed down her face.

"I know that I'm not an easy man," he said, and it took everything in me not to laugh.

"But you make me want to be a better man. You've shown me what it means to truly love someone and to be loved back. I already feel like the luckiest man in the world for knowing you. But if you agree to forever with me, you will make me the happiest man in the world, Emilia. You are my today, my tomorrow, and my forever. Will you marry me, angel?"

"You had me at 'I'm not an easy man,'" she said, crying. "Yes, I would be honored to be your wife, Bridger Chadwick."

He tugged her down and kissed her, and Winnie came out from behind the bush and moved closer, snapping even more photos of them.

After a few moments and some tears, Emilia looked up and smiled. "I was just going to say we need a photo to capture the moment. And here you are, Winnie."

Bridger stood and tugged his new fiancée close as they posed for a few more pictures. Emilia gushed over the setting and the backdrop and they kissed and hugged, and Winnie caught every moment of it.

My girl was all heart.

She loved big, and I just stood there watching her do her thing.

"Okay, I think I've got plenty to work with." She moved forward to hug them both goodbye, and I walked out from the side yard.

"Congrats. I'm so happy for you both," I said, pulling my cousin in for a hug before doing the same to Emilia.

"Thanks for helping set this up, and thanks for making this backdrop and for taking the photos, Winnie," Bridger said, and I was still in awe sometimes at the effect that Emilia had had on him. The dude was all up in his feels these days.

"I'm so happy that I got to be part of your special day,"

Winnie told them. She waved as I took her hand and led her out of the yard.

"Be sure you blow out all those candles before you go inside, Casanova," I shouted, and I heard them both laughing behind me.

"That was amazing," Winnie said with a sigh.

"It was. Thanks for doing all of that."

"Of course. I'm glad I could do it." She smiled up at me. "Now let's go get our girl."

Our girl.

We really were our own little family now.

32

Winnie

The last few weeks had been amazing. I had one book in editing and another that was about to release, and I had a break from writing right now.

Early copies, also known as ARCs or advanced reader copies, had been sent to tons of influencers, and the early feedback was absolutely blowing my mind. People were gushing about this book, and I couldn't wait for it to be out in the world.

Archer was so interested in the whole process, and I loved that he cared. My first two book releases were very different experiences. My father had taken me to dinner both times, because Jaden thought it was silly to chase a pipe dream and thought I should be picking up more hours at the advertising firm I worked at instead of writing.

"So you get to catch your breath a little now. And the first round of edits you got back for this last book were really positive, right?" he asked as he studied me from behind his desk. I'd stopped by his office to drop off some cupcakes I'd made.

"Yes. I didn't have a ton to fix, which was great. Now it's off to copy edits." I shrugged.

"That's amazing. So many moving parts in this business. And *Whisper Sweet Nothings* releases in two weeks," he said. "You'll be traveling for release day, so we'll have to do something to celebrate before you go. Or we can do it when you get back if you prefer."

My breath hitched. He was so thoughtful, and I didn't realize how much I needed that in my life.

"Thank you. Just celebrating with you and Melody anytime will be great."

A part of me wanted to ask him to come with me on the book tour. I wasn't looking forward to being away from them for a week. But my publisher had booked a pretty busy couple of days of signings for me, and I'd be on a plane and on the go the whole time. Melody couldn't miss school, and Archer would need to be there for her, and he had work as well.

I wouldn't ask him to do that. It wouldn't be fair.

Melody was off for spring break next week, and we were hosting Easter at his house.

"Our house" was what he'd repeatedly said to me.

My father was flying in for Easter so he could meet Archer and Melody. They'd FaceTimed often, but it was important for them to meet in person now.

"I'm proud of you," he said.

"For what?" I laughed, an attempt to shrug it off. I'd never been great with praise or attention on me.

"For chasing your dreams, Winnie. For knowing there was something else out there for you and going after it. For leaving a marriage that wasn't working. Tuning out the voice of a weak man who tried to crush your dreams. You know what you want, and you go after it. It's fucking impressive."

"Maybe that's why we get along so well," I said. "I feel the same about you."

"Do you now?"

"Yep. You were in a relationship that was a happy one, and you were thrown a curveball. You didn't hesitate. You followed your gut, and you stepped up to the plate in the most amazing way for your daughter. You built a home for her and a life for her, and she's this amazing little human. And then you started a company from the ground up, and now you employ over thirty-five people. And you never complain about being tired or not having any time for yourself. You just do it all. You're everything to everyone."

"Damn. We're impressive," he said with a laugh. "But I do have the world's best nanny helping me balance my life, so that makes a big difference."

I chuckled. "We're a good team, Archie."

"The best team, beautiful."

"Okay, I need to get going. I have a meeting with Laney, my agent, in an hour. She said she has a lot to go over with me today." I stood up.

He came around the desk and kissed me. "Have a good meeting, beautiful."

He took my hand and led me out of his office.

"Where are you going?" I asked.

"I'm walking my woman to her car."

I'm here to say that chivalry does not only live in the pages of a fictional book.

He helped me into the car, reached over and buckled my seat belt, and then kissed me again.

Normally, I liked to be independent. I would never have let Jaden buckle my seat belt, nor would he have wanted to.

But with Archer, I liked the way he cared for me.

The way he paid attention to my needs.

I had more needs than I'd ever realized, because I'd been so used to taking care of myself.

Archer had taught me that just because I could do something on my own didn't mean that I *had* to do it on my own.

And I liked doing things for him as well.

No one was keeping score. It just came naturally.

"See you at home later," he said as he closed the door.

I drove the short distance back home, where I put a roast in the slow cooker, tossed in some laundry, and then sat down for my Zoom call.

"Hey," Laney said. "I've got big news for you."

"Okay. I'm here for all the big news."

"First off, the preorders for *Whisper Sweet Nothings* are off the charts. The reviews coming in from early readers and all the shares, they've just magnified things. Apparently a few TikToks have gone viral, and needless to say, the publisher is absolutely thrilled."

"Oh, that's amazing. Great news. I've seen a big uptick in sales on my dashboard for the first two books."

"Yes, they said the print versions are flying off the shelves faster than they can stock them." She clapped her hands together twice before continuing. "They've had a ton of stores reach out, and they want to extend the tour."

"Extend the tour? What does that mean?"

"It means everyone is hustling to get you some graphics, assuming you agree to a three-week tour." She shook her head and smiled. "They want you to add New York, Philly, Virginia, North Carolina, and a few Midwest cities, including your hometown of Chicago."

My heart raced. "What? I'd be doing all of that on this tour?"

"Yes. And I'll be going with you for part of it. If you agree to the itinerary I just sent over, we'll get things booked. They have a few news stations that want to have you on as well. So it's going to be a ton of PR for this release. This is so exciting, Winnie," she squealed. "Why do you look like a deer in headlights?"

I laughed. "No, I'm just caught off guard. This is amazing. Very surprising and exciting, and of course, yes, I'll make arrangements to get things covered here. I'm on board with whatever they want to do."

My stomach was in knots. This was incredible news, but I was also nervous about being gone that long.

I had a routine now.

One that I liked a lot.

One where people depended on me.

I was also supposed to start writing again the week that I was scheduled to return, and now I'd be gone much longer.

"Your UK publisher reached out about having you fly out to London for a stop, but I just don't know that we can fit that in."

"London?" I gaped at her, feeling completely overwhelmed.

"Yes. I told them we could plan it for the release of book four. Does that sound better?"

I blew out a breath. This was a lot. "Yes. We can do it for book four."

Was I having an out-of-body experience? My lips were moving. I appeared overjoyed. But inside I was panicking. Things were happening so quickly.

This was unexpected.

My little internal planner self was overwhelmed.

Could you be thrilled and terrified all at the same time?

Yes. Apparently, you could.

"Okay, I'm going to let them know to get it all booked, and you and I are hitting the road in just a few weeks. Time to do some retail damage and get some outfits. You've got a lot of events to prepare for."

"Can't wait," I said. I was still trying to process everything.

I ended the call and sent a text to Archer, even though I knew he was in a meeting. I just wanted to let him know. He replied with confetti emojis and told me he was so proud of me. He even said for me to text the girls and go shopping for some outfits.

He was on board and happy for me.

Me: *Hey. I just found out the book tour is no longer one week, it's going to be a three-week tour with a lot more stops. I need to get some new outfits, where should I go?*

Lulu: *Whattttt! Three weeks! Let's go!*

Lulu: *This is my dream come true. Let me style you for the tour. I promise I'll let you wear a bow every day in your hair.*

Me: *I love this idea because I have no idea what to wear.*

Henley: *Congrats. This is amazing. What if we do a girls' day in the city this weekend? We can all pick things out for you to wear.*

Wren: *Holy shitballs. I'm so happy for you. I'm in for Saturday. I have no fashion sense outside barn couture, but I will go along to cheer you on and eat good food.*

Emilia: *This. Is. Amazing. WINNIE! Look at you go. I'm in.*

Eloise: *First, we get to read the books early, and now we get to shop for book tour outfits. Count me in. All your hard work is paying off. I'm so happy for you.*

Me: *You guys are the best. Thank you. Love you.*

They all responded by saying how happy they were for me, and that they loved me, too.

I was grateful that I'd found friends who felt like family.

There was a knock on the door, and I padded out of my office and down the hallway. When I pulled the door open, I was thrilled to see Isabelle. Archer's mom had been so good to me, and she occasionally stopped by for a cup of tea or just to catch up.

"Hey, sweetheart. I was in the neighborhood and thought I'd pop in and check on you."

I hurried into her arms. My head was spinning, and I was a weird mix of elated and anxious, and I just needed a hug.

"Hey," she said, wrapping her arms around me a little tighter. "Are you okay?"

"Yes, I'm good," I said, pulling back and motioning for her to come inside. We made our way to the kitchen, where I put on the teakettle as I filled her in on all that had just happened. I pulled out two cupcakes from a Tupperware and set them down at the table for us as well.

She just listened as I rambled on about all of it.

I poured our tea into the mugs I'd set out and placed them in front of us before finally sitting down.

Her hand came over mine, and she smiled. "First and foremost, congratulations, Winnie. This is very exciting, and you've worked really hard for this."

"Yes. It's everything I hoped for." I shrugged. "It's actually beyond what I hoped for."

"I get that. And it's going to be a very busy couple of weeks for you. Are you nervous about the travel?" she asked.

"I don't think so. I'm fine with traveling."

"Okay. Is it the book signings themselves that have you anxious?"

Again, I thought her question over. "I don't think that's an issue, either. I mean, I'm still trying to wrap my head around the fact that anyone is going to come stand in line to meet me. But I'm excited for that part. I don't feel nervous about that."

"Are you nervous about leaving Archer and Melody?" she asked as she took a sip of her tea.

"I'm not nervous in the sense that I'm worried they won't be okay." I blew out a breath. "I'm nervous about being away from them. We have a routine together, and I'm used to that. And I'm going to miss them. I'm going to miss them so much. I won't be here for homework or dinner or bath time." My heart raced, and I placed a hand on my chest as the words left my mouth. "I won't be here to hear about Archer's day, or pick Melody up from school. What if they need me? What if they miss me and I'm not there for them."

What in the hell was happening to me?

They'd be fine. I'd be fine.

Why was I panicking?

"Oh, sweetheart, this is what happens when you love deeply. It's hard to be away from the people we love. But that can't stop you from doing the things you want to do in your life. Archer and Melody support you. Our whole family supports you. And love should never mean clipping your wings. Love should allow you to soar. And they will be waiting for you with open arms when you come back."

Love.

She knew what this was.

Maybe I was anxious that we hadn't said it to one another.

And now I'd be leaving.

I nodded. "Yes. I know that. I'm probably just caught off guard because I wasn't expecting this."

"Of course you are. That's more than fair." She squeezed my hand.

I nodded. I knew she was right. It was silly to stress about being gone for three weeks.

Time would pass in the blink of an eye, and they'd barely notice that I was gone.

33

Archer

Melody had asked me if we could host Easter this year, and Winnie was completely on board. She'd wanted to work on the Easter egg hunt, which she was taking to a whole new level. She'd spent hours finding hiding places out in the yard.

It would only be Melody and Cutler looking for eggs later, so it wasn't like we'd have dozens of kids looking for them. But she insisted that was even more of a reason to take the time to hide them well.

Her father had arrived a few days ago. He'd been staying with us, which was awesome, because we got to spend a lot of time with him at the house. He was a great guy, and it was easy to see how close he and Winnie were.

He adored his daughter in a way I could relate to.

Not only because I loved her, but because I adored my own daughter the same way.

I recognized it.

The way he'd assessed me the first night he arrived, the instinctual need to protect her.

But what had really impressed the hell out of me was the way that he took to Melody. He got down on the floor to play with her and brought her a giant chocolate Easter Bunny, because his daughter loved my daughter—which meant he did, too.

I refilled his coffee. Melody was hanging out at my aunt and uncle's house with Cutler this morning so we could get things set up here.

"She's still got dozens of eggs to hide." Sam chuckled from where he stood in the kitchen, glancing out the back door to the yard, where his daughter continued hiding eggs like it was an Olympic sport. "She just cares so damn much about doing things the right way. I'd have just rolled them in the bushes and all over the grass."

I refilled my coffee and topped his off before we both moved to sit at the table.

"Same. Melody and Cutler won't even know what to do now that they'll actually have to search for the eggs. They also used to just be filled with jelly beans, but Winnie's packed them with different candies, coins, dollar bills, erasers, key chains, and a bunch of other goodies." I laughed.

"That's my girl. She's always been that way." He shrugged as he took a sip of his coffee and then studied me for a few beats. "Thank you for being so good to her. She hasn't been this happy in a very long time."

"Neither have I. And there is nothing to thank me for. She's changed my life and Melody's life for the better." I blew out a breath. "I think it's easy to go through the motions and not even realize what you're missing in life until you find it."

I was madly in love with this woman.

I'd almost said it several times, but she was so nervous about leaving on this tour, and I didn't want to do anything to complicate things for her.

So I tried every day to show how much I loved her with my actions, just not the actual words.

Hell, I'd only said it to one person in my life, and that hadn't worked out.

So I didn't want to do anything to make her feel pressured.

Her career was taking off, and she was about to leave on a three-week book tour.

I didn't want to take away from this big moment, so I was waiting for the right time to say it.

Because I never thought I'd be saying those words to another woman.

And here I was feeling all of it.

"I understand that. I was very closed off after my wife left us when Winnie was young. I just poured myself into work and my daughter, and I didn't have much of a life outside of that. And I'm not complaining, because that girl out there hiding every single egg like her life counts on it..." He paused to chuckle. "She's my pride and joy. I'm sure you understand that."

"I do."

"So I came here, all ready to intimidate the shit out of you, throw out a couple threats to keep you in line." A sinister grin spread across his face. "But, I've been pleasantly surprised that I don't feel the need to do that."

I snorted. "I get it. I'm sure it's been hard with you living so far away and not knowing what was going on here."

"Yes. I mean, I trust my daughter, in every way but her personal life. The only guy she's been with before now was a real asshole. When she agreed to marry him so young, it was the only time Winnie and I have ever truly fought. We didn't speak for over a week, and then I came to my senses."

"So Jaden won you over back then?" I asked.

"Hell no. He was a selfish prick, and I had his number." He clasped his hands together. "But you'll learn this very soon, Archer. If you don't want to alienate your child, you have to let them make mistakes. It's the most difficult thing to do as a parent. Never liked him, and unfortunately, he lived up to my expectations. But I had to let her figure it out herself."

"That's got to be rough." I blew out a breath. "I think he's finally moved on now. He hasn't reached out in a while."

"Well, she's got this book release coming up, and trust me when I tell you, he'll be watching. He'll come out of the woodwork because he thinks he's owed something. He guilted her into marrying him because he had zero drive and no plan, and he made her feel bad about wanting things for herself," he hissed. "And he feels like she owes him now, which is crazy, considering she gave him most of her advance for the first two books she published. But what he doesn't realize is that I made sure we got her a good divorce attorney, and he doesn't have a chance in hell of coming after her future earnings. That was worth every penny."

I nodded. "What kind of man tries to take money from a woman he loves?"

"A selfish one. He was always a spoiled kid. Came from a great family, and didn't take advantage of all the opportunities he had. Instead, he sponged off of Winnie until she couldn't take it anymore."

"That's fucked up," I said, shaking my head with disgust.

"I do appreciate you encouraging her to go off and chase her dreams." Sam's voice was laced with emotion now. "She's been made to feel guilty for years when it came to doing things for herself. She's a caregiver by nature. Hell, I had to constantly remind her that I was the parent and she was the kid when she was young," he said with a big smile on his face.

"I want her to do whatever makes her happy. I've officially fired her as my nanny," I said with a smirk. "Felt kind of weird to be dating my employee."

A deep chuckle rumbled from his chest. "Yeah, she mentioned that. But she takes her relationship with you and with Melody very seriously, and she's loyal as hell, so leaving you for a few weeks is difficult for her. I think some of that is deep-rooted, because her mom left her at such a young age, so she often thinks doing things for herself means she's disappointing the people she loves."

Fuck. I never thought of that. She kept bringing up how anxious she was, and I didn't realize where it was coming from.

"That makes sense now. I keep telling her that we'll be fine. And if I could miss work and pull Melody out of school for a few weeks, we'd be going with her. But I know she needs to chase her dreams, and wherever that leads her, I will support her. I promise you that."

I'd be lying if I didn't admit that a small part of me worried that there were bigger things than me out there for Winnie. Hell, I'd been with a woman in the past who'd walked away from both me and her baby girl for her career.

I didn't judge her for it. But that didn't mean that it didn't hurt like hell at the same time.

But I would never be okay with pressuring or guilting

someone into choosing me over their dreams.

Part of me was just hoping that at the end of this, Winnie would still choose to be with me.

But in the back of my mind, I knew her career was taking off, and she might just want to be free once she got a taste of all that success.

And I'd support her either way. Winnie had already spent years living her life for someone who didn't believe in her.

I would not be that man.

I would never clip her wings.

It didn't mean a little part of me didn't wish like hell that I could keep her right here forever. I loved her too damn much to do that.

So I was preparing for the possibility that this tour could lead to other things that she wanted to pursue.

Her UK publisher was already pushing for her to come there for a book tour.

And I'd encouraged her to take every opportunity she wanted to.

"I don't doubt that, Archer," he said after a pause, bringing me out of my thoughts. "I can see it in the way you look at her. And even when she shares her anxiety with me, she tells me how much you support her. She didn't have that in her past relationship, so I'm very glad to see that she has it now."

"She does. I give you my word that won't change." This was why I'd hold back on all these big feelings that were consuming me. Because telling Winnie that I loved her right before she left would only make things more complicated for her. My job was to make sure that she knew we'd be fine on our own.

I wouldn't be a needy asshole.

"I appreciate it," he said, extending a hand and shaking mine from across the table.

"Are you seriously shaking hands after being here for three days?" Winnie's laughter filled the space around us as she came back inside the house. "What's with the formality?"

"Just two men having a good chat," Sam said.

We both chuckled as she came to settle on my lap. I nuzzled my nose into her neck. "Did the egg lady get every single egg hidden?"

She turned in my arms and flicked my shoulder. "Hey, who wants to do an egg hunt when they aren't even hidden well?"

"Most people," her father grunted from across the table. "Kids just want the treats. They don't want to have to use a compass to find a quarter or a sticker."

"I take offense to that." Winnie's mouth fell open. "First of all, there is not one egg that only has a quarter or a sticker in it. They were filled with love. And most of the best things in life come with a little work."

"They'll love it, beautiful," I said. "Thank you for doing that."

"And what have you two been doing?"

"We put the ham in the oven," Sam said as he snorted and reached for his coffee. "I mean, you had it out on the counter and set the timer, so it was hard to mess that job up."

"Such a smartass," she said with a smirk at her father before glancing at her phone. "We've only got twenty minutes until everyone gets here. I need to go get changed."

She moved to her feet, and I followed.

Because following this girl was like following the sound of my own heartbeat.

I changed into a button-up and left my jeans on, while Winnie slipped into a little white dress and some heels, along with a silky white ribbon that she tied on the back of her head, her brown waves falling over her shoulders.

"Come on. I want my dad to take a picture of us before everyone gets here. I need to leave you with something when I'm gone," she teased. I forced a smile, but the reality was, things were about to change.

We walked down to the edge of the yard beside the river, and I twirled her around before pulling her into my arms as her father snapped a few photos of us.

"Do you want me to whisper sweet nothings in your ear, Winnie?" I teased.

"You could give all my heroes a run for their money, Archie," she said.

"Daddy? My Winnie! Sampy! I'm back home!" Melody came racing out to the backyard. She'd spent lots of time trying to decide what she wanted to call Sam. Since he was Winnie's dad, she felt like "Grampy" should be incorporated, and with his name being Sam, she'd come up with "Sampy."

"Hey there, sunshine," Sam said as he bent down to greet her. "We're glad you're back."

"Did the Easter Bunny come and hide the eggs?" she asked as we walked by to see her, just as Cutler waltzed over with all the swagger of a nine-year-old trapped in a grown man's body. My cousin Emerson, her husband Nash, my aunt and uncle, and my parents were right behind him.

They'd all met Sam the night he arrived, when my parents had thrown a dinner to get everyone together to meet him. Of course he'd meshed well with everyone.

Just like his daughter did.

"He sure did. We tried to catch him, but he took off running down the edge of the river," Winnie said, eyes wide and dancing with mischief.

Melody gasped just as my mom walked over and reached for my daughter's hand. "Mimi, we've got to get our baskets ready to start looking."

"Let's go get them. They're in the kitchen." My mom led her inside.

"My Winnie is going to help me find them," my daughter said as they hurried toward the house. "She saw the bunny take off!"

"Hey, Sam." Cutler walked over and held up his fist, and Sam responded with a fist bump.

"Happy Easter, Beefcake."

"So what's the deal with the Easter egg hunt? I've heard there are a lot of eggs this year." Cutler glanced over at Winnie. "You know you're my girl, Winnie. You going to help a guy out?"

Winnie's head fell back as she laughed. "I'll be out here helping you and Melody. But I did hear that there are a few eggs with each of your names on them, because they have something special inside just for you two."

Cutler whistled. "You're a lucky man, Uncle Archie. Your girl's got an in with the most popular bunny in town."

Emerson laughed as she walked over to us. "Seems like the Easter Bunny has been busy this year."

Melody ran over, cheeks flushed and brows cinched together, because she was all business now. "Here's your basket, Beefcake. Let's start looking, and we can help each other."

"Always, Mel." He took her hand and led her toward the large tree across the grassy yard.

"Daddy! Winnie!" Melody could barely speak as Cutler held up an Easter basket that was filled with pink treats and stuffing. And then he handed it to her and picked up the next one, which was filled with white and yellow stuffing and all sorts of treats.

"He brought our baskets outside."

I glanced over at Winnie, who was watching the two kids like they hung the moon. A wide grin took over her face as she jogged toward them, acting like she was completely surprised.

"What? He hid some baskets out here?" she said with a laugh. She dropped down in the grass while Melody and Cutler pulled out all their treats and held them up for everyone to see.

My daughter's body shook the slightest bit with excitement.

Winnie stood and started taking a few photos of them with her Polaroid as Emerson took pictures with her phone alongside my mom and my aunt Ellie.

Music played through the outdoor speakers, and the sun was shining down on us.

It was a perfect day.

Lulu and Rafe walked over and stood beside me.

"You better hold on tight, Archie. I think we're all in love with her," Lulu said with a laugh, and Rafe wrapped an arm around his wife's shoulder and kissed her cheek.

I couldn't agree more.

I just needed to be careful that I didn't hold on too tight.

34

Winnie

I hated the departure lanes at airports. The cars pressing on their horns, and the security guards directing people to move forward. Travelers who were in a hurry moved past me, dragging their wheeled bags behind them.

And I felt this overpowering need to tell Archer that I loved him.

He'd put the truck in park and jumped out to grab my bag. I adjusted my crossbody purse across my chest and slipped my backpack over my shoulders when I stepped out to the curb.

A loud whistle startled me as the security guard shouted: "That truck can't stay there, buddy."

Archer held up a hand in acknowledgment. "Just getting her bag out."

He smirked at me, all sexy and confident.

Do it. Tell him.

It had been weighing on me. I felt it. I knew he felt it, too.

Why were we holding back?

And I was leaving for three weeks. I needed him to know.

"You okay?" he asked as he stroked the side of my face.

I nodded, feeling my eyes well with tears.

Why the hell was I so emotional?

It wasn't goodbye; it was "see you later."

I wasn't leaving forever.

"I'm good, I um…" I said, and my mouth went completely dry. A couple of cars honked their horns as they moved in and out of the drop-off area, and my heart raced with anxiety.

"Okay, beautiful. Happy release day. I'm so proud of you. Be safe and call when you land." He pulled me in for a hug.

"Love ya." The muffled words left my mouth as a loud whistle blew from right behind me, and I startled and nearly fell before I jumped back.

"Love ya"? Is that what I just said?

"I'm going to need this truck moved now, or I'm writing you a ticket," the buzzkill security officer said, and I had a deep desire to flip him the bird.

He'd just ruined my airport "I love you" and turned it into an epic fail.

Archer nodded, leaned down, and kissed me once more before glancing at the man in uniform glaring at us. "Got it."

He jogged around the truck and jumped in the driver's seat. I waved as he pushed the controller to put the window down.

Say it.

For the love of God, please say it.

"You've got this, Winnie," he told me. "Don't worry about us. Have a great time."

"Have a great time"?

I forced a smile just as a woman with an oversized rolling bag slammed into me, and Archer pulled away from the curb.

"Ouch!" I grumped, pulling my foot away after she'd completely wheeled over it.

I replayed the events of the goodbye as I made my way through security and then again through the entire flight to Seattle.

He'd definitely heard me, right?

I'd told him that I loved him, or at least a more casual version of "I love you"—and he'd told me to have a good time.

But from the moment I landed in Seattle, where Laney was waiting for me, I was forced to focus.

Our itinerary was packed, and after my arrival at the airport, we'd gone straight to a bookstore, where I signed fifteen hundred copies of *Whisper Sweet Nothings*.

I didn't have time to think about the fact that I'd whispered a sweet nothing into my boyfriend's ear when we were saying goodbye, and he hadn't said it back.

So maybe I had some time to think about it.

But I forced myself to be present.

It was release day, and I needed to get my head on straight.

Everyone helped by opening the flaps of each cover to make things move along faster. It was exciting and overwhelming all at the same time.

Laney and I made our way to the hotel to change clothes quickly. Then we hopped in a car to get to an in-person signing at another bookstore, with readers who were there to celebrate my release with me.

I glanced down at my phone to reread the text Archer had sent when I landed.

Not exactly what I was hoping for.

Archie: *Did you land, beautiful?*

Me: *Yes. I'm here and heading to the bookstore.*

Archie: *Okay, be safe. I'm watching your rank online and cheering you on.*

Me: *Sorry we were so rushed with our goodbye.*

Archie: *Don't worry about it. Airports are always a little stressful.*

Really? You think?

Try telling a man you love him and have a whistle blown in your ear.

"You ready for this tonight?" Laney asked as we drove toward the bookstore that was hosting the release day signing.

"Yes. I'm so excited to meet Ashlan Thomas. I can't believe she's doing the signing with me."

Ashlan Thomas was one of the most well-known romance authors out there right now, and we were with the same publisher, so they'd asked her to join me for a discussion before we signed.

Once we arrived at the store, everything was a blur. I met my editor, Daisy, whom I worked with at the publishing house, as she'd flown in for the event as well. We'd had many Zoom calls, but it was my first time meeting her in person, and it meant so much to me that she was here.

And then I turned to see the gorgeous woman beside her.

"Hi, Winnie, it's so lovely to meet you. Thanks for letting me celebrate with you tonight. I'm Ashlan." She extended her hand.

"Oh my gosh, I, er, I'm a huge fan." I stumbled over my words and just decided to hug her, which made her laugh.

We were quickly ushered onto the stage, where we chatted about our writing process, and how we'd chosen this profession, and I was just completely in awe of her. Our conversation was easy, and we laughed and had a great time.

When we finished our chat onstage, we spent the next two hours meeting readers and signing books. To say that it was emotional would be a massive understatement.

I must have pinched myself a dozen times before we said our goodbyes at the bookstore, and Ashlan, Daisy, Laney, and I climbed into a car to head to dinner.

I sent Archer a text with a photo from the signing, and he responded with the same sentiment as earlier.

Archie: *So proud of you. Be safe and have a good time.*

Yeah, yeah, yeah. I get it. You want me to have a good time.

We made it to the restaurant and ordered dinner and drinks, and we chatted about how incredible the signing was.

"Oh my gosh. I can't believe this," Ashlan said as she looked down at her phone when it vibrated.

"Is everything okay?" I asked.

"Yes. My husband Jace just texted me. Apparently, we have mutual friends, Winnie. We're practically family."

"What?" I gasped, because I felt like I'd known her my entire life after the signing, so I was thrilled that we had mutual friends.

"Umm… does the name Beefcake ring a bell?"

"Stop it right now! You know Cutler Heart, a.k.a. Beefcake?"

She laughed as Daisy's and Laney's eyes moved between the two of us.

"My cousin is Cage Reynolds, also known as the father of the infamous Gracie Reynolds."

"You're Gracie Reynolds's aunt? Beefcake's girl! How did I not know this?"

"I guess we're like the Kevin Bacon of small towns. I live in Honey Mountain, and my cousin Brinkley is married to Lincoln

Hendrix, and they live in Cottonwood Cove. Lincoln found out that he had a half brother later in life, and his name is Romeo Knight, and he lives with Cutler in Magnolia Falls."

"Yes. Lincoln is the superstar football player, and I know Romeo. He's the famous boxer, and one of Cutler's uncles."

"Correct. So that's how Gracie and Cutler met, and then we met everyone over time as well. And now Cutler's dad married Emerson Chadwick, of the Rosewood River Chadwicks," she said with a laugh. "And here we are."

"What a small freaking world it is," I said.

"I think in the book world they'd call this an interconnected series." Laney laughed. "All of these families appear to have one thing in common, this kid with a very interesting nickname. What is it? Coolcakes?"

Now it was our turn to laugh.

"His name is Cutler, but he goes by 'Beefcake.' He's probably the coolest kid I've ever met," I said.

"Totally agree," Ashlan said. "That boy has more swagger in his pinky finger than most grown men. And he and Gracie are so adorable together. Best buddies, although he has grand plans of marrying her someday."

"He told me all about it. And he is one determined guy." I chuckled, just as Daisy said something to Laney, and they both glanced down at her phone and started talking release day numbers.

The waiter set down our entrées, and I groaned when I took the first bite. It had been a long day, and I was definitely ready for a good meal.

Ashlan glanced at the two women across the table from us, who were clearly talking business, and she leaned forward. "So how are you feeling? This is your first tour, and it's probably a bit overwhelming."

"Yes. It's day one and I'm so excited, but I was nervous about being gone for so long." I filled her in on how I'd moved to Rosewood River, and I told her all about Archer and Melody.

She couldn't get over the similarities. She'd also been a nanny when she'd first started writing. But she'd known her now husband most of her life, as he was a family friend. She understood all the dynamics going on in my life right now, and it was so nice to have someone to talk to about everything.

"I just want to say this to you, because I know where you are and how mixed the feelings are. It's obvious that you're really happy and you've met someone you're crazy about, and that's a good thing, Winnie. And your career taking off is also a good thing. As a woman, I think we tend to feel so much pressure to be everything for everyone. And the truth is, it's not possible. But you can come damn close with a little balance." She chuckled. "That's the key. You've got to find balance. Balance in your life and your career. And it's different for everyone, but I can promise you, I'm a mama of three, and I love my babies like crazy. Jace, my husband—he's my biggest supporter, my inspiration, and my safe place, you know?"

"I love that," I said. I could see how much she adored her family, since it was written all over her face.

"Me too." She glanced at Laney and Daisy before leaning closer and keeping her voice low. "And my career, well that's something just for me. Well, just for me and my readers. But it's something that I love and enjoy, and I had to learn that I can't say yes to everything, but I can say yes to plenty, if that makes sense."

"That makes sense." I sighed. "It's just been a really weird day, so I'm sure I'll feel more settled tomorrow."

She was so easy to talk to that I ended up telling her everything that had happened at the airport.

"Well, we don't know for sure that he even heard you, and it's not like you really said it." She chuckled and squeezed my hand. "You picked a tough time to drop the L-word, and then you sort of turned it into a high school girl's bestie love ya mantra."

"It still means the same thing. I'm sure he heard me." I exhaled. Who was I trying to convince, me or him?

"Listen, Winnie, take it from someone who's been there. It's complicated when children are involved. And you're on this whirlwind adventure, and he's not. At the end of the day, it's not so much saying it, it's living it. And from what you've told me, that man has been loving you for months. You tossed him a 'love ya' that we don't even know for certain he heard, so I wouldn't let that get in your head. Focus on his actions for now, because you aren't there to talk to him."

"That's a good point. And his actions say it. I mean, I feel it every day from him." I reached for my wine glass and took a sip.

Her gaze softened. "It's a lot to navigate for a partner when your career takes off the way that yours is right now. So a little part of him is probably nervous that you'll leave and never look back."

"I would never do that. I miss them like crazy, and I've only been gone for one day."

"I know you do. But you've got to love him enough to trust that everything will be okay."

"Thank you. I know you're right. And my timing was terrible," I said as we both laughed.

"It's stressful leaving. I hate being away, if I'm being honest. But it's also good for my kids to see that I have a career that I've worked hard at, and I just keep my trips short now." She cut into her steak and popped it in her mouth.

"I like the sound of that."

Laney and Daisy rejoined the conversation, and we laughed and talked for another hour over dessert and glasses of wine.

We finally said our goodbyes, since we were all exhausted and ready to head up to our rooms. I was grateful that we'd had dinner in the hotel restaurant, because I had to be up early in the morning to get to the airport, as we were heading to Denver tomorrow.

I hugged Ashlan extra tight, and we exchanged numbers and agreed to talk soon. She'd told me all about writing sprints, and I was looking forward to texting once I was home so we could sprint together.

Once Laney and I stepped off the elevator on our floor, she walked beside me.

"So, your numbers are off the charts with this release, Winnie," she said. "Everyone is thrilled. They want to set up some meet and greets next month, if you're open to it."

"That's amazing," I said as I processed her words.

"Yes," she gushed. "This is just incredible. I'm so thrilled for you. So we'll get you those dates in the next couple days so you can get them on the calendar."

"Sounds good. I just have to be home for Melody's birthday. I promised her I'd be there, and we have a big party planned."

She nodded. "Okay, well, I'll find out the dates and we can work around it. But I'd plan on being very busy over the next few months. You're a hot commodity right now." She winked.

"Thank you," I said.

"I'm proud of you, Winnie. You're adjusting to all of this so well."

Maybe on the outside, but on the inside, I wasn't.

"Thank you so much. Good night, Laney. I'll see you bright and early."

"Yes. We'll grab a bite at the airport."

"Sounds good."

I pushed open my door just as she yelled back: "Sleep well. Love ya."

For fuck's sake. She'd tossed it out there pretty casually.

I'd really botched my first "I love you."

My phone rang as soon as I stepped in the room.

Archer.

I swear the man could read my mind. He always knew when I was struggling.

"Hey," I said, kicking off my shoes. I walked toward the bathroom and turned on the water to the bathtub. I needed to soak my feet, which were sore from wearing heeled boots all day.

"Hey, beautiful. How did it go today?"

I blew out a breath. "It was incredible. Did you know that Ashlan Thomas knows Beefcake?"

I spent the next few minutes telling him all about the connection, and he listened and laughed. I turned off the tub and slipped into the hot water.

"So she's related to Gracie Reynolds. I've been hearing about this little girl ever since I met Cutler. Hell, even Melody talks about her as if she knows her."

"Such a small world, right?"

"Yeah, it is."

"I wish I wasn't so far away from you guys right now," I said with a sigh, because the mix of the hot water and the sound of his voice had me completely relaxing.

"Everyone is fine here, don't worry at all, all right?"

If he told me not to worry one more time, my head might blow off my body.

"Okay. If you say so. How was your day?" I asked, trying not to feel rejected.

"Some major shit went down at school today, and I caught

Melody sneaking off with my phone, so I think she tried to FaceTime you earlier. I told her that you were at the signing. So you can't tell her that I told you, but I think you'll want to hear this."

I glanced at my phone, and my chest squeezed when I saw three missed calls from her. I'd had my ringer off for hours, and I felt terrible for missing those calls.

Those were not the calls that I ever wanted to miss.

"I'm so sad I missed her call." A lump formed in my throat. It was nearly midnight, so obviously she'd been asleep for a long time now. "But you've got to tell me."

"Well, Justine Schwartz, being the little shit that she is, stole Tommy Jordan's underpants."

As soon as he said it, loud laughter escaped, and my mood lightened. "How did she get his underpants."

"Do you remember when Melody told us that he takes a long time in the bathroom?"

"Yes."

"Well, apparently he likes to strip naked if he has to poop," he said, and I could hear him fighting back his laughter. "Justine cracked the door open, saw the pile of clothing, and snatched his undies."

"That girl is really something." I shook my head with a laugh. "So where were the undies?"

"She placed them in Mrs. Groucher's inbox."

"No." I was laughing hysterically now. "Just no. Everyone knows that box is for completed work only."

"Well, I think he completed his work in the shitter, so she delivered his briefs for him."

"So what happened?"

"I guess Tommy went back in the bathroom to put on his undies, and Justine went to Principal Carver's office once again."

"She's going to need a nameplate on his door because she's there so often."

"Agreed. You want to hear the best part?"

"I can't imagine that this could get any better," I said.

"Melody asked me at dinner if we could go buy some tighty-whities for Tommy to keep in his cubby in case this happened again." I could hear the smile in his voice.

I drained the tub water and climbed out, then wrapped a towel around myself and hit FaceTime.

His handsome face came across the screen when he answered.

"Hey," I whispered as I padded out to the room and sat on the bed.

"Hi."

"I was surprised you didn't FaceTime me, and I wanted to see your face before I went to bed."

"I love that face," he said, with a sleepy smile. His green eyes looked heavy. "But I miss it more when I see it."

I nodded. "I miss you, too, Archie."

"Three weeks. It'll be a piece of cake." He sighed.

"Okay." I blew out a breath. I was so exhausted. "I've got to be up in four hours to get to the airport."

"Close your eyes, baby. I'll stay on the phone until you fall asleep."

I didn't want to tell him about the other things in the works that would require more travel.

I knew he'd tell me it was a good thing.

But right now, being away from this man did not feel like a good thing.

35

Archer

Winnie had been gone for ten days, and we'd had a hard time finding the time to talk these last few days because she was on the East Coast. The time difference was an issue, plus she was really busy, not to mention completely exhausted.

Melody and I were struggling because we missed her, but we put on a good front whenever we spoke to her.

It was remarkable that we'd existed for so long without Winnie in our lives, and now, ten days without her felt like some sort of cruel punishment.

I'd stopped calling as much and letting her call me when she had time.

I didn't want to bother her or make her feel pressured. She'd finally opened up to me that she might need to travel again for a week or two after Melody's birthday. I could hear the concern in her voice.

I needed to proceed carefully.

Her life was changing, and there might not be room in it for me and Melody.

I couldn't fault her for that.

But I'd be lying if I didn't admit that I was struggling with it. With not knowing what the future held.

There was a knock on my door, and I glanced at the time, surprised that anyone was stopping by this late, as it was almost ten p.m.

I pulled the door open, surprised to see Bridger standing there.

"It's late. Are you all right?" I asked.

"I'm always all right." He moved past me as if he owned the place and walked straight to the kitchen. He pulled two beers from the refrigerator and popped the tops before handing me one. "Is Melody asleep?"

"Yes. It's almost ten o'clock at night—of course she's asleep."

"Ahh… I see someone forgot to take his anti-dick pill today." He gave me a look. "What's going on with you, Archie? Everyone's noticed that you're not yourself."

"How the fuck am I not myself? Who the fuck else would I be?"

"For starters—let's dissect that response. That's something I would say. Why are you so on edge?"

"I'm not." I scrubbed a hand down my face.

I was.

Of course I was.

Everything was unknown right now.

"The first step is admitting that there's a problem," he said with an evil grin on his face before he took a pull from his beer.

"Why do you seem like you're enjoying this?" I hissed.

"I don't know." He shrugged. "Maybe because I've always been the problem child, and now I'm in therapy and dealing with my shit, so I can easily spot a fucked-up motherfucker better than anyone. And you, my friend… are a fucked-up motherfucker."

"Are you drunk?"

"Drunk on life, maybe." He winked in that condescending way that he knew would get under my skin. "And this is my first drink today. So stop deflecting, Archie. We're talking about you, not me."

"I'm fine."

"Says any man who isn't fine. For fuck's sake, just tell me what's going on."

I exhaled sharply. "It's nothing."

"Really?" he said, pursing his lips. "You skipped Sunday dinner, and you've been MIA on the group texts."

"So let me get this straight… I feel a little under the weather on Sunday and skip dinner, and that makes me a fucked-up motherfucker?"

"Don't forget being MIA from the group texts," he said as he moved to my pantry. He helped himself to a bag of potato chips before sitting back down at the kitchen island.

"I've got a child. I'm doing this all on my fucking own right now, dickhead. If you haven't noticed, my girlfriend isn't here at the moment, so how about you cut me some fucking slack." My words came out much harsher than I'd expected.

"Ahh… there it is. Was that so difficult?"

"Was what so difficult? Telling you why I missed a meal and a few text messages?"

"Oh, Archie, you really are a fucked-up motherfucker."

"And you're an asshole," I snipped before reaching for the chips and grabbing a few from the bag.

"Just admit that you miss your girl."

"It's no secret. Of course I miss her. But I'm happy for her. She's doing amazing, and that's great."

He laughed. "You don't need to put on a show for me. Of course she's doing amazing. She's a fucking rock star. But you are retreating because of some deep-rooted shit, and you need to figure it out. It's not healthy to keep saying everything is fine when everything isn't fine. You're a mess."

"Gee. Thanks. Tell me how you really feel."

"If I tell you what I think, will you agree to do me a favor?"

"Sure." I rolled my eyes.

"I think that Scarlet fucked you up a little bit." He held up his hands when I started to argue. "I know, I know, you don't resent her choices. You wanted a kid, and she didn't, and you don't hold that against her. But that doesn't mean that it didn't fuck you up a little. The woman you loved chose her career over you."

"For fuck's sake. What is this? Some sort of demented therapy? I don't resent Scarlet. She was honest about what she wanted, and so was I."

"I know that. But I also know that she chose her career over you and over Melody. It's her choice. Good on her. But that doesn't mean that it didn't fuck with your head when it comes to future relationships. Which is why you haven't had one until now. And then guess the fuck what?"

"Please don't make me. I already have a headache." I rubbed my temples.

"Your girlfriend, whom you're crazy about, is traveling the world because her career is blowing up. And that scares the shit out of you. So you're doing what you do best—you're suffering in silence and retreating into yourself."

My eyes bulged out of my head. "Who the fuck are you? I feel like I'm talking to the Dalai Lama."

"Hey, what can I say? I'm reading some self-help books and I'm doing a real deep dive into my fucked-up trauma. Boom. There you go."

"Why?" I asked as I shook my head.

"Because I'd like to have a long life with my future wife, and we plan on having children, who I don't want to fuck up with my cold jaded heart. So I'm dealing with my shit." He sighed. Bridger's mother had lost her life giving birth to him, and his biological father soon went off the rails due to grief, so Bridger was raised by his aunt and uncle, who were also my aunt and uncle. He'd dealt with some serious trauma, and I'd been proud as hell of him for dealing with it head on after he'd fallen in love with Emilia. "And you need to deal with yours."

I nodded. He wasn't wrong. Fear was probably at the root of everything I was feeling right now.

"I'm happy for her, and I'm proud of her." I blew out a breath, because it was the truth.

"I know you are, Archie. But she's noticing it, too. She called Emilia this morning because she's worried about you."

"Fuck. That's the last thing I wanted. I'm trying not to put pressure on her. Not to tell her that I'm fucking lost without her. I don't want to hold her back, so I'm just trying to support her. She's got all these opportunities happening, and they just might take her in a different direction. And I will not be the man who stands in her way. I'm not that guy." I stood and moved through the kitchen, then grabbed a glass and filled it with water to keep myself busy.

"There's a big difference between being supportive and shutting down. You're shutting down. You're letting fear take over, and you need to figure out why you're doing that, or it won't be her career that takes her away, it'll be you who pushes her away. You can't just shut down when things are difficult."

I didn't respond. He'd pissed me off, but I knew he wasn't wrong.

"Okay."

"Yeah?" he asked, then stood up and tossed his beer bottle in the recycling bin.

"Yep. I'll work on it."

"You'll do more than work on it. You've got a meeting with Debbie, my therapist, tomorrow morning at eight a.m. Go straight there after you drop the little monster off at school."

"I've got a meeting tomorrow morning," I grumped as I followed him to the front door.

"Yes, you do. With Debbie. Everyone else can wait." He pulled the door open and turned around to face me. "Will you just trust me on this?"

"Well, seeing as I'm a fucked-up motherfucker, I don't have much of a choice, do I?" I said, my voice lighter now.

"Takes one to know one, buddy. Call me tomorrow after your meeting." He held up a hand. "And start responding in the group chat, or you're going to be getting more visits from other Chadwicks."

"Got it." I rolled my eyes as I watched him walk to the end of the driveway and turn toward his house. He lived close, and it was a nice night outside.

I exhaled and thought about calling Winnie, but I decided to wait.

I needed to figure my shit out before I talked to her.

And I was ready to make that happen.

• • •

I'd come three times this week to see Bridger's therapist, Debbie, who was apparently my therapist now, because my asshole cousin had scheduled me for three sessions.

"Does that make sense to you, Archer?" Debbie asked.

"Sure. I mean, I guess I just didn't realize that me being okay with what happened with Scarlet could still mess me up in other relationships. I respect that she knew what she wanted, and she was honest from the beginning. Or at least once she realized she was pregnant."

"Yes, and you've told me that you don't fault her for her decision to give up her rights as a mother," she said. "You've made that more than clear, but that doesn't mean it still didn't feel like a betrayal to you emotionally. You were in love with her. You can understand someone's reasons for leaving, and still be hurt by them."

I blew out a breath. "And you think that me not wanting a relationship for such a long time was because of fear."

"I think you were protecting yourself, yes. And then you met Winnie, who was a big red flag to you, from what you've shared." She chuckled.

"I hired her to be my nanny, not my girlfriend." I snorted. "But yes, she wasn't looking for anything, either, since she'd gone through a tough divorce, not to mention being a decade younger than me."

"Nine years younger now, right?" She had a playful grin on her face, because I'd shared the inside joke with her.

I'd felt lighter this week than I had in a very long time, actually.

There'd been clarity where I hadn't expected it.

Where I hadn't even realized that I needed it.

"I see whose side you're on now," I said, chuckling.

"I'm on both of your sides." She smiled and added, "The question is, are you willing to risk being vulnerable again? There are no guarantees in life, Archer. When you were dating Scarlet, you never had the discussion about children, correct?"

"Correct."

"So when she found out she was pregnant, it forced the discussion. And you realized you both wanted different things. It hurt, but you made your choice, and she made hers."

"Yes."

"With Winnie, it sounds like it's very different," she said. "You started off being cautious and careful, but there were feelings there. And you took your time and became friends first. And you've mentioned that you two talk about everything. What you want out of life. Your hopes and your dreams. All of those things."

"We do. She's very honest and genuine. It's impossible not to talk to her about things most of the time. She sort of makes me talk." I laughed.

"That's a good thing. And it helps to build trust, which is why I think you were able to finally put your guard down."

I nodded. "Trust isn't the issue."

"Right. The issue is fear, Archer. You see these things happening for her, and I know it's a mixed emotion for you. I don't doubt that you're thrilled for her and that you're her biggest cheerleader. You've made it clear that you don't want to pressure her in any way, but my guess is that you're hurting her in a different way."

"How?" I asked, clasping my hands together, knowing she was right but hating it at the same time.

"You've put your guard back up. You're retreating into yourself for self-preservation," she said, her voice softer now. "And I'm sure that's hurting her. You shared that you've been distant with her."

"I know she's busy. I don't want to burden her."

"Is it a burden when she calls you?" she asked as she studied me.

"No. I look forward to talking to her."

"So why would it burden her if you called her?"

I rubbed my face. "I don't know."

"Let me ask you this," she said, setting her pen down on the notepad that rested on her lap. "Winnie's career has already taken off, yet she's checking in with you constantly, even when she's exhausted, right?"

"Yes."

"So why would that end if she continues to have success?"

"I don't know. Maybe she'll want to live somewhere else. Start a different life," I said before clearing my throat.

"Has she talked about wanting to relocate?"

"No." I shrugged.

"All right, so let's just recap a few things." She tilted her head to the side.

"Okay." I nodded.

"Winnie sort of told you that she loved you when she left." She put her hands up to stop the rebuttal that she knew would follow that statement. "She said a casual 'love ya,' but you and I both know what that meant. She was working up the nerve to say 'I love you' and panicked, and you didn't say it back. Instead you told her not to worry about you guys, and you've talked to her while she's been away, but certainly not as much as you normally speak. She's shared with Emilia that she's worried about you, so she's clearly noticed. Can you imagine from her perspective how this might seem?"

"Meaning?"

"Meaning, it sounds like you're the one who's one foot out the door, not her. She shared how she felt, or at least she tried to. She's put herself out there. She's telling you that she feels anxious about being away from you, and you continue to tell her it's going to be fine, instead of admitting that you're also struggling. You're the one who hasn't been honest."

"I made her father a promise that I would never hold her back," I reminded her, because we'd already discussed that conversation.

"So not telling her how you feel, not being responsive—that's your way of making sure that you don't hold her back? I don't think so, Archer. I think you're holding back because you're afraid she'll hurt you. And at some point, you've got to take a risk. I guess the million-dollar question is, is she worth the risk?"

I didn't hesitate. "She's more than fucking worth it. I'm madly in love with her."

She smiled. "Okay. You've told me how you feel, how about you tell her how you feel."

I nodded. "I can do that."

"It's the first step to putting your past behind you and moving forward toward the future that you want."

She was right.

It was time.

36

Winnie

I'd landed in New York this morning, and I was doing this last stretch on my own, as Laney needed to get back to work. I was fine on my own now. And I'd met a different author at each stop, which had been a real highlight of this tour. I'd met so many authors whom I myself was a huge fan of.

It was surreal in so many ways.

I'd just sat on a stage at one of the most iconic bookstores in New York City with Claire Chestnut, a well-known contemporary romance author. We'd had a great conversation, and I'd gotten more comfortable speaking in public over the last two and a half weeks.

We settled at one large table beside one another as we signed books for all the readers who'd attended the event. It was so nice chatting and hearing how they'd discovered our books, or how they'd related to them in some way. I think as an author, that's the best compliment, when a reader connects to your words.

I signed and took photos and talked for a few hours, then hugged Claire goodbye. The bookstore would be closing soon, so I tossed my markers in my green suede tote bag and pulled up my Uber app.

Of course, I checked my texts to see if I had any messages from Archer.

He hadn't been calling as much, but he always sent texts before every event each day.

Archie: *Good luck today, beautiful. Just be yourself. I miss you.*

That was the first time he'd said that he missed me in over a week. My chest squeezed at his words, because I missed him so much.

Just as I was getting ready to type a response, a deep voice startled me.

"Hey, Win," the familiar voice said.

I looked up, surprised to see my ex-husband Jaden standing in front of me.

"Jaden. What are you doing here?" I asked, not hiding the surprise in my voice.

He chuckled, and I could smell the booze on his breath. "I'm in town for Johnny West's bachelor party, and I was scrolling on social media and saw that you were here for a book signing. I tried to make it over for the event, but we were out, so I just snuck away to see if I could catch you."

It was completely par for the course for Jaden to show up to something after it was over. Especially an event that was for me.

Our relationship had been me picking him up over and over

again, yet he never showed up for me.

Jaden had held on tight just to keep me stagnant and in place.

Archer wanted me to chase my dreams, but I wanted him to hold on tighter.

"Well, thanks for stopping by." I chuckled, because I was just getting ready to leave.

"Listen, Win, I'm impressed. I guess I owe you an apology for doubting that people would actually want to read your books."

"I don't need an apology, Jaden. I'm good."

"I can see that," he said as he shoved his hands in his pockets. "I'm seeing someone. We've been together for a few months, and it's good. She's got a great job. Makes really good money, so she helped me get the car fixed, in case you were worried about it."

I snorted. "I wasn't worried about your car. But I'm glad you're happy, Jaden. I wish you the best."

"So, can I get a book signed for my girlfriend? She can't believe my ex-wife is a famous author now."

The woman who'd hosted the event, Vee, appeared out of nowhere, almost as if she'd sensed my discomfort. "We're about to close, but I can ring you up for that book before I shut the register down."

He startled a bit and glanced over at me. "Oh, you don't get free copies?"

"I have copies that the publisher sends me to my home, but this is a book signing hosted by the bookstore. So the books aren't free." I started to reach into my purse for some cash but stopped myself.

Jaden wasn't my problem anymore.

I didn't need to buy him a book.

If he couldn't spare twenty bucks to purchase my book, then that was his choice.

He surprised me when he pulled out his card and handed it to her.

She gave me a book, and I looked up at him. "Who am I making it out to?"

"Coraline," he said, clearing his throat.

She was the woman I was fairly certain he'd cheated on me with.

I should have felt something.

Anger.

Sadness.

But I felt nothing for this man. Only relief that he wasn't in my life anymore.

I'd surrounded myself with people who believed in me. People who respected me.

I quickly wrote her name in the book and signed it before passing it back to him. "My car is here, so I need to get going. Take care, Jaden."

"Yeah, you too, Win." He tucked the book under his arm and held up his free hand before walking out the door.

I thanked Vee before stepping outside and smiling when I slipped into the Uber.

It hit me in that moment how much my life had changed over the last few months.

I'd found a man I loved, and a little girl who had my heart.

I'd landed in the most peaceful town, where I'd made great friends.

My career had exceeded my expectations, and I was on a book tour, talking to readers about a book that I wrote.

I dialed Archer from the back of the Uber, hoping he'd pick up this time.

Melody's face came into view, and I smiled, my chest

squeezing just at the sight of her. "Hi, my Winnie. I'm missing you big."

"I'm missing you, too, sweet pea."

"Daddy's taking a shower, and I'm watching a show until he comes out, but I heard his phone ringing, and I was hoping it would be you."

He's taking a shower? It was six p.m. their time. He usually showered in the morning, and they'd usually be having dinner now.

"It's me," I said. "Guess what?"

"What?"

"I ordered all the decorations for your birthday party."

"Is it still going to be a cowgirl party with horses and pink hats and boots?"

"Of course it is. We're going to make it so cute," I said with a chuckle as the car pulled in front of my hotel.

"I can't wait, Winnie. Justine told everyone that since you were gone, my party is going to be canceled." Her big brown eyes were wide, her cheeks flushed.

I thanked the driver and got out of the car, then stepped toward the hotel and entered the lobby. "Well, that is not true. This party is going to be the best party ever."

"Yes!" She pumped her fist at the ceiling, just as I heard her father's deep voice in the background.

I didn't step on the elevator because I knew I'd drop the call.

"What did I tell you about answering my phone when I'm not in the room, angel face?" he said before he glanced at the screen to see my face. "Hey, beautiful."

"Hey." I took him in. His hair was wet and clean, and he was wearing a black sweater and looked like he was ready to go out. I could practically smell his cologne through the phone. "You look nice. I thought I'd catch you guys having dinner?"

"I'm having dinner at Mimi and Pops's," Melody shouted, and I didn't miss the look that Archer gave her.

Was she not supposed to tell me?

"Oh, that'll be fun. And where are you off to on a school night?" I asked, trying not to sound annoyed, though that was how I felt at the moment. We'd barely spoken on the phone this week. It had mostly been texts, and he'd call and leave messages when he knew I was at the signing, and then he wouldn't pick up when I'd call back.

"I'm, uh, I'm going out for a bit."

"I'll go get my sleepover bag, Daddy," Melody said, and I didn't miss the way he winced. She leaned over the phone and waved. "I love you, my Winnie."

"I love you, too," I said, a lump forming in my throat as my gaze locked with his. "Sounds like a big night out for you."

He nodded and ignored the comment. "How was the signing?"

"It was good. Jaden stopped by."

"Your ex-husband stopped by? Doesn't he live in Chicago?"

"Yes. Apparently, he's here for a bachelor party and saw that I was doing a signing, so he came by at the end."

"How was it?"

"Fine. He has a girlfriend, and I signed a book for her," I said, my voice flat because my mind was reeling.

Why was Archer being so mysterious?

"I appreciate you telling me that he came to see you," he said.

"You appreciate me telling you that he came to see me?" I repeated his words, the sarcasm impossible to miss.

"Yes."

"Well, I'm not the secretive one, Archer." I purposely called him Archer instead of Archie, and his lips twitched the slightest bit as if he was trying to cover a smile. Was this funny to him? "I'm the one who's been open and honest this whole time. And you know what?"

I started walking toward the elevator because I was frustrated and hurt, and I wasn't even sure why.

"Why are you angry?" he asked, his voice completely calm, which only made me more angry.

"I'm exhausted. I'm freaking exhausted. I've been going nonstop, and I just wanted to see your face, and you've been so distant since I left, and now you're going out and I'm going to bed." I sniffed a few times, a desperate attempt to stop the tears from coming. "My elevator is here, and I need to go."

"Don't give up on me, beautiful," he said, his green gaze locking with mine.

What does that even mean?

I wasn't the one giving up on him.

He was the one who'd been shutting me out. He was the one who hadn't told me how he felt.

I'd been putting myself out there this whole time.

"Good night, Archer." I ended the call and stepped onto the elevator.

As soon as the doors closed, I let the tears fall.

Everything hit me at once.

All the travel. The lack of sleep. The hustle and bustle that I'd experienced over the last two and a half weeks.

But mostly my tears were falling because I was in love with a man I knew loved me back.

But I wasn't certain he would ever allow himself to admit it.

I pushed into my hotel room, then dropped on my bed and

kicked off my shoes as I swiped at my cheeks.

My phone vibrated, and I glanced down to see a text from Archer.

Of course, it was cryptic and only frustrated me more.

Archie: *Hey. I'm sorry about that. I didn't know she'd answered the phone. I promise we'll talk tomorrow and I'll explain everything. I miss you, Winnie.*

I didn't reply. Instead, I padded to the bathroom and turned on the water in the tub.

But I was ready to have that talk.

Tomorrow couldn't come soon enough.

37

Archer

I landed in New York after flying through the night so I could make it to Winnie's hotel this morning. Her next stop was in New Jersey, so she'd be staying here another night.

I owed her a face-to-face conversation.

I'd been an idiot, and I was here because she deserved better than what I'd given her.

I could tell that she was upset last night, but I wanted to see her in person.

Bridger had flown me here on his plane, and he even had a car waiting for me when I landed.

"Do you mind pulling over at this flower stand on the corner?" I asked the driver.

"Absolutely, Mr. Chadwick." He pulled to the side of the

road, and I jumped out and bought her the biggest bouquet of pink roses they had.

Thankfully she'd told me her room number. She did that every time she checked into a hotel, because she said if anything happened at the hotel or there was a fire, she wanted me to know her room number in case I needed to send help.

I laughed every time I thought about it.

But it would absolutely make surprising her easier.

Once I was back in the car, we made our way to the hotel. I glanced at my watch, and it was still early here, so she'd probably just be waking up.

"Thanks again for the ride," I said. I slipped him a generous tip before pushing out of the car.

I couldn't wait to get there.

Couldn't wait to see her.

Hold her.

Kiss her.

Tell her everything I'd been holding in.

I glanced around, grateful when a man who looked like he was coming from the gym stepped onto the elevator, and I followed him in. He swiped his key, and I asked him to hit floor seventeen for me. It was one of those hotels that required a key to get to the different floors.

He gave me a nod and stepped off on floor five.

I sent Winnie a text as the elevator continued to move.

Me: *Hey. Are you up? Do you have time to chat?*

Winnie: *Yes.*

She was being short. She was annoyed with me, and she had every reason to be.

Hell, I was annoyed with myself.

I'd thought I was doing the right thing, and it turned out I was doing everything wrong.

I stepped off the elevator, walked to the end of the long hallway, and stopped in front of her door.

I knocked twice, holding the flowers in front of my face so if she looked through the peephole, she'd see the flowers and not me.

The door opened just a crack, with the chain still engaged.

Atta girl.

"Can I help you?" she asked.

I pulled the flowers away from my face and smiled. "Is now a good time to talk?"

"Archie? Archie!" she gasped, and she pulled on the door several times before realizing she needed to close it to take the chain off.

Once the door opened, I expected her to give me the cold shoulder, but she didn't. She lunged into my arms, and I lifted her off the ground, her legs coming around my waist as she buried her face in my neck.

Little sobs escaped her throat, and I dropped the flowers on the dresser as the door slammed shut behind us. I walked us to the bed to sit, then settled her onto my lap and wrapped my arms even tighter around her.

"Hey, hey," I whispered. "I've got you, beautiful."

She just stayed right there, crying and hugging me for probably two or three minutes before she finally pulled back to look at me. Her hair was in a loose braid falling over her shoulder with a thin white bow tied around the bottom. I glanced down to see that she was wearing her white sleep shorts and matching top. My hand glided up her thigh, beneath the loose-fitting bottoms, and grasped her ass cheek.

Her head fell back as she laughed. "What are you doing here?"

"I owed you a conversation. I thought you were mad at me." My other hand moved to the side of her neck and face.

"I am mad at you. But I'm also happy to see you."

I swiped the tears from beneath her eyes with my thumb. "I'm happy to see you, too. I was on my way out last night to catch my flight here, and I wanted to surprise you. Leave it to Melody to answer the phone."

Her lips turned up in the corners. "So, you weren't going out looking all clean and handsome?"

I laughed. "Haven't been out once since you left. Everyone's given me shit for it. Apparently, I've been very withdrawn."

She nodded before moving off my lap to sit beside me on the bed.

"No touching me until we finish the conversation. You know I'm weak for you. So, tell me why you've been so weird."

"Honestly, I didn't realize it was that noticeable. But, after talking to Dr. Debbie, I can now understand how I gave you a lot of mixed signals."

"Who's Dr. Debbie?"

"Bridger's therapist. He made me go see her a couple times this week. He'd already psychoanalyzed me, and she was much kinder about it." I chuckled.

"Tell me."

"I truly thought giving you your space while you were on this adventure was the right thing to do, Winnie. Your father and I spoke a lot about how Jaden hindered your growth, and I would never want to do that. So I wanted you to go spread your wings, and see what opportunities were out there. But apparently, it was fear-driven, and pretty selfish of me."

She snorted. "'Fear-driven,' huh? You don't say?"

I blew out a breath. "Yep. It's taken me a long time to want to have a relationship again. I never held Scarlet's choices against her, but at the end of the day, she chose to leave. I've been fairly guarded ever since Melody was born, and you're the first person I've opened up to outside of my family. And I was hesitant to tell you how I felt, because—" I shook my head, trying to find the words.

"Because you were afraid that I'd leave you," she said as her hand found mine. "And you were afraid to talk to me about it because you thought that you'd be pressuring me to stay."

"Wow. You're good at reading me, huh?"

"I'm a woman with abandonment issues of my own. So that's why it's important to have the hard conversations. But I'm open to having them, Archie. Because this isn't casual for me. This"—she motioned between us—"what's happening here between us? It's not like anything I've ever felt before. It's so much stronger, and it's so worth the risk."

"I love you, Winnie. I love you so fucking much that it's actually painful. I haven't been sleeping, because I missed your body in my bed. I missed your laugh and your smile, and I missed your cooking. Definitely missed your cooking." My gaze locked with hers, and I chuckled.

"My cooking, huh?"

"Well, among other things." I sighed. "I missed you. Our home doesn't feel right anymore when you're not in it. And I don't want to scare you off, but I came here because I need to tell you these things. I need to tell you that I want forever with you. I want to build a life and a family with you. I know that you've been married before, and I won't pressure you in any way to do that again if that's not something you want, but I want everything you're willing to give me, Winnie."

"First of all, I'm not against marriage. I'm against being married to an asshole." She shrugged. "I actually love marriage, and I see that with you. I see all of it. A love that goes the distance. A family that we continue building together. A life. One that feels right with you."

"Yeah?"

"Yeah, Archie. So next time you go quiet on me, we're going to talk about it, okay? Because I am thrilled that my career is taking off, but that doesn't change the things that I want with you. I can write romance sitting on our front porch growing old together, because you've given me the inspiration to do it. You've shown me what it feels like to love a man deeply and to be loved back the same way. Even if you hadn't said the words, I felt it. I felt it right here." She lifted my hand and settled it over her heart.

"I promise to say it to you every day moving forward. I'm sorry it took me so long to figure out my shit."

"You were worth the wait, Archer Chadwick. Even if you made me say it first."

"You didn't say it first. You said 'love ya,' and it was all muffled and during a very stressful time. I was freaking out that you were leaving, and then you dropped a casual 'love ya'?"

Her head fell back in a fit of giggles, and I swear it was fucking music to my ears. "I do love ya, Archie."

"I love you." I stared at her, and she smiled back at me.

"Love you, too."

I slipped her spaghetti strap down her shoulder, letting her top fall just below her breast as my finger grazed over her hard peak. "Damn, I missed these tits."

"What else did you miss?" She pushed the other strap down her shoulder and fell back on the bed, taking me with her. "Because I've missed you so much."

"I've missed everything about you, beautiful." I leaned down and kissed her. I kissed my way down her neck and over both of her breasts.

She was perfection.

Soft and sweet and everything that had been missing from my life.

I dragged her pajama shirt down her body, along with her bottoms. She was lying there bare on the bed, and I tugged my sweater over my head as I took her in.

"I could stare at you forever, Winnie. You're so beautiful. I want to memorize every inch of you."

She smiled up at me as she reached for the button of my jeans, then pulled down the zipper. I stood up, kicked off my shoes, and shoved my jeans and briefs down my legs before kicking them off to the side. I crawled onto the bed, settling between her thighs as my fingers dipped in, swiping across her heat to find her soaked.

I hissed out a breath as I gripped my cock, and I teased her entrance as she nearly arched off the bed.

"Please," she groaned. "I need you right now, Archer."

Her words were a plea. Desperate and needy.

I thrust into her, and her arms wrapped around me, nails digging into my back as I pulled out and then drove into her again.

Over and over.

She met me thrust for thrust as she begged for more.

And I couldn't get enough.

I'd never get enough of this woman.

We found our rhythm as her hips bucked up against me, and I

gathered her hands and pinned them above her head. I held them there as she arched her back and groaned, and my lips came over her nipples.

Sucking and licking and flicking them with the tip of my tongue as her breaths came hard and fast.

We were both covered in a layer of sweat, but we kept at it.

I reached down between us and put the slightest bit of pressure on her clit as the sexiest moan left her lips.

"Archer," she cried as her entire body trembled beneath me. I slammed into her one more time before I followed her into oblivion.

The sounds leaving my throat weren't even human. We rocked back and forth against one another, riding out every inch of pleasure as I released her hands.

Her breathing slowed, and she tangled her fingers into my hair.

My forehead fell against hers.

"I love you, Winnie."

"I love you, too." She smiled up at me.

"Do you have any obligations today before the signing tonight?" I asked as I stroked the hair away from her gorgeous face.

"Nope. Today is a catch-up day." She shook her head. "Do you have to head home this afternoon?"

"No, beautiful. I'm here with you until you come home. We've got the next few days together."

Her eyes widened as a big smile spread across her face. "Really? You're staying? What about Melody?"

"She's with my mom and dad, and she was thrilled that I was coming to be with you. I didn't tell her until I dropped her at my parents' house, because she definitely would have spilled the beans." I laughed. "But we'll be home soon enough. Right now, I want to be here to support you these last few days. I'll be the dude in the back whistling and cheering you on, if you're okay with that."

A tear rolled down her cheek. "I'm definitely okay with that. Thank you. I'm so happy you're here."

She wrapped her arms around my neck and hugged me tighter.

"Me too, baby. And I'm not going anywhere. I'll be right beside you whenever you need me."

And I meant it.

This woman completed me.

And I was ready to start forever right now.

38

Winnie

Archer and I had wrapped up the book tour and flown home. Having that time with him was magical. We'd explored New York and New Jersey, then traveled to Boston and DC, and he'd come with me to each signing. Every time I'd look out in the audience, he was smiling at me. And then he'd hang out afterward and talk to readers, and all the exhaustion that I'd been feeling would shift. Because he was here with me, which just made the long days a lot easier.

And the sex. Don't even get me started. We'd never been in a hotel room together, and we didn't have to worry about being quiet or walking around the room naked.

And a laid-back Archer Chadwick, dropping his towel on the floor after his shower and showing me the goods—that was a visual I'd hold on to for a very long time.

But being back was just as good, because Rosewood River felt like home. I'd missed Melody. We'd been busy working on her birthday party, which was today. We invited her whole class, including Justine, much to the chagrin of Archer and his brother and cousins. I'd had to remind him that excluding her would be stooping to her level.

And at the end of the day, Melody wanted everyone at her birthday, which I loved about her. She was the kindest little girl, with the most forgiving heart.

"Which one is the little shit who messed with my girl?" Bridger grumped as he and Emilia walked over to where Archer and I were standing.

"Bridger." Emilia shook her head and laughed. "She's a child."

"A child who bullied Melody. At least let me glare at her a little."

"I believe you bullied me for years," Emilia said. "But we can all grow, right?"

"Sorry about that, angel. But this girl told Melody she wasn't lovable. I was just a dick because I thought you hated me. This girl is out of control."

"This girl is six years old. Trust me, I'm not her biggest fan, but it's a birthday party and we're not glaring at children," Archer said, and Emilia and I both chuckled.

"Can I trip her? Put mustard on her cake?"

"Bridger!" Emilia gasped. "Stop talking like that, or I will withhold sex for a month."

Bridger frowned. "Fine. I'll leave the little gremlin alone."

Rafe and Lulu walked over, with Henley and Easton right behind them.

"What a party," Henley said. "This is so cute. You went all out."

"This is all Winnie." Archer winked at me. "I had nothing to do with it."

"You don't say?" Easton said with a laugh.

"What gave it away?" Rafe tapped his chin and smirked. "The giant pink balloon cowboy hats? The pink-and-gold balloon arch and the cake that's shaped like a pair of pink cowboy boots?"

"This is my kind of party," Wren said, leaning over and giving me a hug. "I love this theme."

"Damn. There's a lot of kids here," Axel said.

"All right, I'm coming over to hide out. Our fathers are both in the jumpy house." Clark shook his head with disbelief, referring to my father and Uncle Keaton.

"Well, they went in there to help Melody, but then I think they started jumping and they liked it."

"Beefcake is monitoring the door, so no kids will be going in while the grown men jump around for a little while." Clark took a sip of his water.

"Why is it so loud?" Bridger said, sighing.

"I don't know, because there are like thirty children here?" I said with a laugh.

"Winnie!" Melody called from the yard as she stood next to Justine and Tommy. "Justine doesn't believe that the cake is real. She thinks we don't have a cake."

"I guess we just figured out which one is the bully," Bridger said under his breath.

"Takes one to know one." Easton smirked as I walked toward Melody.

"Hi, sweet pea." I bent down in front of her. "The cake is real, I promise. And we have ice cream and whipped cream and sprinkles, too."

"My mommy lets me have all the sprinkles I want. Sometimes she gives me the whole bottle." Justine popped a hip and pursed her lips all at the same time.

"My Winnie wouldn't want me to do that because it would give me a tummy ache." Melody's hand found mine, and a little part of me wanted to call Bridger over to glare at the little heathen who was giving me attitude.

"That's right. We don't want to get a tummy ache."

"That's because Melody is a baby." Justine laughed, and I glanced over at her mom, who was on her phone.

"Oh, Justine, your mom is calling you. You better go see what she needs."

Justine cinched her brows together. "I didn't hear her call me."

"I did," Tommy said. "She called for you twice."

Justine stomped away, and Tommy wagged his eyebrows at me and Melody giggled. I covered my mouth to keep from laughing.

I went to get my camera and spent the next hour snapping photos of the kids doing potato sack races, and I got several photos of Melody getting her face painted like a butterfly. We'd set up a little photo station with the Polaroid camera, because that was Melody's favorite, and Lulu was working that booth and passing out photos to the kids.

"All right, I know we aren't allowed to act on it, but that little Justine is playing with fire by picking a fight with me." Lulu crossed her arms over her chest and glanced over at the little girl who was now yelling into the bounce house and demanding everyone get out so she could jump alone.

"What did she do?"

"She just asked me if I was a real blonde or a bottle blonde."

Lulu gaped at me as she adjusted her silk headscarf.

"What did you say?"

"I asked her if she was a real redhead or if she used a package of Kool-Aid to get that color." She smirked. "You go low, I'll go lower."

I snorted. "Don't tell Bridger. He's ready to lose it on her."

"Trust me, I won't say a word. But she best not come at me again or I'll dish it right back at her."

"I would expect nothing less," I chuckled as Melody came running over to ask if it was time for cake.

"Let me go get things ready, and I'll bring it out here and we can sing and eat cake." I kissed her cheek and jogged into the house.

I'd just entered the walk-in pantry to grab the party plates when an arm snaked around my waist. "Hey, beautiful. Are you having fun?"

"I'm having a great time, how about you?" I turned around in his arms, then pushed up on my tiptoes and kissed him.

"What did I do to deserve you?" he whispered, and my breath hitched in my throat. "Thank you for making this day so special for her. She's never had a party like this."

"It's been a good day. I love seeing her so happy, you know?"

"I love seeing both my girls so happy. Every time I looked over at you today, you had this big smile on your face."

"Maybe that was because I was looking back at you."

"Wow. Impressive. Are you a romance author, by any chance? You've got a way with words."

I laughed. "You can always whisper sweet nothings to me."

He leaned down, nipping at the sensitive skin at my ear. "I'd love to dip my fingers beneath this little skirt you've got on and check between your legs to see how wet you are."

"Well, seeing as we're hosting a six-year-old's birthday party, I don't think that would be appropriate." My words were breathy. His hand moved to my ass, and he tugged me up against him, and I groaned when I felt how hard he was beneath me.

"Well, what do we have here?" Rafe's voice startled me, and I jumped back.

"For fuck's sake," Bridger grumped as he came up beside his brother. "We're ready for cake, and you two are getting busy in the pantry?"

I laughed, and I could feel my cheeks heat as I grabbed the paper plates. Archer swatted my ass when I hurried past them to leave the pantry.

"You assholes have terrible timing," Archer said.

"We're waiting for cake, and you two disappeared a while ago." Rafe raised a brow as I set the ice cream, whipped cream, sprinkles, plates, and silverware on the tray I'd set out and reached for the cake.

"It was two minutes," Archer said, laughing.

"Yeah, two minutes too long. That Justine kid keeps shooting me daggers, and some other little boy just hit me up for twenty bucks." Bridger took the tray, and Archer carried the cake, while I handed Rafe the lighter and the cake knife.

"It's probably Tommy. Justine keeps stealing his undies, so he probably needs the cash to buy some new ones." Archer snorted.

"Man, I'm glad I'm not a kid anymore. This shit is a lot to handle." Bridger pulled the door open, and we stepped outside.

We set everything down on the table, and I called Melody over. Cutler was right there beside her like the protective cousin he was.

"Nice cake," he said as he tossed me a wink.

I lit the candles, and we all sang happy birthday to my favorite six-year-old on the planet.

Everyone was there, and she was surrounded by so much love.

I was surrounded by so much love.

And it hit me in this moment, as Emerson and Isabelle helped me pass out cake and Archer scooped ice cream onto the plates.

Happily ever after isn't just about finding your soulmate or the love of your life.

Happily ever after is so much bigger than that.

It's about what you create together.

The life that you build.

The love you have with your partner. The people around you. Celebrating the little things and the big things.

Archer looked up at me, then walked over and swiped at my cheek before licking his finger. "You have some frosting on your face, beautiful."

"Yeah?"

"Yeah." He leaned down and kissed me.

In the middle of a birthday party, with the sun shining down on us and the water splashing from the river as it glided by.

We were creating this beautiful life together, and I loved every second of it.

I'd found my happily ever after with this handsome, charming, stubborn, wonderful man, and his amazing daughter, and incredible family—and it was all right here in Rosewood River.

My future.

My heart.

My home.

Epilogue

Archer

ONE YEAR LATER

"Mom's crying again," Axel said over a mouthful of biscuit. "Mimi, it's happy tears, right?"

"Of course. The happiest tears I've ever cried. I just can't believe it all happened. I'm just really happy for all three of you," my mother said, glancing between me and Winnie as she dabbed her eyes with her napkin.

"It's really wonderful," Aunt Ellie said as she sniffed a few times.

"You've got your mama now, too, Mel," Cutler said from across the table. He, Emerson, and Nash had come home to celebrate the adoption.

Winnie and I had tied the knot six months ago in a very small outdoor ceremony with just family and close friends. But it was important to her that she adopt Melody before we started growing our family. She'd grown up without her mother, and she just felt strongly about making it official that she was Melody's mother legally, as well as emotionally.

I'd reached out to Scarlet for the first time in seven years. She said she'd expected this call to come at some point, and she was happy that I'd found a partner who wanted to be a mother to Melody. We kept the call very short, and she happily signed everything required by the state to make the adoption legal.

"Me and Beefcake both found our heart mamas," Melody said.

"Yep. And my mama has my whole heart," Cutler said, and Nash rolled his eyes.

"How about you save a little piece of that heart for your pops."

Cutler laughed. "I'm all heart for you, too, Pops. But you know that Mama is my girl."

Winnie hadn't stopped smiling since the paperwork arrived.

"Is Auntie Lu going to read 'The Taylor Tea' tonight?" Melody asked, since even she looked forward to the weekly gossip column now.

"Oh, of course I am. It's a special one today," Lulu said as she reached for her phone. Her chair was pushed back from the table to allow enough space for her growing belly.

"'Hey there, Roses, Rosewood River's favorite family is keeping us well fed this season,'" she said in her most dramatic voice, then paused to explain. "'Well fed' is hipster talk, meaning we are the entertainment of this town."

Everyone chuckled, and Henley snorted as she rubbed her

own pregnant belly. “Thanks for the sidenote, Lu. Keep going.”

“‘Our royal family must be drinking some special water, because it’s hard to keep track of all these pregnancies.’” She chuckled. “They make a good point—look at us.”

I glanced around the table. Lulu and Henley were both six months along, and they claimed they didn’t plan on being pregnant at the same time, but the fact that they were both due only two weeks apart seemed suspicious. Emilia and Bridger had shocked everyone with their no-fuss courthouse wedding almost a year ago, and she was three months pregnant now.

“We’re not the only people in town having babies,” Bridger grumped.

“Well, we do make up a good percentage,” Wren said as Axel wrapped his hand over hers. They’d been married in a small outdoor ceremony nine months ago on their property. They’d just told us last weekend she was pregnant, and everyone was thrilled.

Clark placed his hand on his wife’s stomach and winked at her. He and Eloise had eloped in Las Vegas ten months ago, and they were due any day.

“Fine, continue telling us everything going on in our family.” Bridger rolled his eyes.

Lulu cleared her throat. “‘We all know that it was big news when our favorite single daddy was no longer single. But word on Main Street is that today is a different kind of celebration, because after he rode off into the sunset with his beautiful heroine (pun intended), they’ve made it official, and she’s adopted his little rosebud. They’re a family of three, and this town celebrates that kind of special love.’” Lulu paused and sniffed a few times before dabbing at her eyes with her napkin. She turned to look at me and Winnie. “It is a special kind of love.”

"It's better than fiction," my mother croaked, and everyone laughed.

"It definitely gives me all the inspiration I need," Winnie said as she leaned her head against my shoulder.

Lulu looked back down at her phone to finish reading. "'So, we'll leave it on that special note. We'll be back to spill some more Rosewood River tea next week.'"

"That was a good one," Emilia said as she also dabbed at her eyes.

I glanced around the table, noting that everyone looked a little weepy, aside from Bridger, who was piling food on his plate.

"I feel like 'The Taylor Tea' loves Archer and Winnie," Henley said. "It's always very complimentary of you two."

"They are, aren't they? And Oscar was a famous author, so he's clearly good with words." Lulu gasped as her eyes widened. "Do you think he could be writing 'The Taylor Tea'?"

I felt Winnie's shoulders stiffen beside me, and I glanced up to see Bridger dropping a biscuit on his plate.

The table was quiet, with everyone clearly processing her words.

"Oscar? Are you kidding me?" Bridger said. "It is definitely not him. This has a woman written all over it. Dudes don't give a shit about who's pregnant and who's sleeping with who." Melody pointed at him for cursing, and he chuckled. "I've got credit in that jar."

"That's a good point. But maybe it's Edith adding the woman's touch," Henley said.

"Nah. I fixed their computer for them last year. Those two can barely work a laptop. I've already ruled them both out." Bridger reached for his beer and took a long pull as if he wasn't giving it another thought.

"I think it's a woman, too," Emerson said with a chuckle. "It's so detailed, and it normally tends to hate on the guy a little."

Everyone threw out their guesses, and I looked up just in time to catch Bridger winking at Winnie.

He'd never shared what he'd seen on that laptop over a year ago. It had stayed among the three of us, as far as I knew.

"I kind of like that we don't know who it is," my mother said. "It makes it more fun."

"And I could't care less who it is," my father said as the table erupted in laughter.

"We've got a good life." Aunt Ellie held her glass up. "And if people want to spill the tea about all the things we have going on, so be it."

Everyone raised their glass.

"Cheers to the Chadwicks. May our tea be overflowing until the end of time," Lulu sang out as we clinked glasses around the table, most of them being water glasses, since a fair percentage of people at this table were pregnant or children.

"I'll drink to that," I said.

I glanced over at Winnie. My wife. The mother of our daughter.

And I'd never been more grateful than I was right now in this moment.

• • •

SIX MONTHS LATER

"Remember the first time I caught you out here eating ice cream?" I said as I gripped her hips and lifted her onto the counter.

"I sure do. You came out in those sexy gray joggers and no shirt." She wiggled her eyebrows at me playfully.

"And you were licking the ice cream off that spoon very seductively, Mrs. Chadwick."

I scooped some mint chip ice cream onto my spoon, and she opened her mouth for me to slip it inside.

"Damn, that's good," she groaned.

I leaned forward and kissed her. "So minty and sweet."

She took the spoon from my hand and scooped a little on there and fed it to me.

"I have a surprise for you, Archie." Her voice was full of tease.

Damn, I loved this woman.

"Are you going to strip naked and cover your body in mint chip ice cream and let me lick it off of you?"

Her head fell back on a full-bodied laugh as she jumped off the counter. "We could make that happen. But this is something else. I got you a little present. I wasn't going to give it to you until your birthday, but now I'm too excited."

"Oh, I love presents from my wife." I leaned over the counter and watched as she hurried over to the laundry room and came back with a little black gift bag.

I reached inside and pulled out a tiny onesie that read: I LOVE MY DADDY.

My eyes nearly bulged out of my head. "What? You're pregnant?"

"Yep. I took a test this morning, and then snuck out to get this cute onesie." She bit her bottom lip.

She'd gone off birth control a few months ago, but we hadn't been trying that long. I was elated. We wanted to grow our family, and we were both ready.

I tugged her against me and wrapped my arms around her.

"This is amazing, beautiful." I kissed her hair.

She tipped her head back to look up at me. "I love you, Archer Chadwick."

"I love you more."

She sighed and stepped back. "Melody is going to be such a good big sister."

"She is. And you're going to be an amazing mama," I said, brushing the hair back from her face. "And the timing is okay with your writing schedule?"

"It's perfect, actually." She blinked a few times, and her eyes were wet with emotion.

"What are you thinking?" I asked.

"I get to write happily ever after for a living. And when I started this journey, it was an escape for me. I was living vicariously through my characters." She blew out a breath before continuing. "And now I'm living it. My own happily ever after."

"Me too, baby. I'm the luckiest man in the world," I said as I tipped her chin up to meet her gaze.

"I'm so happy I get to do this life with you. My forever love."

"My forever love," I said before giving her a chaste kiss. I turned to put the ice cream in the freezer, and then I scooped her into my arms.

She chuckled. "Are you going to carry me everywhere now?"

"For as long as you'll let me." I set her down on our bed and climbed in beside her.

She slid over and settled on my chest, and I leaned down before whispering against her ear, "I love you, beautiful."

"I love when you whisper sweet nothings to me, Archie," she said, her words sounding sleepy.

I wrapped her up in my arms and held her tight.

My best friend.

My wife.

My love.

My forever.

Extended Epilogue

Archer

TWENTY YEARS LATER

"I can't believe we're finally breaking ground," Cutler said as he glanced around at the expansive land, surrounded by the most beautiful mountains. Water splashed against the shore in the distance, and I breathed in the cool air.

"It's one of the best things he ever talked us into," Bridger said after ending his phone call and walking over to us.

Twenty years ago, a gorgeous plot of land had become available in Blue Sky Bay, and I'd called everyone in my family immediately. It wasn't something I could afford on my own, and Bridger had offered to buy it for everyone, but we all wanted to invest in it together. So, my brother and Wren, and all my cousins and their significant others, chipped in, and we purchased the land together.

All with the idea of building on it someday.

But then we got busy having babies, and watching our kids grow, and sending them off to college.

The land appreciated, of course, and Emerson had come out here to help Cutler move into his new home two years ago. She'd planted the seed about us finally building on this land.

My nephew had expanded on his father's construction company and opened his own ROD Construction in this quaint little town that sat between Rosewood River and Magnolia Falls, right on the bay. It had always been a secret little place that not many people knew about, but now this town was booming. It was the place to be. Cutler went to college not too far from here, and he'd gone on to architecture school, and now here we were.

He'd gone on to get both his contracting license and his architecture license. He'd designed the family home that we were about to break ground on, and now he'd be building it as well. Emilia had offered to provide some guidance on the interior, but she was busy running her own business back home, so we'd need to find someone local. The exciting thing was that we'd all share this place, which would become a generational home that we'd pass down for years to come to our children and then to their kids.

It was time.

"You don't think we're going too big on this?" I asked as I scratched the back of my neck.

It was going to be a mammoth home, with twelve bedrooms and just as many bathrooms, not to mention the gym and the game room and the movie theater.

"We want to be able to all use it together, too, so I think the size works." Bridger shrugged.

"You know what they say, size matters." Cutler laughed. "Go big or go home, boys."

"Of course that's what you'd say, hotshot." I clapped him on the shoulder. "Those plans you drew are something else."

He was a talented kid, no doubt about it. He'd always been the coolest kid I'd ever met, and to say he'd grown into an even more amazing man would be an understatement.

Cutler Heart was as good as they came.

"Thanks, Uncle A," he said. "We're ready to get started. It's going to take some time, because it's an enormous home, but it'll be worth the wait."

"All good things are," I said.

"I disagree," Bridger grumped. "I like microwave popcorn, and that's fast. I prefer a short movie to a long movie. I am always a fan of short conversations versus long ones. And I can make money in minutes. So, there you go."

I rolled my eyes. "I know Emilia is going to be as involved as she can be from a distance, but do you think we should find a local designer? We'll have a lot of decisions to make, and if we don't want this to take years to build, then it might be wise to have someone who's here."

"No chance you can get Gracie to take this on?" Bridger asked.

Gracie Reynolds was Cutler's best friend. Hell, she'd become family over the years, and they were very close. She'd even spent two summers living in Rosewood River and interning for Emilia's company, as she'd gone to school for interior design.

"That's doubtful. She's still in Paris and dating that pompous douchebag, Gabriel." Cutler's jaw clenched, and I didn't miss the way his shoulders tensed.

"Yeah, Emilia and I took them to dinner when we were in Paris a few months ago, and I didn't like the dude at all," Bridger added.

"Well, you do hate most people," I chuckled.

"True. But Emilia didn't like him, either, and that's saying a lot, because she loves everyone. The guy was a piece of work. He talked about himself the whole time, and I'm fairly certain he hit on our server right in front of Gracie. She tried to play it off, but I could tell she was upset." He shrugged.

I glanced down to see Cutler's hand fist at his sides. "I'd like to knock that fucker out. I don't know what she's doing with him."

"You should have dated that girl years ago." I gave him a look, because we always gave him time about it.

"Nah, we decided we were too good of friends back when we were in high school. We didn't want to risk messing that up, not when we're so connected through our families." He blew out a breath. "But she's my girl. Always will be."

"I get that. And you've always been a bit of a heartbreaker, so you don't want to go there." I winked at him.

Cutler smirked as he shook his head. "Now you sound like Gracie."

Bridger clapped him on the shoulder. "Well, if you can't get her back here, you need to find someone to take on this job, because I don't want Emilia to feel like she has to do it."

"I got it. Let me see who I can find," Cutler said, but now he looked a million miles away. As if talking about Gracie Reynolds had taken him far away.

Hell, she was in Paris, and he was here in Blue Sky Bay.

I knew he missed her, and the look on his face told me it was worse than I'd thought.

He hadn't been the same since she'd left.

His phone vibrated in his back pocket, and he reached for it.

His entire demeanor changed when he looked down at his screen.

"Speak of the devil." A wide grin spread across his face. "It's my girl and she's in Paris, so I need to take this. I'll be back."

He walked off, and I looked up at Bridger, who was staring out at the water. "You ready to build our family a home that we can all enjoy?"

"I am. I think we're all ready." I moved beside him as we walked along the property.

"Every bathroom is getting a badass toilet in this home," he said. "I want to warm my ass in every bathroom in this house."

"A palace filled with golden shitters sounds about right for the Chadwick family," I said with a laugh.

"Now you're speaking my language."

"It's a good life we've all built, isn't it?" I asked as I turned to look at him. I was a lucky bastard. I had a wife I loved more than life itself, and a daughter and a son I was incredibly proud of.

"It is a good life. Minus the fact that my teenage daughter wants to spend a summer abroad with her girlfriends, and I'm not Liam fucking Neeson and I'm terrified of letting her go."

Laughter bellowed from me. Bridger was an over-the-top father when it came to his three daughters. He was ridiculously protective, and we all made fun of him.

"You worry too much. I'll have Melody talk to her." I sighed as we both stared out at the waves crashing against the shore.

Some moments felt like life was moving too fast, and others felt like life was just beginning again.

And Blue Sky Bay was going to be a place we could all come to relax and be together.

As a family.

Just the way we liked it.

Acknowledgments

Greg, thanks for the fairytale. Love you forever!

Chase & Hannah, you are my reason for EVERYTHING! Love you so much!

Nat, I am ENDLESSLY grateful to have you in my life and right beside me on this journey. You really do complete me! LOL! Thank you for always having my back and stepping up in any way that I need. Most of all…thank you for your friendship!! Love you!

Mom, thank you for reading everything that I write the minute I finish it! It means the world to me. Love you!!

Georgie, I'm truly so grateful for you. Thank you for believing in me and supporting me always! Thank you for keeping me calm when I'm spiraling. Thank you for being an endless support system to me. Love you so much!

Willow & Catherine, love my love chain forever! So grateful to be on this journey with you both. Love you endlessly.

Kandi, Ahhh…you are such a bright light in my life. Thank you for always being there to cheer, to listen, and to be a huge inspiration to me. So grateful for YOU. Love you so much!

Pathi, endlessly thankful for you! Thank you for all of your support and encouragement! Love you so much!

Jessica Turner, I'm so incredibly grateful for you. Thank you for believing in my words, and these characters, and cheering me on. Seeing my books in bookstores is a dream come true, and I'm so thankful for you! Xo

Sarah Rifield, thank you for working so hard to get my books out in the world, and being an amazing cheerleader and support system. I'm so grateful for you!

To the amazing team at Entangled Publishing…thank you for making my wildest dreams come true! I appreciate you all so much!

Katie and Kim at Lyric Audio Books, thank you so, so much for all that you do to help bring these books to life! So grateful for you!

Kim Cermak, You are such a rock star. Thank you for always remaining calm, and supporting me, even with last minute requests! LOL! I love you my Bravo sister! Truly, my world is so much better with you in it! Love you!

Christine Miller, Kelley Beckham, Tiffany Bullard, Sarah Norris, Valentine Grinstead, Meagan Reynoso, Amy Dindia, Josette Ochoa, Ratula Roy, Jill McManamon, Jaime Guidry, Megan Cermak, and Emma Walczak, I am endlessly thankful for YOU!

Tatyana (Bookish Banter), thank you for being such a support, and such an amazing friend. Love you!

Paige, I adore you. So grateful to have you in my life. I love our decorating DM's and being on this journey with you. Love you my sweet friend!

Abi, thank you for beta reading, and cheering me on, and stepping up whenever I need help! Love you so much!

Stephanie Hubenak, thank you for always reading my words

early and cheering me on. Our daily chats are my favorite. And the GRAPHICS!! You are endlessly talented my friend! Love you!

Kelly Yates, thank you for always stepping up and reading my words early! So incredibly grateful for your friendship!

Logan Chisholm, I'm so grateful for you, and all of your support. Thank you for creating the most gorgeous videos for me! Thank you for always saying yes to anything I need! It means the world to me! And a little shoutout to your supportive mama, Tina, who is the cutest!

Kayla Middlekauff, thank you for making amazing content! I am so thankful for YOU! I still remember the first time we met (I was dazzled by your cute outfit!), and I absolutely love being on this journey with you. Love you!

Janelle (Lyla June Co.), thank you for your support and friendship! I'm so grateful for you!

To all the talented, amazing people who turn my words into a polished final book, I am endlessly grateful for you! Sue Grimshaw (Edits by Sue), Bill Siever, Hang Le Design, Sarah Sentz (Enchanted Romance Design) and Jaime Ryter (The Ryters Proof), thank you for being so encouraging and supportive!

Crystal Eacker, thank you for your audio beta listening/reading skills and for always coming through for me when I'm in a state of panic! So grateful for you my sweet friend!

Erika Plum, thank you for the adorable bookmarks! You nail it every time!

Jennifer, thank you for being an endless support system. For running the Facebook group, posting, reviewing and doing whatever is needed for each release. Your friendship means the world to me! Love you!

Rachel Parker, so incredibly thankful for you and so happy to be on this journey with you! My forever release day good luck charm! Love you so much!

Gianna Rose, Diana Daniels, Rachel Baldwin, Kristina Maysonet, Sarah Sentz, Ashley Anastasio, Kayla Middlekauff, Tiara Cobillas, Tori Ann Harris and Erin O'Donnell, thank you for your friendship and your support. It means the world to me!

Dad, you really are the reason that I keep chasing my dreams!! Thank you for teaching me to never give up. Love you!

Sandy, thank you for reading and supporting me throughout this journey! Love you!

To all the bloggers, bookstagrammers and ARC readers who have posted, shared, and supported me—I can't begin to tell you how much it means to me. I love seeing the graphics that you make and the gorgeous posts that you share. I am forever grateful for your support!

To all the readers who take the time to pick up my books and take a chance on my words…THANK YOU for helping to make my dreams come true!!

Doubling the Trees Behind Every Book You Buy.

Because books should leave the world better than they found it—not just in hearts and minds, but in forests and futures.

Through our Read More, Breathe Easier initiative, we're helping reforest the planet, restore ecosystems, and rethink what sustainable publishing can be.

Track the impact of your read at:

CONNECT WITH US ONLINE

@Entangled_Publishing

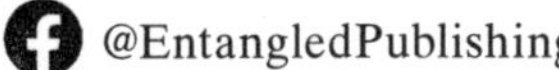
@EntangledPublishing

@EntangledPub

Join the Entangled Insiders for early access to ARCs, exclusive content, and insider news! Scan the QR code to become part of the ultimate reader community.